SIGNAL TO DEPART

SIGNAL TO DEPART

A Novel

~ ~ ~ ~ ~

M. H. SALMON

~ ~ ~ ~ ~

HIGH-LONESOME BOOKS
P. O. BOX 878
SILVER CITY, NEW MEXICO 88062

ISBN # 0-944383-32-7 (softcover)
ISBN # 0-944383-33-5 (hardcover)

Library of Congress Catalog Card # 95-95042

~ ~ ~ ~ ~

First Edition

Dedication

This one is for young son John -- a.k.a. "Bud" -- with love

Signal To Depart is a work of fiction. All names, characters, places, issues and events are fictitious or are used fictitiously, and any similarity to real people, places, issues or events is purely coincidental.

~ ~ ~ ~ ~

Books By M. H. Salmon

Non-fiction

Gazehounds & Coursing
Gila Descending
Tales Of The Chase

Fiction

Home Is The River
Signal To Depart

"No propitiation availed to bring back the harmony between man and sky and soil. All had failed, and in the failure the old men and the priests, interpreters of the wisdom of the Ancients, read the signal to depart."

Ross Calvin
Sky Determines

Prologue

They came into the valley as a tattered band just ages ago. They came afoot, the entirety of the forced simplicity of their lives contained in the packs on their backs. And they came up from the south, off the harsh deserts of what we know as Mexico; and finding slender runs of clear perennial water coming off the mountains to the north, The People settled into the valley and soon into other *vegas* along the various streams where they had water and lengths of level land for crops and yet could reach either the deserts or the mountains in a day's hunt. It must have seemed a glory of a find. For here between mountain and desert was a measure of land without great cold and yet relieved of great heat. Four gentle seasons invigorated by mile-high elevation, healthy breezes, and a bracing arid climate, where nonetheless a modicum of water flowed for every need. In time The People prospered in ways beyond their best imagination. Each generation was gradually more numerous than the last, until their villages dotted the prime lands along the available streams. And each generation was better fed, housed and clothed. In time only campfire narratives, spoken by the Old Ones and passed down from the Ancients, could remind them of the hard scrabble in a harsher land. Geological time would hardly mark their passing. By our time they lived a thousand years. And near the end, an end they could hardly see coming, a measure of primitive leisure and a verdant land and life yielded a generation or two of dreamers, the artists of their time.   With a written language they would have left a great literature.   But they could only scratch on chosen walls of native rock, and with home-made paints mark on those chosen walls and on their pots and bowls of fired soil, and there they made an art at once crude and timeless and highly perceptive.   Art of power and sadness, and death and fun; of venetic pursuit of game large and small, and the seasonal cycles of crops; of satire and lust; of love and birth and the creatures with whom they shared the chain of life. With their art they would reach everything, from the raunch of pornography to the mysteries of the cosmos.   And then, some eight centuries ago, they faded away.   Many died.   Those who lived gradually dispersed.   The *vegas* were left empty of humankind. Only featureless trails led away...to where?   Among the artists, priests, and the Old Ones there must have been some who understood what had gone wrong.   But it was too late; change couldn't help them now, and not even the spirits could save them. With a written language they would have left a great story for us to read.   But they were artists who could only scratch on native rock and mark on fired soil with natural paints.   Perhaps some of the answers lie there.

Signal To Depart

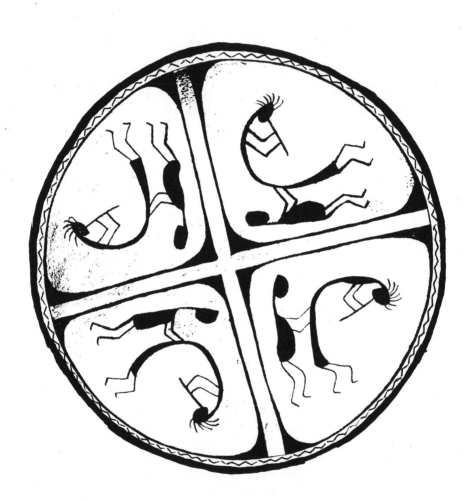

PART I

Chapter 1

I am a dreamer; something of an artist of my time. I can't scratch effectively on native rock, or paint at all well on native rock, or fired soil, or canvas, or anything else, with home-made or store-bought paints. But my writings continue to mount. Few of my dreams have been left unrecorded. They almost equal my readings and my books! Largely a fantasy life, as written by myself, and others. It hasn't been so bad. And on rare occasion I have sought to go beyond fantasy and make a dream come true...

Perhaps there was no more reason to have finally gone there than to have missed the town all those years. I'd seen it on the maps, and much can be inspired by the maps so much needed by one who spends his life on the road. For a dreamer, an entire community can spring to life from a spot on a map. And often I had seen the town on a map and envisioned its life and setting: a town of easily knowable size, too proud to die yet of scarcely recognizable growth, with neighborhoods marked by modest yet distinctive houses, and fine old buildings downtown preserved by people of taste, with pretty women walking uncrowded streets, and unhurried shopkeepers awaiting patiently and without complaint the proceeds of each day; the entirety set 'neath the shoulders of hills, and along a valley The People themselves once knew, surrounded on three sides by hardscrabble ranches and expanses of hilly rangeland and, further out, mountains clad with pines; the slender *Rito Gavilán* running through and declining into the flat desert to the south; a heritage and history as rich as all its variegated cultures and topography could leave behind, and all of it overlain by clear, sun-bright Southwest skies. At least that's the way I imagined it. I knew it might be something different. I couch my fantasy life with a day to day realism that, time and again, can leave me in sharp disappointment over the real thing. A helpless romantic, hopelessly and happily out of harmony with his own time? Yes! Of course! Yet I did know something of the town and its history and a good deal of its natural surroundings from my life with books, and it sounded good.

Books. That's where the most of the dreaming comes from. No one whose life is books -- and I know many who, like me, have to have them -- can envision more of the world contained between respective hard covers than I. I read it, and almost make it real. The right words, and I'm almost there. But even one lost in dreams and confirmed in a love of books would admit in an honest moment that dreaming is not the same as experience. It's not the same as being there, and doing it yourself. I have my honest moments. And I can admit, further, to a vague notion...over the years I have marked out a few spots on the map of the greater Southwest that I have been saving for a time when I would not travel but would make for myself a home, *mi querencia*, that place, as J. Frank Dobie wrote, and only that place, "that gives natural man contentment." And over the years I have, without real planning, finally found myself in several such places, and have found them wanting. Not surprising. The fact is it's all going, and going fast, and we all know it. And almost all of us, it seems, couldn't care less. Only in those special books can we find what was, in near-perfect form -- the Western Myth, as imagined. By writers and readers alike. The perfect naturalness that The People had known. The perfect primitiveness that later settlers -- Apache raiders, Hispanic farmers, Anglo mountain men and men of the range who saw all that grass and brought too many cows -- had etched upon the land. And of course the failed Western Myth of our time, which even the imagination can't save, as we come to the Great Southwest in droves, seeking surcease from crowds, traffic, the crush of humanity; from crime, fouled nature, racial discord, and a myriad of human social aberrations; drawn by a more perfect past, and a hope for a better future. In this of course we fail miserably, merely reproducing in our numbers what we sought to leave behind. No one knows how to stop this. And few can resist it; even the best it seems are seduced by the time which has come. That's why what I do is so important. Only in books can we have the Western Myth in near-perfect form; the Western Myth, as imagined. The necessary antidote to the present; surcease from the modern, the urban, and the trendy. And many of these books, like

The Myth, are all but gone. I find them, long out of print and lost away in dusty attics and lonely alcoves, unread for years or even generations, and make them available to those in a new generation who care. Keeping The Myth alive, to know what was, and perhaps, in part, could be again; that the past might inform the future. And turning a nice profit in the exchange.

I'd been disappointed, by even the relatively good places, relieved to be once again on the road. The town I contemplated now in my mind's eye was perhaps the last best place. It was almost easier, and more tempting, to go around the mountains, stay down on the desert, and skirt the *Rito Gavilán*, holding that perhaps last best place safe, as a dream for the future, rather than come to know it as a real and current disappointment. I was on the interstate, headed west from Tucson, perhaps half way to El Paso. The exit and turn off were just ahead. Tobosa, New Mexico! Pretty name. Ugly town. I had passed it countless times, always went straight on; perhaps there was no more reason now to think of change. But I let the engine slow itself, then geared down and eased off the four-lane onto the exit ramp, and turned onto the narrow, empty two-lane, headed north. To my left the sun set deep in the West. The sparse lights of Tobosa, New Mexico soon fell away behind me. Along the roadside, tobosa grass, grama grass and yucca were giving way to piñon, juniper, and oak. As yet unseen ahead were the lights of my destination, just over the Mule Mountains looming in the dusk. The old bus began to chug. We were climbing. I was alone. Me and all those books.

~ ~ ~ ~ ~

I pulled off the road at the peak of the high hill as the town came into view in the valley below. It was quite dark now and there was nothing to see but the lights. There was a concentration of stationary lights of different colors in what looked to be the center of town, and along the narrow, winding Tobosa Highway leading away from town other, many-colored lights spaced out until they gave out in rural darkness. Along the streets in town and out on the highways a scattering of late-night cars were moving white lights. The great monolith of the *Mondragón* Range loomed in silhouette to the north of the town. I got out of my bus and stood in the darkness and shivered in the cold as I looked at the lights of the town in the valley below. It was somewhere between late winter and early spring and it was quite cold at that elevation in the dark. But it was pleasant to stand there for a while and shiver in the cold and look at the lights and imagine the rest of the town hidden in the dark. Neither cold nor heat in the out-of-doors is unpleasant so long as you know you don't have to put up with it any longer than you want to. I have never been one to place myself any distance from the creature comforts of modern life, and I stood and shivered and looked below and dreamed about it all until the sharp cold went from pleasant to unpleasant and then I paused to take a long steaming piss before stepping back up into the bus. I turned the overhead light on, picked up a certain piece of security from where it hung on the hook beside the seat, then walked down between the shelves filled with books to the living area at the back. I turned the overhead light off with the other switch as I turned on the night light in the living area. This was home for most of the year -- a sink (very small), stove (very small), fridge, shower and comode (all compact, well placed and functional). Only the bunk was of near-normal size but I'd found room for that too, plus a small, antique desk, room for some paper work and the manual, portable typewriter. Under the desk and stuffed under many of the bookshelves were a variety of wooden boxes, built to fit, holding my literary works, my writings. One book length piece in particular, my current novel in progress, had it's own box right under the typewriter and desk. I'd built all this to suit myself. A tiny apartment and writing studio at the back of a private library on wheels, separate from that library when the door was closed. Everything fit and all was neat and in order. I always keep everything neat. And well protected. On the hook by the seat up front, during the day, or on the hook by the bed at the back, at night, was the holstered revolver, that *certain piece of security*. The "single-six" in .22 magnum. Always close at hand. Not a big bore, and single action, but it does nicely. In our time such a thing is necessary. The first time I needed it, all I had to do was cock the hammer. He heard that and knew what it meant. The other time neither the cock of the hammer nor a verbal warning of what was about to happen to him caused flight. The .22 magnum hollow point did. He went off packing a leg but leaving enough blood behind that you wondered how it would all turn out for him. I suppose I should have said something about that. When you shoot someone in our time you're supposed to report it to the appropriate government authorities, but of course I never said a word. I have little use for any government authority, aid, or business. The less those sons-a-bitches know about you the better. I hung the holstered revolver on the hook by the bed.

I looked down the bus to where the books in their shelves disappeared into the dark front of the vehicle. Then I turned and stripped and showered and then to the sink where I brushed my teeth and I dried standing and combing my hair. I always keep myself neat and clean. And despite an inactive life borne of dreams over experience, I'm in pretty good shape. I could see in the mirror that I was holding up nicely. Lately I had started holding my books further and further away to read them and so recently I had given in and picked up some reading glasses at a drug store on the road. Other than that, I figured I was good as new.

I got into bed and looked to the two hardcover volumes on the night stand. One of these was my own book. Of course, everyone would like to write a book. To have something of your own to add to the literature of the Southwest, that was the thing for me. To have something to say to the world. Not necessarily a great work -- only time would determine its ultimate place in the ratings -- but something that at least could hold its place on a shelf, and contribute to The Myth. Something that could take hold of the past, and contribute to the future. My book didn't have a dust jacket for that is a needless decoration, a modern affectation. Better, it's pages were hand-sewn, by me. And the boards were of an old-fashioned solidness covered, by me, with a dense brown cloth of a quality seldom seen on books anymore, with a genuine leather strip melded by my hand over the cloth of the spine and a portion of the front and back covers of those cloth covered boards. A gilt inlay, my own stamp and dye, an artist's depiction of the roguish Mimbres character, Kokopelli, was the only cover decoration. That's all it needed. He was my man. A legendary figure, a focus of the mythology of the Ancients, Kokopelli was depicted by the art of The People over many centuries and many lands, variously ardent, joyous, mischievous, most always lusty and phallic. He is often hump-backed, not a deformity, but rather humped by a pack wherein he carried seeds that could produce crops, jewels and crafts and art objects of the day, and other items of trade. Like me, he carried what was really needed in his time. He was a trader and a raconteur, a not entirely mythic figure based beyond doubt on an actual elite of those times, real men who traveled from valley to valley and tribe to tribe, bringing valued goods to isolated peoples; and, so the legends and art tell us, exacting sexual tribute for his goods, and luring nubiles off into the bushes. Alone and no doubt lonely much of the time, he was voracious in his pleaures whenever he found them. An adventurer-vagabond not laughed at but loved, not feared but liked; many lamented his leaving and all, it seems, awaited his return. He often carried a flute or a prayer stick, which helped him interpret his times for a mystical race, and, not infrequently, a bow and arrows, for Kokopelli was a great hunter, too. He was fertile: of crops and meat; of sex and lust and procreation; of the primal thrall of the chase. My own favorite depiction of Kokopelli is to be found on an ancient bowl, cracked and fractured but still visible of a man: he is humpbacked with precious goods, yet still fluid and athletic; he brandishes his hunting bow in his left hand and from his ears sunspots dangle. His eyes are bright and twinkle and radiate the rogue. In his right hand he lovingly cradles his own fabulous cock. He was loved and understood then as he can't be understood now: as a symbol of fertility, for we moderns are largely divorced of where our food and sustenance comes from, and cannot know the word *fertile* in a time when food is always plentiful and most of the young live rather than die. But Kokopelli can still be loved today as he was then, and understood then as he can still be understood now: as a representation of inconsequential sex; that is, the pursuit of it, and the lurid satisfaction of it, without consequence. For the pure joy of it. The only kind that doesn't hurt. What every age has dreamed off. And who better to represent it than the vagabond trader bearing rare and valued goods. For such a traveler has many opportunities, I know. I have seen the actual bowl, in a museum, that depicts my favorite Kokopelli. He's my man, and I put him in gilt imprint on the cover of my book. And inside the covers were nicely marbled, decorated endpapers, molded to fit by me, and on the first fly-sheet of the seventy pound richly textured natural bond I had inscribed in my very small, very precise hand: "Jason Niles -- his book." Of course this was a book of fiction but there was truth to it, I felt, nonetheless. And a very nice looking book of my own design and make, a very fine book, a far better looking book, a more substantial book, than the mass of cheap productions that come off the presses these days, and I felt I had every reason to be proud of it. As I often did at the end of a day, I reached over and took hold of my book, and handled it with pleasure. Then I exchanged it on the night stand for my current reading.

More correctly my current reading was for me a re-reading of a classic volume I hadn't looked at in years. The author, Will Comfort, was a story in himself. He had been a hack writer most of his life, a few flourishes of a larger, greater, talent, but mostly dated stuff you wouldn't read today for money. Then, late in life, he was inspired by a great and yet nearly incomprehensible man long since gone. The Apache chieftain, *Mangas Coloradas* (Red Sleeves), born in the mountains overlooking the Spanish copper mines, two days' ride west of the *Rio Grande* and not twenty miles from where I camped, rose from humble beginnings to capture control of his tribe of Apaches by virtue of unusual height and physical prowess, a force of personality and confidence arisen from a mystical nature, and a native statesmanship that could see beyond short term victory and defeat. He was, perforce, a dreamer, and yet a man of action, too. And, too, like any Indian of the time, he took women who didn't belong to him (all Apache women of the time belonged to somebody), married thrice for pleasure and power, using the polygamy to broaden and consolidate his political hold among various Apache tribes; and, once the whites brought in the firewater, was not above going off at times on a monumental drunk. Even shit-faced, they said, he had a certain dignity. Years after his death in 1863, and the death of his tribe, by the most shameless gringo treachery, cavalry officers who had known him were still talking about him with some awe, and left that feeling in memoirs of various literary worth. But it took a dreamer, a congenital sleepy-eyed boy with a wild edgy mind, to capture the

man for posterity.   And so Will Comfort, *reading* about Mangas
Coloradas, by a leap of faith *became* Mangas Coloradas for a time,
and told his story in words, with all it's romance, mystery and
shame, and collected his character on pages, with all it's honor and
contradiction, in a novel called *Apache*.   Comfort had always been
a dreamer; he found talent for his imagination, from out of nowhere
it seems, late in life.   And now I held this book once again in my
hands, a rare first edition, a "fine" copy, as we say in the trade,
with a "fine" wrapper.   A valuable book, priceless in its way, that I
would sell one day at a hefty profit.   But that night I read it myself
from the first edition, camped and comfortable in the land Mangas
Coloradas hunted, and roamed in flight from the soldiers; in the
land Will Comfort roamed in pursuit of the ghost of Mangas
Coloradas.   I knew by heart the good sentence that began the story:
"Two days' sun to the east of the Copper Mines was the Big
River," the author wrote.   A straight sentence, competent and
compact, unextraordinary on its own.   But once you'd read the
book you knew that was the only sentence that could start the story
right.   Outside a cold breeze glanced harmlessly off the windows.
Inside I read with pleasure until I fell asleep.

Chapter 2

There could be no doubt that I would stay a while in Del Cobre,
New Mexico.   How long I couldn't say, but I was going to give it a
go.   Less than a week in town, and I was already the proud owner
of a bookshop!   Well, I didn't own the shop, I rented it, but I
owned the books, and the rental on the shop was in the form of a
one-year lease so clearly I had made a commitment, of sorts.   Other
towns where I had tried to stay I never got so far as to open a shop.
I had worked some small business out of the bus as I had tried to
get a feel for the town, whether or not to stay, whether or not there
was a good opening for a shop.   Either the town didn't feel right, or
I couldn't find the shop.   Or maybe it was both.   Here, I had
stumbled into the shop straight away.   I knew it was a good deal as
soon as I knew I liked the town.   The landlord, a friendly codger in

a crotchety sort of way, peered over the top of half-glasses as he showed me around the shop and talked:

"You'll like Del Cobre," he said. "They's too many Mexicans but you'll like it. Everybody gets along. And you need to be *here* with your bookshop. You seen our town museum in that ol' building up the street?"

"Yes sir," I said. "I've seen the sign out front."

"That's the only thing to see and visit downtown, if you're a tourist. And you've been to the Piñon Cafe, down at the corner the other way?"

"Not yet," I said. "I'm going down there this morning."

"They's several good cafes downtown, as far as a good meal, but the Piñon's the only one that's got enough tone to draw a tourist. 'Course locals go there, too. But a tourist hasn't much choice. If it's downtown Del Cobre they're going to visit, they're going to visit the museum, then they're going to walk down the street to eat at the Piñon Cafe. Or they'll eat at the cafe and then it's the museum. They're three blocks apart and you're right in the middle so they're going to walk right by your bookshop either way. So this is the street you need to be on, and, what's more, you need to be on this side of the street."

"I guess I lucked out," I said.

"You damn right you did."

With a promotion like that I was surprised when his declaration of... "this is what you'll have to pay to do business here"...was followed by a number that approximated what one might expect to pay per month to park the bus in the alley behind the shop. And the price included the apartment -- the back room, in effect, of the shop -- between the shop and the alley, where I would live. It was a small "efficiency" apartment but it was still bigger than living in that bus. I held it in and said nothing as I counted out the first month's rent plus the deposit in cash but he was perceptive and added, "this ain't Santa Fe, you know."

"Or Scottsdale, either," I said.

That made him smile for the first time at something I, rather then he, had said.

"No, for sure it's not Scottsdale. And they ain't no charge to leave your bus in the alley out back...I just decided that."

He clearly liked being paid in cash and he hungrily stuffed the money in a pocket not knowing that I could have and would have happily paid a good deal more. But a book trader never bargains to hurt himself.

I started down the street to the Piñon Cafe. It was one of those early spring days in the Southwest when the sun arcs through the whole day without a cloud, the breezes are light, and it feels a little too warm when you have your coat on and a little too cool when you take it off. The streets were narrow and clean and the buildings were old with various brick or block or adobe construction with no two the same and in varying states of repair, or disrepair, and I'd seen enough of the shops and various mercantile affairs downtown to understand that no one was terribly busy in Del Cobre but no one appeared desperate either. This was a fair-sized town by the standards of rural New Mexico. There was a stoplight located at a strategic crossing here and there but there were no parking meters and you could park for as long as you wanted when you found a place. You wouldn't have to drive far to find a place and from there you could reach anything downtown in a walk. I could reach anything downtown in a walk from my shop and had no need of a vehicle downtown because there were a number of cafes, several bars, a bank, a grocery store, the post office, a stationary store, laundromat, and the like, all within a reasonable walk. All said, Del Cobre was just the right size -- maybe 10,000 people; it had the important physical and cultural amenities of a city, while retaining the more important social and cultural amenities of a town. It was the size every town in America would be, it we just knew when and how to stop. I stopped at the crosswalk to wait for the light before crossing the street to the Piñon Cafe. A police car, the only car at the crossing at that moment, pulled up; he had the green but he pulled up anyway and motioned me across against the light with a nod of his head and as I crossed in front of him he nodded again and raised a faint wave with an index finger like when you pass a rancher on a lonesome country road. This was my kind of town.

I bought a paper from the self-serve box outside and went into the Piñon Cafe. It was in an old adobe building but everything inside was new. You could see where what had been a large room had been walled off with half walls and arches and *vigas* to make three rooms which were something like indoor courtyards or *placitas*. The *vigas* were of a size that they must have been brought down from some old growth way up in the high-lonesome and the thickness of the walls and arches told you it was real adobe with the usual white-plaster covering which yielded a bright, pleasant Southwest motif more like what you'd expect in northern New Mexico or even Old Mexico itself. It was all new and clean and understated and well done and did have a certain "tone" like the codger said, and a glance at the menu showed a range of selections from traditional Mexican dishes to Bar-B-Q to standard middle-American cafe fare. Prices ranged from reasonable to downright cheap, there was a decent selection of beer and wine, and I knew that this was where I would come to eat most of the time. I ate a selection of *huevos rancheros* with tortillas and beans and strong coffee, and read the paper. It was a good fill with the added sauce of good appetite and then I walked back up the street. I had a week's work ahead before I could consider hanging the shingle out front of the Roadrunner Bookshop.

~ ~ ~ ~ ~

There was the matter of the floors. My shop had, or once had, fine hardwood floors, but they had become dreary with scuff marks, sunbleach, and the other declines that good wood can suffer from age, and I called a man in with the equipment to sand and refinish the floors. While he worked on the floors I worked on the walls. They were a good rough stucco but had been painted years ago a dull autumn tan which had gone into a sour brown color with age and dirt. I painted it all two coats of fresh white and got done about the time the man with the equipment got done with the floors. The white walls brightened the room and the stucco gave the southwestern flair while the floors were dark and solid and subdued and rather Victorian and with the refinishing you could read the wood. I bought two Mexican-style space rugs for the floors but otherwise let the wood be its own decoration.

I built the bookshelves myself. I got some pine, some good inch-and-a-half planks. It was not expensive wood but it had nice knots and swirls and whorls -- wood with character -- but would need the right stain to really bring it out. I put each shelf together

on the floor then hefted it up and bolted each to the stucco wall.
Then I built a long bookshelf to stand in the open space in the
room. When they were all up I gave each shelf two coats of oil
that brought out the difference in each plank and would preserve
the wood. The shelves were not so tall but what an average-sized
person could pull a book off the top shelf, and I got a three-legged
foot stool like you would set on to milk a cow for the short people
to stand on to reach the top shelf or anyone to sit on while perusing
a lower shelf. I left just enough room under the lowest shelves for
all those boxes filled with my manuscripts and literary works in
progress. I bought a small table that was underpriced from the
antique store around the corner and I put it where you'd see it
walking in the front door. This was for display books. I bought a
smaller antique table that was also underpriced from the same store
and put it in the one corner of the one-room shop that didn't have a
bookshelf. I put a small two-burner heating unit on the table with
a perk coffee pot on one burner and a whistling tea pot on the
other. The coffee pot would perk strong Mexican coffee with
chicory that you would smell when you walked in the room and the
tea pot would heat water that anyone could use to make the half
dozen varieties of teas that I would stock. I got the tea and several
cups. Real cups. That same antique store again provided a
compact easy chair that set to the side of the table with the coffee
and tea pots. It was a comfortable chair and had flat arm rests, the
kind of chair that someone who reads books wants to have for the
purpose. My codger landlord came by with a desk one day that I
might sit behind and I built a small shelf with a glass door up on
the wall over and behind this desk where I put my own book and
several other books -- those ultimate books -- that I would not part
with under any circumstances. And I put a variety of western art,
everything from Remington to O'Keefe reprints, on any wall that
was open and above the top shelves. Then I stocked the shelves
from what I had in the bus. Of course I won't have anything to do
with a telephone, or, worse yet, a television, but I did install a good
radio that, wired to a certain metal pipe coming down the wall,
picked up the Public Radio signal from far-away El Paso, nice and
clear. Then, out front one morning, I hoisted a middling-sized
wooden sign of a rustic motif I made myself. It said *Roadrunner*

Bookshop. Underneath what it said was the outline of one of those remarkable tough, taut, comical predatory birds that range the entirety of the Southwest and perhaps more than any fauna or flora you could name defines the region in boundary, image and character. It took all of a week for everything and when I was done I had a bookshop for booklovers, a fit compliment to what I would offer in books, a place where good books of the Southwest, and a special few from elsewhere, could be perused in pleasure whether you bought one or not. I had some hope that some would buy and a certain satisfaction that anyone who liked books would like the shop.

Chapter 3

In a month's time there was no great influx of people in the Roadrunner Bookshop. The codger came by one day and told me not to worry. He said that it was still snowbird season and snowbirds don't come to a town over a mile high in the winter. He told me that in a month or so it would start getting hot in the snowbird country of the Southwest and that then Del Cobre would look pretty good. "It always picks up in May," he said. That sounded reasonable but I wasn't worried. There wasn't a lot of tourist traffic but what there was went by the store from the museum to the Piñon Cafe -- or from the cafe to the museum -- just like the codger said they would, and some of them did stop in. There were more lookers than buyers but with a bookshop it's never any different anywhere. Some of the tourists did buy and now and again a local would come in too. They were even more inclined to look. Some clearly had never been in a used book store before, other than one stuffed to the ceiling with mass-market paperbacks and similar schlock, and more than one commented on the fact that most of my used books cost more than new books of a similar size. Of course size has nothing to do with it but I merely nodded, yes, and asked them where else they were going to find a copy of that title. That always gets them straight. And a few locals bought too, often someone from the college, or someone from one of the older local families, and usually upon spying a book that they'd heard about or read once long ago and that they were sure no longer existed anywhere. Then there would be a great focused interest on this book and a long story about how they'd been searching for this title for years and seldom then was price a problem. That's always fun for a book dealer. You put away the cash and feel at the same time like you just gave someone a present that no one else could provide. And I knew the reading would no doubt do most of them some good. There wasn't a lot of traffic in the shop but there was some, and at the end of the first month I had just about gathered in the rent. That was fine because I had other ways to make money from used-and-rare, antiquarian, and out-of-print books.

~ ~ ~ ~ ~

I had been an itinerant book dealer for a many years and was always behind in finding the particular books people wanted. I had always tried to serve that interest because it's fun, a kind of treasure hunt, to find a special book for someone, and it pays too and I had done a lot of it but I was always behind. I always had more requests than my search service could handle. Now with business slow and my work no longer on the road I had the time to work at my desk right there in the shop while most of the traffic went by the window. I rifled through my extensive collection of three by five cards carrying individual titles -- "books wanted" -- as well as the heaps of catalogs I've always got, and ads in the weekly Bookmans and other trade journals, and I ran some ads therein myself under "books wanted," and every day stacks of post cards went out with information to buy, sell or trade. I always work through the mail so it's slow but I wasn't in any hurry and by month's end I was getting hard-to-find books, and money for hard-to-find books I had found, every day in the mail. Too, I began to work up my first book list, another thing I never had time for on the road. My list of buyers was honed down to those who really want books and know the genre I work in and will pay for that special book. I began to work up a list of the best books I had. I had some awfully good stuff, individual books costing three figures and occasionally four figures, as well as very moderately priced books which were nonetheless unusual or unique in their way, some of the best of it in my storage in El Paso. I went down there one day in the bus and brought back fresh stock. On the list I described each book meticulously, as to condition and content and character. I had read almost all of them myself.

Those were leisurely days without much overt business which was fine. I would wake up early when the first light would ease through the one little high window in my apartment in the back of the shop. There was plenty of good, hot water and though the bathroom was scarcely large enough to turn around in it had one of those old deep tubs sitting up off the floor on clawed feet with a shower head above, if that was the choice, and I would soak in that tub, or shower, then shave, and about the right time walk down the street to the Piñon Cafe for breakfast. Maybe nine days out of ten the sky was sharp blue and cloudless and the overnight frost would be leaving fast that time of the morning. Once in a while when the wind was right, or I should say wrong, an acrid odor would be noticeable in the air. That was from the copper mine and smelter -- Felps-Dodd, Inc. -- south and west of town, I was told. I was also told by one resident that, "the pressure is really on the sons-a-bitches and they're going to have to clean it up." In a year or two, they said, not even an occasional whiff of acrid air would mar my morning walk to the Piñon Cafe. And that time of morning other people were up and about too, and folks coming downtown to shop, and merchants opening their shops, and people on sidewalks empty just a few hours before, but nobody ever seemed in any big hurry, no more than me. On the tenth day, give or take a few, the dark clouds would move in somewhere in a twenty-four hour span -- often at night -- and put some snow on the streets. Laying in bed early in the morning I would somehow know when snow had fallen though I couldn't see the ground out the high window without standing up. You can sort of feel it, and then the sun would hit the snow and the whole town was extra bright for a few hours till the snow burnt off. The Piñon Cafe was so handy sometimes I would round a block or two to get there, or take a longer walk up through the hilly, older part of town where all the brick Victorian houses were, where the Anglos lived; or through the hilly, older part of town where all the dirt adobe houses were, where the Mexicans lived. And up in the midst of the Victorian homes was the college. I'd make a walk there too, on occasion; it, too, offered more old buildings than new, the architecture appearing oddly more Mid-western than Southwestern for the most part, the pace very leisurely, not contentious, and all in all right out of the 1950s, my favorite decade. There couldn't have been more than 2,000 students, total, but half of them were women and at least half of them were something to look at. Pretty coeds. And some of their instructors were women and some of them were pretty too. That was worth a walk to the college now and again, and a certain anticipation. Whenever I would get to the Piñon Cafe for whatever meal the food was invariably good, the days in town cool to warm but never hot, and the nights cold, though you could feel spring coming on. I had been an itinerant bookseller for many years and as I settled into a new life in a kind of town I thought didn't exist anymore the relative leisure began to capture me and suddenly it seemed to me no great mystery why I had come here to try and find a home and maybe stay; I was so tired of being on the road.

Chapter 4

There was a striking elderly woman that I would see from time to time in the morning at the post office. She was tall and angular with faded jeans and a ranch shirt with pearl snaps instead of buttons and whatever hair she had -- you couldn't really tell how much -- tucked up underneath a battered felt hat. Despite the cowboy flair and masculine get-up there was no doubting this was a woman of still pleasing form, a fine looking woman, even if your first sight of her, like mine, was from a distance. She was very brown and weathered in the face with bright snappy blue eyes that would smile at whoever would smile or wave or say hello to her in passing, including me. What was most striking, she came to the post office horseback. I would see this sorrel animal standing on the grass just on the edge of the post office parking lot, sometimes saddled but most often not, with the reins hanging loose to the ground -- ground tied -- and no more inclined to wander off than a parked car with the emergency brake on. A little blue-heeler dog with longish hair and one blue eye and one brown was always close by with the horse, and where the horse would toss her head and nibble grass in her own little world the dog waited expectantly and oblivious to the rest of us for her master's return. Once I saw this woman standing by these animals while talking to someone, and the dog's eyes would go from one speaker to the next, like she understood every word, and it made sense that the old woman was the one with the horse and the dog. But for a long while I never could tell where she came from or where she went; she was always in the post office getting her mail out of the box or out front visiting and that horse standing there off to the side like she'd just been set there from above and another time. Then one day I stepped out of the post office with my mail and that old woman was swinging up on that horse, bareback. She was smooth and effortless and she grabbed the mane and mounted in one easy motion and reined her around and took her but a few steps; she reined her off into the trees that lined the creek, *Gavilán* Creek, that ran behind the post office through town. I walked over and she and that horse were already down in the creek bottom, the dog running alongside, the horse clip-clopping downstream in the water at a good trot. It wasn't much of a creek but over time it had made quite a deep ditch through town and it ran all year, I'd been told, and I watched her for a while but not for long because she and the horse and the little blue-heeler dog were soon lost in the trees along the creek.

~ ~ ~ ~ ~

About a week later she came into my shop. She didn't say anything right away but she smiled at me with those bright snappy blue eyes and began to peruse the shelves. She didn't have the battered felt hat on. She had pulled her gray hair back and tied it behind her head and it reached in waves halfway down her back. It had gone from near-black to mostly gray but it was thick and full as the hair of a young girl. You don't see that on an older woman. She was singular and tall and well formed and retained a certain athleticism and it was clear that in her time she had been a great beauty. Even with those bright eyes though there was a lot of age there and I took her to be past seventy years old. After a while she came over to the desk empty-handed and said, "Oh child, I've got a whole house-full of books like these."

Signal To Depart

~ ~ ~ ~ ~

I carried her directions carefully in my mind; they were simple enough. I walked east down the street three blocks, past the Piñon Cafe to the post office, and just to the south of that building I found the horse trail descending to the creek. It was nearing noon of a warm spring day full of sun but it was much cooler down under the trees along the creek. High up in mountains to the north the snowpack was feeling the warmth and the creek was running high and not quite clear. Still, it was just a creek and easy enough to follow down and where I had to change sides I could jump across or find a rock to step on and make it to the other side without getting my feet wet. A smattering of small trout and other fish would flit and flare away as my shadow and form crossed the creek. The trees were cottonwoods, hackberry, and willow, mostly, and it being well into spring they were leafed out that pale green so typical of young leaves, making a heavy shade in the creek bottom. There was all manner of bird life chattering along the way. Some were not happy with my intrusion on their spring nesting. I moved along steadily and didn't bother anyone. Early on in my walk there was some trash and other detritus along the creek, and graffiti written on the rocks and cliffs above -- the usual adolescent sexuality finding its usual crude literary release -- but as I worked my way south and east of town human sign dropped off and it was like I was up in the big woods in the big mountains to the north of town, where this flow of water came from. I would have been remiss not to note a certain literary connection. For it was in those mountains to the north that Aldo Leopold had marked out nearly a million acres that he felt should be kept forever wild. He had spent some time there himself, packing in horseback and hunting with self-made bow and arrow, and it was this wild country, the great range that fed the creek where I walked, plus his restored farm in Wisconsin and the then untrammeled Sierra Madre of Mexico, that had stimulated his fertile mind to produce the greatest literary work of American conservation, *A Sand County Almanac*. The book that explains why every community needs wilderness in juxtaposition. Of course I had read it time and again; indeed I had my own copy, a first edition inscribed and signed by the man himself. Not inscribed to me alas (that would have been quite impossible), but inscribed nonetheless and one of the few books I would never sell. And just as surely I had never been into the great wilderness to the north that fed the little creek, or any place like it. It wasn't like me to have an adventure in such a place, but I felt a connection to it, and to its literary spokesman, as I walked the shady creek it fed.

As well, early in the walk, when I had stopped to listen, I had heard the sounds of the town above the lip of the ditch; but then that fell away too. I took my time and it seemed a pleasantly long walk. In fact I couldn't have gone much over a mile when I stepped over a barbed wire fence and soon the walls of the little canyon began to break away from the creek and I could see there was open land out beyond the trees and running water. I left the creek and stepped out from under a big cottonwood and there was the valley held gently between ragged cliffs, not high, to the left and right, and the rolling hills beyond and all stretching away downstream to the south and east. I wasn't a mile from town and it was like I had traveled way out Beyond The Divide to the Big Country. A rich narrow ribbon of trees and growth, more spaced out now, followed the creek on down, and on either side a strip of the valley floor was flat and green. This was a typically dry spring in the Southwest and the apparatus of controlled irrigation was not present along the creek. It was natural sub-surface irrigation that made the narrow strip of green. Just out of the bottom, at the next level, a shelf of land followed the contours of the creek, between the creek and the cliffs, on down. This shelf of land was mostly open with patches of piñon and juniper and scrub oak and mesquite here and there, growing in clumps and rubbing up against the cliffs. And above the cliffs, not high, the rolling hills were great shouldering grasslands on to the south and east and west, with a piñon, juniper, oak or yucca here and there to wart the ridgelines. Behind me, the great *Mondragón* Range loomed snow-capped, blue-black and forested. On a far hill to the southwest, a large building, more than a house, was visible, but nothing else human was in conflict with the natural landscape.

I followed the creek on down, in the bottom between the creek and the cliffs, in the kind of reverie a dreamer knows who has wandered into a great surprise. For a time a pair of great dark birds, rare Mexican Black Hawks, came out flapping from their high cottonwood nest and scolded a sharp-pitched, prolonged and unmusical note over my head. But I liked it. I knew all about them, as I have studied every book ever published on Southwestern birds. But I had never seen a Mexican Black Hawk before. I couldn't take my eyes off the scolding, soaring hawks, until the voice came out from well across the valley behind me: " Oh honey, I'm over here!"

I crossed the bottomland and up the slope onto the shelf of land that ran along and against the low cliff and jumbled rocks and in a nook there was the low rambling adobe home. A wall of adobe about hip high to keep the stock out -- though it didn't work for all the bright, colorful chickens -- encircled the front of the home with a swing gate opening into the *placita* shaded by two enormous cottonwoods under which she had returned to sit in the shade with a tall glass of iced tea. I came through the gate and that little blue-heeler dog was beside her and growled and was going to take me head on when the old woman said, "Stop that, he's a friend!" I never had much use for dogs or cats or anything you might call a pet, but this blue-heeler herd dog was impressive. So far as I could tell she had no name. But just as surely she waited knowingly and patiently out front at the post office and now, as well, she heard and understood just what the old woman said as she lay down and put her head on her paws by the old woman's chair, that quickly comfortable with the presence of a stranger. And then the old woman was smiling at me with those bright eyes and she said, "Honey, you would have walked to Mexico if I hadn't of caught you."

Her hair was down but this time not tied in the back but just down over her shoulders and beyond and it was even more evident that this had been a woman of enormous beauty who retained a certain loveliness and a singular style. I couldn't argue with what she said and I was a little sheepish saying, "Jason Niles," and I introduced myself to "Claire Callahan." Her hand was large and strong and callused, her grip firm, and she had my iced tea there for me on the small table at the other chair and I sat down.

"This is all so lovely," I said, a bit dazzled.

Signal To Depart

She threw her head back and cracked a wonderful spontaneous laugh in seeming great joy and surprise and said, "Darlin', Bingo would never say it that way, even if he liked the place."

"Bingo?"

"My son. Don't think we named him that. His name is Clemson, same as my husband. He's dead. He was always Clemson but our son was Clem to most people. Then my husband died and Clem started all his business hereabouts. Started as a young man. He makes jackpot deals, most all good ones, for himself. After one big jackpot folks started calling him "Bingo." I wasn't happy about it at first but Clem, he liked it. And, well, it does fit him. So I call him Bingo now, too. It's a shame but I do. He would never say *lovely*; not on his life. You would be about his age."

I was still cooling off in the shade from the walk and I drank half a glass of tea and said, "What sort of deals?"

"It's land, honey. He buys it, develops it -- that's what he calls it -- sells it. He has apartments in town, too. You hear that?"

I'd been hearing a deep distant engine noise way off to the southwest that would come and go with the breeze and I nodded my head and said, "sounds like a dozer."

"That's Bingo's D-8 cat. That's his project these days. Over the hills here behind the house is the city dump. They say landfill nowdays but it's a dump. Sometimes you'll hear a dozer run there too but that's not Bingo. Over the next hill is the southwest pasture of the old ranch. Only it's not part of the ranch anymore. After Clemson died...some years after...we sold it off for the country club -- you probably saw it off that way, up on the hill -- and the golf course...nine holes. It was Bingo had me do it. And then the pasture between went to the city for the dump. That's when I wouldn't sell any more, not even for Bingo. Anyway, Bingo has that dozer and it's a big 'un. He got the contract for the landscaping for the club and all the nine holes, then he got the contract to build the club plus what we got for the sale of the land...it sure wasn't worth that for pasture. Now he's got a housing development going over there, just off where they play that silly game. He's clearing and leveling for new housing and all those double-wides folks like to live in nowdays. That's what you've been hearing. One thing about Bingo, he gets out and does it. He's all *go*. He has plenty of hired help and some of them can run a dozer too, but not like Bingo. Callahan Construction at work! He could carve a sculpture with that dozer, if he ever had that in mind. But he won't be making any sculptures. He'll be making jackpot deals. And uncovering surprise treasures where and when he can with that machine."

"A pot hunter?"

"Honey, The People were all over this country, up and down this valley and along the other waters from the Willow River over east to the *Rio Jalisco* over west. Bingo knows what to look for and he can just *peel the surface* on the first pass with that machine. He has took home lots of treasures The People left behind but his big jackpot is turning the land into something where people today can live. I can't imagine living that near with other folks myself but over the hill here he has several parcels sold already, and the double-wides to go with them. Seems like lots of new folks moving in these days. And he gets it all himself ever since he broke off with his partner, Jensen, because he cheated him."

"Jensen cheated your son?"

"No, my son cheated Jensen. That's Bingo."

The wind had come around and though I tried I could no longer hear the dull roar of the dozer. I said, "What's left of the place here?"

"A quarter section plus forty acres. It runs all along the creek here and up in the foothills on either side and that includes the house and barns."

"Two hundred acres."

"And one hundred acre feet of water right. Nobody but Felps-Dodd and the city itself has that kind of water right around here."

This was all coming fast and open and almost unbidden. It seemed but one more question was just hanging there in the air that would round out the story. I said, "Does Bingo want the rest of the ranch for the other nine holes and some more of those double-wides?"

Again she threw her head back with a certain style and produced a great musical laugh. "That's Bingo," she said. Then she turned to me and said, "Oh honey, it was a wonderful ranch. I came out here with my folks in 1919. We came in from Oklahoma with all we owned in a mule-drawn wagon, the rest of the animals and us kids trailing behind. People now don't think anyone came West that late in a wagon but we did...lots of folks did. I had two older brothers. During the twenties each one died in his own way. During the thirties momma and poppa died too. I was late -- they were older when they had me -- so it's not like they didn't have a full life. And I had married young and Clemson and I, we stayed on. We started here with about what we have now -- just a homestead. Through the thirties and forties and fifties, little by little, we added twenty sections. Not a big ranch but big enough for us. Some years we didn't make much money. Some years we didn't make any. But we had a milk cow, and beef, and a few hogs and goats, chickens and eggs and the fruit trees you see over there in front of the barn and a big garden full of vegetables and a corn crop and hay crop and permanent pasture down in the bottom there. How much money do you need? We moved the cattle around and moved the crop around and raised grass as much as cattle and never pushed it too hard. Today it's too many living-room ranchers."

"Living-room ranchers?"

"That's where they do most of their ranching, darlin'. There, or driving around in a pickup or talking over coffee in the cafe. They let their cattle gather around the tanks and water holes and along the creeks and don't take the time horseback to move them around. We were herders, me and Clemson and my friend Santos; one of us was out with those cattle most all the time. We slept on the ground with them. And imagine having all that cattle and then buying your beef in a store! But that's what they do anymore. And that's where they get their eggs and vegetables and fruits. Imagine you have even just a few acres and not have a garden, or go and buy your meat and eggs and milk in a store! So many have come to be just like city folks. And they's lots of ranches now where them that own the ranch don't even live on the place. So many have lost their roots in the land and they show it plain enough. And the land shows it too."

"Your place here is pretty as a picture," I said.

"We never managed for this year's money. We managed for the long haul. And we had but one child, my Bingo. But Bingo, he never liked the ranch. He's a hard worker, terrible hard, and he was doing a man's work when just a boy. He's good with machinery but we didn't have much machinery; we had horses and mules and one old tractor. Bingo loved that tractor but he would lose his temper with those animals. An animal, even an old draft horse you worked all his life, is a little different every day, just like a person. Bingo couldn't ever understand that. He can make a machine do what he wants but you have to get to know an animal and treat him soft or hard, depending, to get him to work. Bingo would abuse an animal so he wouldn't work at all. By the time he was twelve years old he could abuse an animal pretty bad. Clemson would whip him and he would sull for days but he never was any different with stock. I don't know what we did wrong but with most kids nowdays they're mindless and aimless and you wish they had some direction, but with Bingo it was just the opposite thing. He was pulling away and bulling ahead with his own direction when he was still just a kid and this little ol' ranch wasn't near big enough for him. Then Clemson, my husband, he died. Killed in a horse wreck right over there by the barn. The horse went over backwards with him and squished his breastbone under the horn. Clemson and I was already losing control of Bingo and after Clemson was gone nothing I said meant anything. And Bingo was seventeen and just out of school and he could see already you can only make so much money off a ranch. They's no limit to what he can make now, as far ahead as he can see. I thought when he married that nice girl it might help. She's ranch raised and she used to come out here all the while and visit me and she's a hand, too. We had a wonderful time. I felt she was like a daughter to me. But she's not my daughter, she's Bingo's wife. She doesn't come out much anymore. After the baby came, the first year or two, she'd come out once a week to bring that little girl to see her grandmother. Oh, honey, she's a darling little girl, all curly red hair and blue eyes like her mother. But if I see her these days it's generally that I go there. They have that fancy brick home in town now, with a furnace in the basement and sprinklers to keep the lawn green all year and that big tub on the porch where they sit for hours steaming in a swirl of water without taking a bath."

"A hot tub."

"That's what they call it, honey. Anyway, after Clemson got killed I kept Santos on and we ran it full time for a good while, till Santos and Bingo had that run-in and Santos had to leave. I'm still here and I'm down to nine cows with calves, these chickens you see, and one milk cow...just because I've done it twice a day long as I can remember and that raw milk makes my stomach feel better. And a little garden, and my one horse. She can still work a little but I can't hardly anymore. I've got plenty to do, not much time, and Bingo looks after me in his way. And now you! I go to the post office or the store and I hear there is a new man in town with a bookstore but there must be more than that. Tell me what you've done. Tell me about your family."

I waited until she had refilled her glass and mine from the pitcher on the table. The sun was going behind the hill behind the house and it was just pleasantly cool with a light breeze that would ruffle the feathers of one of those colorful chickens perched on the hip-high adobe wall. The blue-heeler dog was down on all fours and quiet but worked her eyes to look intently and with seeming understanding at whoever talked. Now and again the drone of that dozer would float in from the southwest and then the breeze would come around and you couldn't here it anymore. I drank tea and said, "There's not much to say about my family...I don't know much about family, at all. My folks...well...I always had the feeling that somehow I wasn't what they had in mind. But when I was still a youngster in grammar school I would check books out of the school library and read them in math class, in social studies class, in English class. Once in a while in English class we would be assigned a book I liked and then I would know it better than anyone. But day by day I would read and read what I liked and neglect what I didn't like and no one could stop me. Otherwise I never was hard to get along with. But my friends were books and I read what I liked and it caused trouble, at home and at school, because I neglected everything else. I was living in a big city, so of course I read mostly about life in the West and the Great Outdoors. Nothing that was happening in my life could equal it. Even before

Signal To Depart

I left I was a kid on the run with trappers and cowboys and Indians and hunters and homesteaders making a life on the land. Well, somehow I made it to high school for a year or two. I began to try to write books of my own and to send stuff to the school paper and write for magazines, hoping I could sell what I wrote, and I began to trade books in order to get other books I wanted to read. No one wanted to buy my writing and even the school paper had no use for what I had to say, but it was a great revelation to me when I found I could buy, sell and trade books and acquire a volume I wanted and still mark a profit or at least a valuable asset at the end of the deal. I knew a good book and could trade it for a profit well before I was of legal age. So there I was in school, trading books at a profit and finding the books I wanted to read and I'm thinking: why should I be spending my time doing anything else? I had acquired an old car and I knew enough about cars to keep it running and one day when I was just about old enough to have a driver's license I loaded it with all my books and went out on the road. I never looked back. I went from a car to a pickup to a bus now, operating from Houston to L.A. and up into Oklahoma, Colorado and Utah. I cover the ground and buy, sell or trade books. I like small towns and work them whenever I can. But I have to work the big cities too. I make my way around, from bookshop to bookshop, to estate sales and to private dealers, and I work book fairs and gun shows and the like and I buy books and I have them shipped to my post office box in El Paso. I also have warehouse space there, to hold my stock. El Paso is right in the middle of the Southwest and I go through from time to time and refill the bus with books and get the mail. I've got some five thousand volumes in stock there, I can carry another thousand with me, and I've got a personal collection of two thousand volumes, also at the warehouse, that I keep for myself, though there's just a few of them I wouldn't sell at the right price. That's what I've done. Now I've got a homestead of my own, not to compare with yours, but I've got a shop and a place to camp in the back room. I hope to stay awhile. Not much of a life, once you get beyond the books."

She was looking at me intently and smiling and she said, "Would you like to see mine?"

We went into the house. She told me how they had built it themselves, told me when, and said it was "shabby but solid and it's home." There was electric and a fridge and a good wood stove and some gas space heaters for heat, but the sink was just one faucet with gravity feed from the windmill and the tank, hot water was what you heated on the stove, and the bathroom was the backhouse located, not surprisingly, out back. "Bingo offers to bring the plumbing inside but there's no reason to change now," she said. In the living room were the books.

She had about 500 volumes in good condition or better on nice shelves that she explained had all been purchased or acquired by her husband. It was mostly Western Americana, though very few "Westerns," per se, which suited me, and there was also a rare array of old agriculture books, from beef husbandry to fruit farming, poultry, hogs, various crops, soil health and regeneration, homesteading in an arid land and a variety of others from the days before factory farming and agri-business. Indeed, the entire library dated back to before he was killed by a horse and so by their age the run of books had good value for that reason alone. She had made a list of each and every book -- title, author and publisher and year of publication. I took the list and told her I'd look it over and come back with a price.

"Clemson bought them and read them and I never paid much attention," she said. "He was the thoughtful one. All I did was work. But these last years, I find I like to read, especially things that happened around here."

"Mrs. Callahan, if I take your books, we'll make some good books from my shop part of the trade. You can come by and pick whatever you like."

"Oh I need something new to read," she said.

We drifted back into the kitchen where she opened the fridge and handed me a quart bottle of milk. It was one of those old quart milk bottles used back when milk was delivered to your door, with a round cardboard stopper for a cap and the cream was thick in the top third of the bottle just like you used to see back when it was real milk, not pasteurized, and was delivered house to house. She said, "You take this, honey. She's a Guernsey and she gives just the best, richest milk. It's been so good for me these last years but it's gotten now where it doesn't help much anymore." Outside, under the cottonwoods, the breeze had come up and the shade from the hill behind us was starting across the valley. The great blue-black *Mondragón* Range to the north overlooked everything; there was nowhere on the place you wouldn't know it was there. The Mexican Black Hawks had returned to their tree and lay hidden at their nest but there were half a dozen ravens down on the flat, flapping around and squawking over something. I could see three deer near the cottonwoods along the edge of the field and a number of jackrabbits had appeared and were feeding along the flat north of where the ravens were flapping around. You couldn't hear the dozer at all, couldn't hear anything but the sound of the wind in the trees and those ravens squawking but the wind was bringing a few early cottonwood seeds down around us, fluffs of white you could see but hardly feel; one in a billion would produce a giant. Lovely was the word, but if it came to her as it came to me right then, she, like me, was too self-conscious to say it. She did say, "You know darlin,' The People were right here before us. All up and down *Gavilán* Creek but especially right along in here. They knew this was the best place to be, even back then. If you walk up the first side canyon on the way back, the first one on this side of the creek, you'll see. Look along those rock walls. Some of it is not so nice, I suppose, but who are we to say?"

I told her I would stop at the side canyon and look for the signs The People had left. I turned and gripped her hand and then stepped away as I thanked her and told her I'd be back with the price.

"Oh child, do," she said. "And come soon...I'm with cancer you know."

I turned away from the woman and the dog who sat alert and close and noble and faithful beside her and started down the hill.

~ ~ ~ ~ ~

Though the evening shade was well along, the petroglyphs and pictographs of the Ancient Ones, "The People," were readily visible on the rock walls up the side canyon. These were reddish granite rocks which, when chipped and rubbed a certain way with other rock, left pale markings of a life before our time. Along a twenty foot span of flat rock wall the Ancient Ones had left a variety of hieroglyphics, the meaning of which could be known only to them, and a number of more literal signs depicting that which interested them and which could be interpreted even now. Clearly, natural history and hunting was of interest, as deer, bighorn sheep, and stylized hares were in evidence, some alone, others in a relationship of pursuit by curious stickmen armed with bows, throwing sticks, and other weapons. And near the end of the wall was a large, ancient *objet d'art* that by a certain modern viewpoint was, to be sure, "not so nice." Here, art had been produced not with rock scratchings on rock but by application of a kind of home-made paint of a dark reddish hue. Wind and rain had been at work for a thousand years yet nonetheless in the cover of overhanging rock there was clearly that fellow Kokopelli again, his ardent cock fully erect. Facing him off, also standing and ready to receive his tumescent urge, was the object of his desire, a woman whose raised arms and bent legs indicated this was no pliant, indulgent female, but rather an active lover, eager for consummation. The forms showed an aching lust; the faces a hint of fright. Tantalizingly, they did not quite touch. It is generally acceded that the art of the ancient *Mimbreños* was largely if not entirely woman-made. I looked at a love scene for ancient or modern times in which the urgent organ and eager forms depicted neither a fanciful, cheap, nor overly hopeful male or female fantasy; but rather, I felt certain, a true depiction of the awesomeness and power of the act itself. The lovers were not quite there. They would be soon. It could be great; it could be a peck of trouble.

At the end of the wall, and lower down, some modern artists with considerably less skill, thought and perception, had mocked and mimicked, in words and pictures, the rich pornography of the Ancients with white, store-bought, paint. There wasn't much to look at there but, mercifully, none of the ancient art had been directly compromised. I took my eye back to lovers who had no written language, then back down the wall as I followed the canyon's return to the creek. Soon, in the gathering dark, I was opening the door to my bookshop and home.

Chapter 5

Sometimes young women would come into my shop. This would draw my attention from whatever I was doing, even if what I was doing involved a good book. As with any customer, I would be carefully polite, suggesting by tone more than lengthy explanation that I would be helpful if they were looking for a particular title, while not pressing upon them should they prefer to browse. Meanwhile I would just as carefully look them over. And I'd hope for something of that transcendent appeal that would enrich any physical attraction. Looking them over was sometimes good, but that transcendent appeal was hard to find, especially when their disappointment became evident to me, upon their realization that I was selling a literary heritage based on a time and way of life that was largely gone, and that I had no romance novels, no "best-seller" trash, nor -- even worse -- any of that self-help, coping, or new-age effluvia that modern American women, and men, seem addicted to that they might make it through to the following day. With one exception...

This woman was not looking for romance novels, a best-seller, self-help, coping, or new-age effluvia. She came into the shop as a graduate student in American literature, one of a handful of students in the masters-in-literature program at the college, and she came in seeking books in the one field the college program seemed oddly remiss in promoting -- the literature of the Southwest. "My professor told me there is no such thing as Southwest literature," she said to me on her first visit to the shop. "He said: 'Southwest books, yes, Southwest literature, no...but don't waste your time on *regional* material.'" She allowed as how she wanted to believe he was incorrect. Her name was Carla Aguilar and she was particularly interested in Hispanic literature of the Southwest, not so much books about Hispanics, most of which, she knew, are written by Anglos, but books of the region by Hispanic authors. She herself being of Hispanic descent, I was particularly pleased to tell her that her professor was quite simply full of shit and invited her to quote me in his presence if she liked. And if she didn't I no doubt one day would. I took her around the shop and pointed out a number of Southwest volumes that were literature in anyone's language, and that were "regional" literature only in the sense that the narratives therein had to take place somewhere. I told her that the literature of the region was, recently, particularly fertile of Hispanic authors, and as I happened to have a some good titles on hand, I made a sale. We had plenty to talk about and not all of it, I could tell, would be congenial. I detected in her conversation a certain correct political stance and race consciousness that afflicts so many of the young of "minority" status today; and that, I'm sure she could detect from my conversation, I would be happy to challenge. I got the feeling she would as happily accept that challenge. She was interesting. She was pretty -- soft and brown with wondrous dark eyes behind horn-rimmed glasses that made them look even bigger, and splendid straight dark hair that went way-way down in the back.. She was bright, feisty in a guarded, soft-spoken sort of way, with plenty of spunk. She was somewhat overweight and moved very carefully on her feet, as if not quite sound, which vulnerability didn't bother me a bit and which in fact I felt in her was becoming and ultimately could be very fine indeed. She spoke without the trace of what an Anglo would call a Mexican accent, yet in a vaguely formal way that largely avoided modernisms and almost like she was translating from some romance language as she went along. By the time she walked out the door with the first of her books I was fairly desperate to have her.

Bless her, she came back. A couple of times. And we talked books and authors and literature and pretentions of literature and she agreed with me about half the time. In honest conversation, this is about all you can expect. And the second time she stayed past closing, the streets outside the shop window got quiet as the cars and horns subsided, and the stray foot traffic disappeared as dusk came on and downtown Del Cobre mostly went home.

"Would you join me for supper?" I asked her.

She looked at me for a moment without tipping her hand. "If I buy mine and you buy yours...I don't want a boyfriend."

We walked down the street to the Piñon Cafe. It was almost dark. The cafe was perhaps half full and we got a table out of the way of anyone, so we could talk. She ordered wine and I got a beer. I told her the flat, beef enchilada plate, with red chili and sour cream and an egg was the top of the line for me at the Piñon Cafe. She said the cheese enchilada plate with green chili was the top of the line for her. And she added: "I'm a vegetarian."

"That's too bad," I said

"I don't think I miss anything. I'm just more comfortable with a diet free of meat."

"Denying yourself meat is like denying yourself sex," I said. "You can do it with a mind stretch but your body will still know something's not there."

"Well, I'm not comfortable with sex anymore either," she said. I said, "I'm sorry to hear that, too."

We told the waitress what we wanted, with and without meat, from the menu. While we waited we had the wine and beer to amuse ourselves and we dipped chips into the *muy picante* salsa that centered the table.

"Why don't *you* write? she said.

"I have a book," I said.

"What's it called...do I know it?"

"It's privately printed," I said. "A special book, literally made by hand. A collector's edition. It's not available yet to the public."

"I'd like to read it."

"Maybe someday you will...and what about you? Will you write?"

"Reading those books makes me ask myself the same question," she said, showing some facility of her own for evading direct response. "I knew of some of the people you told me to read but I was made to see them as *regional* writers. Their works do not qualify for class instruction and I was encouraged not to read them. As if I would lose the ability to know good writers from bad if I read them."

"Well, now you know they're good. Which ones do you like the best?"

"Of what I have read so far, I like the Fabiola Cabeza de Vaca book, and everything by Rudolfo Anaya."

"Excellent choices. Fabiola captured the Hispanic rural/pastoral ambiance while it still flourished, and she captured it very well. The work is a bit dated by sentimentality, but this is perhaps inevitable for the time. And Anaya of course is a great talent. The thing you have to watch out for, with many of the modern *minority* writers, is the touch and tone of the *victim* running through the work -- that simpering, angst-ridden character known as the *whiner* who is just sure the world has singled him or her out for servitude and endless trouble just because your ethnic this or ethnic that. I hope you'll avoid that put-upon air when it comes your turn to write."

She flushed at this, the anger showing right up through her brown skin, and her dark eyes flared, as she chose to react to the ethnic swipe rather than my plans for her as a writer.

"Maybe there are victims whose stories need telling," was all she could muster in response.

"There was a time when that argument would hold up," I said. "But with all the programs and special deals in place to compensate, I can't imagine there would be too much to complain about now. Besides, that put-upon air tends to rob a good story."

"The achievement of any Hispanic who succeeds in the Anglo world involves overcoming many obstacles that you could know nothing about. This land was all ours; now you have it."

"Let's dust that one off. The way I see it, there are more indulgences than obstacles facing the minority individual today. And the indulgences may in fact be the more debilitating. But the question remains...did the greedy, aggrandizing Anglos take it, or did the passive, feckless Hispanics let it get away?"

"Maybe it was some of both. To compete with you we would have to be like you, and maybe we don't want to."

"I would hope that you wouldn't," I said. "But here's the thing. North of the border, this is an Anglo world. If you want to succeed, you have to be just as smart and tough as the honky next door. That's success in the economic realm. Socially, culturally, you can still be whatever you want; it's a free country after all. And of course it's all in decline. Look at our youth. For white youth, American culture is MTV, the worship of unwashed, anemic looking men with stringy hair and wielding a nihilistic message and phallic guitars. I would take country music over that. It's sappy, maudlin and has gone uptown, but at least it's not degrading. For black youth the heroes are sinister dudes in baggy pants who rap mindless, vicious, ultimately self-destructive anger. The heritage of black music in America is rural gospel, and jazz; there is soul, passion, and compassion there, the very contradiction of this urban hate music. They moved to the big city and within two generations they're pissing on everything, including themselves. And then we have our exhalted *Native Americans*. Christ, the whining and simpering that gathers around that gasbag of ethnicity. I mean, these were people worthy of respect and study, in a kind of rough harmony with the natural world, living off the land without changing it much. We all could learn something from their lives, and the culture of the hunter/gatherer. But that was some time ago. Now we have *reservation* Indians. *Sovereign nations* they call them. Sovereign welfare enclaves is more like it. Never has so much been given by so many to so few. And with so little result. The indulgences are killing them. And what about you folks? The heritage of Fabiola Cabeza de Vaca lost their land, went to the big city, and now Hispanic culture is losing the *vaquero* and the *corrida,* and is replaced by the *cholo* or *pachuco,* a weird dude, almost as sinister as his black counterpart, with clown clothes and a goofy hat, driving a boom box with a clearance that renders it useless. Sell your land, lose your language, buy a car! And then we have my own ethnic group -- the *Anglo*?, *Euro-American*? -- who knows what to call us? We tend to do well, in an economic sense, so what we whine about is ourselves, spending all that money on self-help books that presume to tell us how to cope, or make love, or make money, and looking in the mirror all the while. Coping. Coping with what? Coping with stress. The only real stress is deprivation. Most of us have never known it...and you know where it all went wrong?"

"I can hardly wait for you to tell me."

"When the country went to the city, when the urban overtook the rural. Time was when a kid had a normal life, whatever the race, with both folks at home and chickens to feed and a crop to gather, running the fields with a frog in his pocket and hunting and paling around with the family dog. Like *Old Yeller...*"

"*Old Yeller*? she broke in, and behind her glasses her wonderful dark eyes were even bigger now, with both anger and incredulity showing at my extended diatribe, flip provocations, and apparent lowering of the literary echelon, "I think I saw the movie when I was a kid."

"That was Disney. It was all right but I'm talking about ol' Fred Gipson's book. I read *Old Yeller* when I was a kid. But it's not just a kid's story, and it's not just a dog story. That was a family. And a life on the land rendered true by the writer. I think maybe the woman was the real hero, her grit and grace as she took care of that family while the old man had to be away. There was the life I wanted when I was a kid -- the adventures and the lessons growing up -- and still don't know much about. And I probably never will. That was frontier, and nobody wants to go back to that, strictly speaking. But *something* of that life could be retained. Something good. I somehow never had much use for dogs myself, but if I ever have a son I'm going to read him *Old Yeller*. And give him a hound-dog puppy. One of those old-timey kind of hound-dogs, with sad eyes and lots of loose skin and ears down to here -- looks like he left his brains in his socks -- and faithful and constant as the rising sun. If every kid in America had a dog like that to hunt with and pal around with and run the fields with, why, we'd all be a lot better off. But kids don't grow up with a hunting dog anymore, or with a field to run in, or chickens to feed, or a horse to ride, or a crop to gather, or a pond to fish in, or anything else that connects them with the natural world. Instead, they grow up with video games, and that goddamn MTV. No wonder the country's going to hell in a handbasket."

"You are very harsh," she said. But I noticed as I was spouting off and being flip that her flaring eyes softened somewhat and had mixed with a slight smile, especially toward the end when I got on that hound-dog kick, and she continued, "and you are a terrible curmudgeon, an uncompromising elitist, and an unrepentant racist and a misanthrope. But at least you have divided your venom up, so everybody gets some."

"I demur only partially," I said. "I am a terrible curmudgeon and am sometimes sorry. I'm an uncompromising elitist and not the least bit sorry. The masses need an aristocracy of merit and good taste to show the way, at all levels of society. Sadly, that aristocracy is now almost against the law, ruled out by autocratic egalitarianism that's rooted in the most common ways of life. And of course the masses, less well off and poorly educated, overbreed and overpopulate, compounding all social, economic and environmental ills. Of course I'm an elitist. As for the racist/misanthrope label, I think I am not, at least not in the sense commonly applied. In fact, as I dislike the human race, *en masse*, I equally dislike all races, *en masse*. But within each race is a heritage worth preserving, and any number of great talents and beautiful human beings."

She let that all soak in a moment, then continued: "And," she said, "I think you are quite a whiner yourself -- whining about everybody else."

This made me smile, because of course she was absolutely right.

Our plates came and we went after it with relish. For it was awfully good. Certainly mine was. The enchilada offered rich layers of beef, cheese, blue corn tortilla, topped by sour cream and an egg, and of course that savory red chili. The waitress had told us the red was hotter than the green. I could only hope for her sake the green was no hotter than the red. It brought sweat to my brow, cleared my nose right up to the sinuses, and threatened to blister my lips. God yes!...it was in fact just what I'd ordered and hoped to receive.

"So what will you write?" I said, refilling her glass.

"You expect me to know?"

"Yes."

"Until a few weeks ago I could only hope that I might teach some day, talking about writing to students. I never thought that I would write myself."

"A lot's happened in the last few weeks. You've read some new books and had some new thoughts, I know. A good book can do that to you. That's why I'm in the business. That's the good I do in this world...disseminate good books that give people a new, or maybe an old, look at things, and maybe get them started on something good."

She went back to her meal and she was thinking, I believe, about how much she might want to give away, and then she said: "I have thought about something that I might write."

"Tell me."

"It wouldn't be like a regular book. I mean I think of a regular book as when the author tells a story, a kind of narrative, drawn from her own life. I don't think I've lived enough to have much of a story to tell but someone I know well has had a very interesting life. He's my uncle. He's an old man and the doctors give him pills for his heart that he won't take, but still he's spry and sharp and he can sit by the fire or under the shade of a tree and tell the most wonderful stories from his life. He's been a *vaquero* in Mexico and all around here, too. He also worked in big cities and he's worked in the mines, working underground, not the strip mines of today. He can recall a time as far back as what Fabiola Cabeza de Vaca wrote of, and yet he's still alive and knows our time, too. So he is a link between what is now and what is gone forever. My thought is that I could let him talk to me as he has since I was a little girl. He talks to me in English and in Spanish and I would just let him talk only now I would write it down or record it some way and when I had it I would weave it together into a book of some sort. I guess I would be more of an editor than a writer. A chronicler with perhaps some literary license thrown in. But do you think something like that could be a book?"

"It's as good a way to make a book as any. Sounds like rich material."

"Think so...?"

"Yes, I do."

"He is a fascinating man to me. He's a natural story-teller. And he's a great spirit. And wouldn't you know, his name is Santos."

At the name, it was my turn to pause to eat. And I finished my meal, as did she, without saying anything more. Then we ordered another round. I considered that in this part of the world the name Santos could not be so uncommon. But then I couldn't recall having heard it much, even in the Great Southwest. And that was just recently. And Del Cobre was a small town. She had noticed something.

"Do you know him?" she said finally. "His name is Santos Aguilar."

"I don't know him. And it's probably nothing. But the name Santos came up in a conversation I had last week."

"A conversation with whom?"

"Mrs. Callahan, the woman who comes to the post office horseback."

She gave her head a nice little turn and rolled her wonderful eyes. "Well," she said, "there you have life in a small town!"

I said, "Mrs. Callahan told me about having a hired man, Santos, at her ranch after her husband died. Then she said something about a *run-in* between this Santos -- she never said a last name -- and her son, Bingo. She said Santos didn't work there anymore after that."

"It was a *run-in* all right," she said. Then she paused, knowing, I believe, that if she told me even a little, she was going to end up telling me an awful lot. She took a little more wine and said, "Do you want to hear all this?"

"I'd like to hear whatever I can about that woman. She's a great one. And your uncle sounds like a piece of work himself."

"Well," she said, "the outline of the story is pretty well known to the whole town -- at least anyone who's been around that long -- so you may as well hear it from me, because I know it as it really happened...

"My grandparents owned a small ranch south of town...south and east of where the country club is now, just over a couple of hills and east from the Callahan ranch. And part of the ranch bordered the Callahan ranch. After my grandparents died, Santos got the ranch and my father and my uncle Jaime got some money and went to work in the mines. This was what each man preferred. So Santos and the Callahans were neighbors and like any neighbors in the ranch business they would help each other during spring roundup and branding and the fall roundup, too. But little by little the Callahans would buy up portions of Uncle Santos' ranch and in time they bought it all, including the ranch house and the buildings. But Santos stayed on at his old headquarters. He leased the house and five acres from the Callahans and he would work for them a good deal and for other ranches around here. As I grew up and heard the stories of how the Callahans ended up with the family ranch I was bitter. But the sad truth is that Santos was a real rounder in his youth. His life in those days was one big toot. He could be cold sober for months and then stone drunk for weeks and that's when he made bad business deals, and decisions, and in reality the Callahans didn't take his ranch. They just took advantage of the fact that he was unable to keep it.

"Then Mr. Callahan was killed in an accident on the ranch. That left Mrs. Callahan as the owner of the ranch. But her son Bingo was around and he was becoming a very strong-willed young man. He began to have a great influence on her. He drifted off into other business in the county but he still had a hand in the ranch, though as he got older he seldom worked there. The work was done by Mrs. Callahan and Santos. Santos worked there more or less full time after the death of Mr. Callahan. And, in time, he and Mrs. Callahan became lovers. Not so that anyone would know. In those days, in this town, a Mexican man with a *gringa* just wasn't done. But they were lovers and Santos wanted to buy back the family homestead. Mrs. Callahan would have been happy to let him have it, and to sell him some of the old ranch to go with it, but Bingo wouldn't let her do it. Of course he couldn't really stop her. To this day, it is my understanding that that ranch is solely owned by Mrs. Callahan. Bingo has never owned it, but in a sense he owned his mother and made the major decisions regarding that ranch. And then one day Bingo found them together, enough to know what was going on. It must have been a terrible, terrible fight. If there had been weapons, someone would have been killed. But they fought and Bingo was much bigger, and younger, and in the end he beat Santos nearly to death and ran him off the ranch. He wanted to run him off the old Aguilar family homestead, too. Mrs. Callahan wouldn't do that. It seems she and Bingo and Santos reached a kind of agreement, an unwritten truce, that Santos could stay on at the old headquarters but would have nothing to do with the Callahan ranch, and especially Mrs. Callahan. All this was some years ago. And every year, Santos renews the lease. Of course Bingo will one day end up with that ranch. That day may not be far away. Then surely, Santos will have to leave."

I said, "Sounds like Bingo Callahan kicks ass in everything he does. I didn't get a much different reading of the man from Mrs. Callahan herself."

"He is her only child. She loves him because I think it would hurt her more not to. Yet I feel she has few illusions about him. How do you know her?"

"She came by the shop, wanting to sell me the family book collection. I went out to the ranch to look them over. We had a nice visit. I'll be going back out there with an offer. It's a fair offer and I'm sure she'll accept it. She let on that she's not well."

"She's dying, Jason. I have a friend who works at the hospital. She goes there for treatments."

"So she would be tying up loose ends, making amends if she has any to make, making arrangements to pass things along. One arrangement would be the disposition of the family's books. I suppose another would be the disposition of that ranch, which, like you said, would go to her only child."

"That seems likely. But I wouldn't think it would please her very much. She knows what is going to happen to that ranch when Bingo gets it."

"But who else could she leave it to? Any other relatives?"

"Not to my knowledge..."

And then Carla Aguilar was thinking, and I watched her with pleasure, because she seemed such a serious sort, but this thinking she was doing was causing her the most marvelous mischievous grin and her great eyes smiled too as she raised a spoon and tapped the air with purpose while she pondered.

"...Listen, Jason, do you and Mrs. Callahan get along well?"

"Yes; she likes me. And I like her."

"Do you think she trusts you?"

"I'd guess she does. She tells me everything, without my asking."

"And what would you do with the Callahan Ranch if you owned it?"

"I don't know. I don't guess I'd know what to do with a real piece of land. But I know what I *wouldn't* do with it."

"Do you think you could convince her of that?"

"I don't think I'd have to. We've talked; we know that much about each other already. But just a damn minute here...she's not going to leave that ranch to me."

"Probably not. She would feel a certain obligation to Bingo in her will. But you could offer to buy it. She would then sell it to you, which would make her happy. And she would then leave the money you pay for the ranch to Bingo, which would satisfy her obligation there."

"What makes you think I could buy a ranch -- even a 200 acre ranch?"

"You are a man of means."

"Think so?"

"Yes. I'd bet on it. I've been in your bookshop. And I've listened to you when you've told me about books, and the kind of books you handle and what some of them are worth, and what they mean to you and what you do with them. I'd bet money myself that a lot of it passes through your hands in a year's time."

"Not bad. And of course I keep most of it."

"This is not a surprise either, my friend. You are frugal. And I've also been listening to your attitudes about things. About society and government and stuff like that. So I think you probably make your own rules, and cheat on your taxes."

"They would call it cheating. The goddamn government. I figure I give the government just what it deserve on that given year. I figure up what they think I owe, then I deduct forty percent, fifty percent, sometimes even seventy-five or eighty percent, depending on how bad a year they've had giving our money away to self-serving defense appropriations, our vacuous space program, pork barrel water projects, corporate polluters and the like, and indolent ne'er-do-wells who keep having children they can't care for."

"You might get caught."

"Not likely. That's the beauty of being in business for yourself, a cottage industry with no employees and lots of cash sales. The government has no way of knowing what I'm doing, and that's as it should be. I think I could disappear entirely as far as they're concerned and still do a stroke of business. But I want to be a good American so I pay my taxes to my country. Just what it's got coming that year. It's a point of honor with me."

"So you are a man of means."

"I don't have a lot of money in the bank. Whenever I get ahead I invest in books. I've got a good asset in my stock, and especially my private book collection."

"How long would it take to liquidate that collection?"

"No time at all; there are standing orders to buy the whole library. But I would have to want something awfully bad to turn loose of those books. My whole life is up on a shelf."

"I can understand that. I can understand a love of books. I can understand your love for certain books, that retain what you call *a certain heritage in literary form*. But that ranch is the same heritage in living form. It's the real thing, a kind of living remnant. Of course I have my own reasons here. I'm thinking about family, blood relations, and justice."

"Don't tempt me."

"I'm tempting you."

"Well damn you for tempting me. Because I'm tempted. I could come up with some money. Quite a bit. Maybe enough. But I would have to want to do this awfully bad. And she would have to be willing. More than willing; she would have to want it just as much, or it wouldn't be right."

"It would be right, believe me my friend."

"Where do you come up with this stuff? I'm a book trader; I spend my time cutting deals. But you're a grad student in literature, not some real estate slicker."

"Jason, I've been around the whole melodrama all my life. It's part of my family history. And it's like you said, maybe we Hispanics need to learn to be as smart and tough as the honky next door."

"I like that, Carla; I like hearing you say that. But that doesn't mean I'm going to do it. I could get in way over my head on a deal like that."

"Think about it," she said.

"Oh I'll think about it," I said. "Damn you for bringing it up...I can't help but think about it now."

I paid for mine. I tried, but she paid for hers. Then we stepped out into the street. It was a weeknight. There were two bars downtown but not much happens during the week. The Piñon Cafe was closing up behind us. The streets were quiet with a wanderer here and there making their way home. And the night was dark and cool, but not cold, for these were no longer winter nights. We started down the street for the Roadrunner Bookshop. I touched her hand and then I took it and it had been so long for me it was a wondrous sensual shock when she squeezed back and held on to my hand. Inside the shop I did not turn on the light but I turned to her and we held with both hands now and surrounded by all those books I knew already what was going to happen, and I said, "Will you stay with me?"

She looked up at me with those wonderful eyes lost behind her glasses in the dark and said, "Don't tempt me."

"I'm tempting you."

"Well, damn you for tempting me. I told you I don't want a boyfriend."

"And I don't want a girlfriend, as the name commonly applies. But I would like a friend like you, a woman, and pretty and smart, and able to talk about things of interest, and open to certain pleasures."

"Certain pleasures lead to trouble."

"Not if you don't expect too much of them."

Gently then, I reached and took her glasses off. She continued to look up at me, even more vulnerable, as even at short range her world was now a blur.

"Once that starts it gets complicated," she said, "it gets *involved*. Like boyfriend and girlfriend. That's trouble."

"We won't give it a name. And I'm immune. And hopefully you're smart enough not to lose it over a guy like me."

"And what kind of guy are you?"

"A loopy book dealer. And fantasy writer. And congenital itinerant. Open to certain pleasures for the first time in a while."

She dropped her head momentarily, resting against me now, lifted it again and said, "Will you make me feel beautiful?"

"Absolutely beautiful."

"It's not easy. I'm not a centerfold. I'm small at the top, and big in the bottom."

"By morning," I said, "you'll be showing yourself off."

She smiled, I could tell, and said, "Well I'm not going to let you undress me here by the window. And you'll have to lead me now, or give me my glasses back."

"I'll lead you," I said.

Through the next door into my apartment, I stooped in the dark and lit the gas space heater, giving us a small blue flame for warmth and a touch of light. Then we took turns with each other, peeling it off and looking on favorably, and anticipating more. Of course, I had been with Hispanic women before. They are not essentially different -- how could they be? -- but, still, there's nothing quite like it. And Carla Aguilar was startlingly fine; brown to the eye and smooth and soft to the touch; a plentiful and ethnic form, sublimely female. Carla was naked now, and I was appreciative. And it showed. And on the bed she was already coming out of it; her shy body and great vulnerability stretched and spread before me in a great erotic yield. In time I went to all her shy places. It took forever, there was so much so good, and all on display now, and in the end I let her finish as she would, sweat pooled and spread between us, her voice whimpering like a hurt bird against my chest, her big bottom pumping shamelessly under my hands.

Later, laying by my side, she came back to me. Her fingers drifted up and down, finding contours. "You are slender and firm. Like a younger man."

"An accident of nature. The luck of a benevolent metabolism. This is the only physical act I know. And not a regular exercise of late."

"Let's see," she said. And she took me in her hand. Vision was muted discreetly in the small, dim room, soft, flickering light parting the darkness here and there. She watched directly and close, focused on the act, now the bold one. I could not. And as I looked away I saw our selves in the act, the shadowed, lurid, obscene play moving on the wall, faster, building to frenzy. I could only watch vicariously, and I did. It had been a long time for both of us and she shared my exhaltation and would not be stopped in her furious stroke -- with a long groan three great streaming gouts pumped out in paced succession.

"Oh Jason, look what you have done!"

It was my pleasure to put her to sleep that night, rubbing her fine, tawny backside. And there I found, just above the erotic crease, a scar that did not surprise me, from the careful way she carried herself.

"Are you all right?"

"Yes, lovely."

"I mean this."

"I had a lot of pain for many years. Since the surgery I'm much better. I just have to be careful."

I rubbed her backside until her breathing came slow, steady; in perfect peace it seemed. It was a peace unlikely to last, I knew. This had to happen. And it was good. But could it end well for all? Not likely. Of course, I was immune; well protected by long experience. You get to where you think you can't live without one, and then she gives you the business. A most unpleasant business. Never love something you can't have. Did she know that? Not a chance. She would know the pain of loving something you can't have. That was ironic, for surely she was more worthy of love. I was going to hurt her. I'd known it hours before. I should have warned her about that; I guess I sort of did. But this had to happen.

My fingers went down her spine. I sought to soothe the scar. And with my touch I gently marked the route and fold of the erotic crease of her fine and ample ass. It was so good. But I wasn't going to get lost over it. Nobody was going to give me the business. She would have to be from another time. Something out of a myth. Like you would read about in a book. Not much chance of that. It was surely too late in time for anything like that...

...This one will be tricky though. For this brown-skinned girl has designed a plot and invited me to act it out. An inspired plot, yes. But scary. A challenge that it would be unlike me to accept. Better that I should decline. Better that I should read about such things. Better that we should focus on *her* opportunity, that she would produce a work of literary merit, right here in Del Cobre, New Mexico. Something to add to the myth...that would be more like it.

With pleasure I stroked her to sleep that night -- her tawny back, large and splendid ass, erotic crease and vulnerable scar, the soft, heavy, yet not unshapely legs. All so brown and fine. The *Mestizo*. It was a long racial line that brought her here, an admixture of mystical Indians, who looked to the stars and winds and the cycle of seasons for answers, and hard, obdurate Spaniards who conquered them, then looked to God for absolution. Now she slept with a white man, an *Anglo*, one of a race who had conquered and slandered them both. At the moment, we were all here together, like it or not. Who could say how that assimilation would evolve? There were too many of her people coming north now, and too many of my people already here. We would both have to be careful, and look for answers, and hope for the best. There was a certain future in our hands.

Chapter 6

The next day I followed the roads to the Callahan Ranch, rather than trail the creek. I walked with a small knapsack not very heavily laden with some of my goods. Two blocks east to the Tobosa Highway, narrow and winding as it left town, then south and west on that road, mostly uphill, out to the edge of settlement, then east on a dirt road that would be rough sledding in a passenger car. It got rough and then rougher as it wound through the hills, leaving ad hoc housing developments behind, crossing a cattle guard and down a slope and around a bend to the ranch and Mrs. Callahan's adobe home. Carla had drawn me a map. She also told me to forget about buying the Callahan Ranch. "I must have had too much wine to suggest a stunt like that," she said. "Owning that acreage would take up most of your money, all of your time, and put you on the wrong side of Bingo Callahan. I wouldn't wish that on an enemy." Without saying so, I agreed. It was an inspired plan the night before, but I'd had a little to drink myself; in the light of day I could scarcely contemplate letting go of my collected library for 200 acres I wouldn't know what to do with anyway. At the same time I told Carla that, if I owned the ranch, I would see to it that her uncle could stay at the family homestead as long as he wished. "That would mean a lot to both of us," she said, "and I'm sure we would offer to buy it. But don't do it; I had too much wine." Apparently she hadn't regretted the rest of it though, and as I hiked to the ranch I thought of how we had talked that morning about her literary project. We remained enthusiastic about that and there was a good feeling there for both of us. There was a good feeling about everything we had done. We would see each other again.

Mrs. Callahan was home. There were two fenced garden plots a quarter mile from the house, down towards the creek, and while the larger one had not been worked up this spring the smaller one had and she was there, placing small shovelfuls of compost around rows of lettuce, carrots, and squash. Her little blue-heeler dog watched her every move, unconcerned this time by my approach.

"Honey, you're just in time. I was wanting an excuse to do something else for the rest of the day."

She was sweating profusely and as she shoveled out the last load of compost from the wheelbarrow I could see she was having some pain. She would have none of my helping however, and she wheeled the empty wheelbarrow up to the barn herself. Then we adjourned to the shade in front of the house. She had me sit while she went inside to fix the tea and then she came out with it, placed it on the table between us, and sat down. We just sat there for a while and cooled down and looked on down the valley and then I told her what I could offer her for her library.

"Oh child, that's too much for just a bunch of books."

"There are two ways to price books," I said. "One way recalls the old horse trader who said, 'I never lie about a horse, but I don't always tell all I know.'"

"Oh I've known lots of horse traders like that!" she said.

"Well," I said, "a horse trader like that will cheat you if you don't know horses; if you don't know what to ask. You wouldn't get cheated 'cause you know horses but I wouldn't know what to ask and I could get cheated bad. It's the same with books. With someone who doesn't know what their books are worth, a sly book trader will bid low, offering not what the books are worth, bought for resale, but what they think the owner will let them go for. I've bought some that way myself, when I didn't think much of the person I was dealing with. They almost always let them go too low because very few people know books, about as many as know horses. But, by rights, I offer about fifty percent of what I think I can sell them for out of my shop or on a list. So that's how I arrived at my offer to you."

"Well you know books, not me. If that price is good business for you, it's fine with me; I'm well pleased."

"And if I ever go to buy a horse I'll take you along to be sure I don't get cheated."

"Oh you really ought to have a horse," she said. "A person needs a horse, even in this day and age."

Then she said, "I guess you know by now that everything I have will belong to my son Bingo not too long from now."

"Yes, ma'am," I said, "I do. But whoever it goes to down the road, I want to offer you a fair price."

She looked right at me and said, "Just keep this in mind in whatever business you and I might do: I can't take it with me, and my son Bingo doesn't need it."

"I'll remember that," I said.

"Then we have a deal on the books," she said, and reached across the table and shook my hand. Directly I wrote her the check and we agreed that one day next week I would ease my bus down her ranch road and we would load the books. Then, the deal closed, I reached to the knapsack beside me and took out the three books inside and handed them over.

"Call this your *pilón*," I said. "You said you needed something new to read and I'm hopeful you'll like these."

She looked them over, was obviously pleased, I think as much by the thought as the goods, and then she focused on one volume: *Some Recollections of a Western Ranchman*, by Captain William French.

"I've always wanted this one," she said.

"It's a wonderful book," I said. "No one else lived through that time and came away with his perspective, humor, and balanced look at all that went on. He was one of the few men who fought the Apache and wrote of the Apache without expressing a hatred of them. And you'll read in there about the time he goes off on a scouting expedition with some Navajos and the Navajos break away to hunt some deer. They were mostly armed with bows and arrows and at the end of the day they came in with 84 deer slung across their saddles. That was just north of here, about fifty miles. Think what this country was like to produce 84 deer in a day's hunt with bows and arrows. Right now, you couldn't get 84 deer in a day up there with poisoned bait. That's what's happened in one hundred years. This book tells us what this country was, what it was like, and what has been lost. Yet in many ways those were hard times. Times you will understand far better than me. But he remained an even-tempered man with a wink in his eye in whatever he did. He was a rare gentleman. When his book was published in 1928 many of the copies were bought up and burned by some neighbors who didn't like some of the Captain's comments about how some of their kin had done business with cattle. So it has become a rare book and of course it all happens right around here."

"Oh child, I know...I'll love reading this one...thank you so much."

She was in fact just a bit teary at this moment and I went on to say that there were more books in my shop and that she was welcome to any of them.

"I maybe have time for these three," she said. "I'm going to read this one first, just to make sure."

She set the books down then and gathered herself up so she wasn't teary anymore. Then she said, "Honey, will you let me show you around my ranch?"

We went to the barn. There were sundry corrals, pens, watering tanks and troughs, her pickup truck, a tractor and implements and a loading chute outside, and inside more pens, horse stalls, feed room, tack room, and six dairy stanchions. On one wall of the barn was an old style saddle like you see in turn-of-the-century photos with the deep, flat seat and high cantle. It must have been a very old saddle but it's leather looked smooth and brown and well kept. And adjacent on the wall was some heavy duty harness, still sound, dating from the days, she told me, when they did most of their farming with a team. I looked at all the leather and buckles and straps and traces and told her it appeared beyond comprehension to me.

"Almost nobody knows how to hitch up and work a team anymore," she said, "but it's easier than keeping a tractor running if you ask me."

The sorrel mare she rode to the post office was in one of the stalls. We went into the stall with the mare and she slipped a curb bit into the horses mouth and the headstall over the ears in one easy motion. She tied the throat latch and then led her outside and showed a flash of deep pain as she grabbed a piece of the mare's mane and swung up bareback. She apologized for not having a second horse for me to ride or, in the alternative, for not being strong enough to accompany me on foot. I told her I liked to walk and admitted without pride that I didn't know how to ride a horse.

"Oh you could learn," she said. "You're young and you can learn. A good horse is a good thing to have, even now."

We got up into the hills where we could see the property and began to circle the ranch. The horse climbed easily, methodically. She paced the horse for me and it was no trouble for me to keep up. And the dog, excited by the adventure, ran up ahead of us and jumped and spun a twist in the air a couple of times and barked her pleasure before going on to sniff about and hunt, but checking back periodically with the woman she always wanted to please. And up top you could see how the town and the houses and mobile homes, the dump and the golf course, had encircled most of the ranch. Yet all developments were held off into the second or third row of hills by the remaining 200 acres of the Callahan property, so that when you were down along the creek the only sign of development was the Country Club headquarters on a far hill. We wound our way over the hills, headed south, and went to the south end, to the fence line, then east down the hills and across the valley and across the creek and up into the hills on the east side. At a high point there we stopped for a time. Across the valley you could see the house and barns, the corrals, loading chute and various outbuildings, and a few scattered cows down along the creek, everything looking very small for the distance and the elevation we were at. It was green down along the creek. The hills were brown but nonetheless with good grass and beside us the longer grasses were waving in a nice breeze. Overhead a few soft clouds were moving with the breeze and rolling patches of shade across the hills and valley. We looked in silence for a while and I thought I had never seen anything so fine and when I turned and looked up at Claire she was beyond teary and some big ones were streaming down her face. Although she was horseback there was still some exertion for her in the ride and it was clear that any exertion put her in a lot of pain. It seemed clear to me, too, that there was all kinds of pain in those big tears. I said, "Mrs. Callahan, is your doctor doing all he can for you? Do you have something for the pain?"

"Oh yes, honey, I have a good doctor. And I have pills, but I try to leave them alone during the day because I can't hardly work when I take them. I can only lay around and read and maybe sleep a little. That's okay for the night but in the day I've still got things to do."

"Can't they do more for you than that?"

"No honey, not anymore. It's to the pancreas. Once it's to the pancreas you just as well tidy up behind you as best you can and step through the door."

I turned away from her and looked out across the valley and then her hand touched my shoulder and she was pointing and she said, "Darlin', look from the house on south along the rim, passed the barns, on south to where you see all that mesquite and juniper growing along the cliff." I nodded and she went on... "That's where The People lived when they were here. Of course the trees grew in much later, but that is the only better homestead from where we put ours. When we arrived in 1919 we began to cut those trees and we were going to clear and build there. We hadn't gotten far when papa discovered that a village was there in ruins under those trees. He didn't think it was right to disturb those who were there before. He said, 'The Ancient Ones have earned their peace.' So we moved up the valley a half mile and settled in and let the brush and trees grow up as it pleased where the village was. Over the years it came to where only Clemson and I knew what was there, and when Clemson died it was left to me."

I stood looking off across the valley for a time, trying to think of something to say, and when I couldn't I turned around and looked up at the old woman horseback. She was looking off across there too, and she was still crying quietly and I put one hand up on the neck of the horse and the other I rested on the old woman's knee. She reached down and took my hand. She pressed my hand against her knee and then she squeezed it, and I can't say I was too awfully surprised when she said, "Oh honey, let me sell you my ranch." This was all more than a little too much for me and in fact I was getting teary myself, something I thought I had learned not to do, and directly I turned back to the valley below, leaving one hand on the neck of the horse. Neither one of us said anything for a while but it was clear to both of us why she wanted me to have this land and it was clear to me at least that I was already in way over my head with no turning back now. Still, as we slowly worked our way down through the hills and back towards the house, I offered some lame remonstrations about not having ever saddled a horse, milked a cow, strung a fence, or plowed a field, admitting with no pride that my link to the heritage of the Southwest was all fantasy, dreams in my head or reveries strung out over numberless printed pages. She came back that two hundred acres wasn't that much, that I'd pick it up all right because I was young and strong, even if "a little bit bookish," that there wasn't much to the place as a ranch anymore, but that what there was ought to stay. Then there was the matter of the money and there was no easy way out there either because she made it clear she would sell it to me for a dollar an acre if that's what I could afford. We decided it was worth probably four hundred dollars an acre as an agricultural unit, at least five times that as land close to town ripe for development, and that I could probably come up with fifty thousand dollars upon the sale of my private book collection. We went around and around in a peculiar way, with me trying to offer more than she would take and she trying to give it away, until we settled that I would buy the original homestead of the Callahan Ranch, including the house and all the buildings, livestock, machinery, water rights and improvements, for two hundred dollars an acre or forty thousand dollars. "That will leave you some of your favorite books," she said, "and help you get started and it will allow me to leave something in proceeds to Bingo." Of course we both knew we were doing none of this on behalf of Bingo Callahan but it was easier not to talk about that. We both had our reasons.

Back at the ranch Claire swung off the horse and in one easy motion undid the throat latch and pulled the headstall back over the mare's ears and slipped the bit out of her mouth and turned the horse loose. I caught myself trying to note how she had done it, as well as trying to remember how she had so easily bridled the beast two hours earlier, and we watched as the mare nodded her head contentedly as she walked down into the flat to graze and spend the evening doing whatever else horses on their own do. Claire said, "Now honey, you meet me at Lawyer Wynn's office at nine o'clock Monday morning so we can tell him what-all we want on the paperwork."

The shadows were deep across the valley now and I said, "Are you going to be all right?"

"Oh yes, I'll be fine. I suppose I won't see it all again like I did today and this was the nicest way to say good-bye. Now I'm going to go lie down for awhile and read my new book and I might take one or two of those pills."

"I'll stay," I said, "and fix you some supper."

"Oh no child, I won't hear of that. It's Saturday night and you're a young man. I won't have you spending your evening standing around a kitchen boiling up soup for an old woman. I can do that myself. You know there is something going on up the hill there tonight at the Country Club. Bingo and Sarah will be there. He's heard about you and knows about our little book deal. He and Sarah both want to meet you. I've already started writing a letter that he will receive when this is all over that will explain to him why certain things were done. So don't you worry about that. You just walk back up the hill behind the barn, up where we just went, only go a little further west and you'll cross a good cow trail. Take the trail south to the stock tank in the draw and just above it is the fence and the gate and the north-south road that comes in north to the dump. But you take the road south and it will wind up the hill to the country club. You go on up there and have a good time, maybe meet a pretty girl."

I stood and watched her walk on back to the house, her head down and her long gray hair limp to the small of her back, and that perky little dog trotting alongside. She walked slowly and with a certain strain -- only a hint of that athleticism I'd seen remained -- and she turned once and waved and I waved in return. When she had disappeared into the house I turned away and started on foot to the southwest, the lights of the big building up on the far hill in the distance.

Chapter 7

There was a party going on all right. I could hear the country music band as I climbed the last hill and crossed the parking lot full of cars. Through the door I stepped into an extraordinary place by my reckoning, the sort of country club you would expect of a town many times the size of Del Cobre. And maybe I hadn't fully realized it before, but what I sensed about Del Cobre right then was money, quite a lot of money, in this case money holding a base in the copper mining industry, and big agri-business ranching, and accrueing real estate...and a certain kind of ambition; all emanating from the kind of people who are ill-suited to standing still, or accepting of modest contentments, and who would insist at all times and costs, that if some is good, a whole lot is better.

I stepped up to the sign-in book that led to the dining room, bar and dance floor. The sign-in book had a column on the left for "Members" and a second column on the right that said "Guest/Guest Of," and under that second column I wrote "Jason Niles/Bingo Callahan." I didn't hesitate with any of this and the keeper of this sign-in sheet eye-balled what I wrote and as I stepped past shook my hand and offered a big grin and said, "Welcome to the Del Cobre Golf and Country Club." I was not quite as hearty in response, but I tried, and then I headed for the bar. This bar was at the back of the room with a large dining area going off to my left as I walked in, and the dance area and lounge going off the other way with a partial wall separating the two. The dining area was thinning out but the area of the bar, lounge and dance floor was packed and even before I got to the bar I saw a guy standing off a ways who I knew even then had to be Bingo Callahan. And there was a woman beside him that had to be his wife, Sarah. Of course I was trying to take everything in as fast as possible in this new environment and I got a beer right away so I would look like part of the crowd, but all the while one eye was on this guy standing off a ways who had to be Bingo Callahan because of the way he had drawn a crowd around whatever story he was telling. I knew he was telling some kind story or joke because of the way all these men were around him and leaning in with their ears, trying not to miss a single word. He had a great physical presence standing over there. In fact he wouldn't have been the tallest man in the room and indeed did not appear to be a whole lot taller than me. But he was very large and I guess *burly* is the word, comfortably disheveled in a bright print shirt that hung loose outside khaki pants, the expected high-heeled, tooled, Western boots, and up top a balding forehead that showed the tan line of a guy who's outside a lot and always wears a hat. His wife was tall and snaky-lean in the hips and legs -- a hardbody -- and made the more so by tight jeans wrapped over tight buns and tucked down into cowboy boots, looking like a country-girl singer on stage; high-breasted, a good, straight back and a fine head of curly red hair hanging loose to her shoulders and beyond. She was leaning in on this story too, with freckles across her nose and big blue eyes, and when the punch line came there was a big burst of laughter that rose above the rest of the noise in the room and the boys roared and guffawed, and poked and slapped each other -- but nobody poked Bingo -- and gradually they fell away from the storyteller well pleased, admiring even as they shook their heads in disbelief. And it must have been pretty dirty too because the woman flushed and pretended to try not to laugh and rolled her eyes and punched ol' Bingo a couple times in the stomach and feigned disgust, and it all more than anything else showed she was pleased to be with a guy who could command that kind of attention, tell that kind of a story, and pull it off so well. I took my beer away from the bar and walked over to one of the nearby picture windows, all looking out to the east.

There wasn't much light left in the sky. Some of the higher hills still caught some colorful yellow streaks but the valley and the creek and the trees along the riparian zone were almost in the dark. Still I could see a lot because this was the highest hill around. The golf course was down there, nine holes going off to the east and south. And to the east and north was the Callahan Ranch. I could barely make out the buildings of the ranch and one interior light that would have to be the ranch house and Claire, probably reading her new book. South and back west a ways from the ranch I could see a portion of the dump. I traced the route Claire and I had taken earlier in the day, up west into the hills above the barn, south along a ridge to the property line, east and downhill to the valley floor, across the valley and the creek and up into the hills on the east side. I could see just the spot where we stopped and talked. She had pointed from there to the west across the valley and told me about the secret Mimbres site. I could see that, too; that nondescript clump of brush and trees along the cliffs, from the country club window, as my eyes went west across the valley, then back east to the spot on the hill where Claire and I a few hours before had made our deal. And I noticed, looking out the window, some open, undeveloped space over east of where we'd talked, and below where we'd talked -- a small house, outbuildings, windmill and corral, and some nice cottonwoods in a little cut just above in the hills. This homestead clearly was not part of the new developments dotting the hills beyond the boundaries of the Callahan Ranch. Claire and I had not quite topped the hill over there or we would have seen the place below, but I could see it now and I realized it was the old Aguilar homestead at the southeast corner of the Callahan Ranch. All seen and told, it was a rich geography indeed that presented itself from the high hill and the picture window of the Del Cobre Golf and Country Club. It was shortly thereafter that a large hand was placed on my shoulder, and as I turned my head Bingo Callahan said, "It seems I have a guest here tonight."

I turned the rest of myself and we shook hands and started to talk. The man was all charm. A kind of a business-like charm to be sure, but charm nonetheless, with an ever-present, personable, we're-in-this-together grin and mannerism that rather overbalanced, if you weren't careful, a small, deep pair of straight-ahead, interrogating eyes. I am pretty good myself at looking someone in the eye when I talk to them but Bingo was a natural at the same thing as the conversation went here and there, and it was all I could do not to drop my gaze from time to time and let him have it. But I held my eyes on the man and in fact we were about the same height, if not heft. Clearly we already knew something about one another and wanted to know more. And wherever the conversation went it had some link to money.

"I've been wanting to thank you, Jason, for buying my mother's books. I'm taking it that you are going to buy them, if you haven't already, and it means something to her to have the family's books go to someone who has a feel for that product. She's not well you know."

"I did buy them," I said, without blanching at the word *product*, or his mother's impending death, "this afternoon. It's a nice collection. Too nice a collection to end up at a library sale for fifty cents each."

Bingo liked the ring of that and it brought a new reach to his smile.

"You understand," I went on, "that I'm going to turn around and sell them at a profit to someone else. A collector, most likely. He, or she, will handle them carefully, read them with pleasure, profit from the knowledge obtained, and value them for what they are."

"Oh I highly approve, I highly approve. The principal of highest and best use should apply to books, land, water, whatever. I don't know a damn thing about books or the book business, but I'd make an educated guess that a book that is no longer in print has got to get increasingly scarce over time. And anything that gets scarce gets in demand and the price goes up. Land is my business and I would suspicion the principal is the same with books or land. Certain types of land become in a sense scarce. Then the price goes up. You take this land out the window here. You were looking at it, and you were liking it. I like looking at it, too. My guess is we aren't looking at it, or liking it, quite the same. That's fair. But you take all you can see out there and move it ten miles south, it's hard-scrabble. It's piss-ant country. Where it is, it's prime. The key is location. And in real estate, the three most important factors are: location, location, and location. What you see is the equivalent of what you'd call, I believe, rare-and-out-of-print."

I could smile at that, and I did, but I said, "Drawing a parallel between land and books would necessarily have some kinks in it, Bingo. Some of your mother's books are fifty years old and are worth no more now than the day they were printed and sold. Inflation hasn't touched them. They may be out of print and scarce, but as literary or collectable properties they were trash then and they are trash now. There is no parcel of land in New Mexico that you could buy now for what it sold for fifty years ago. You couldn't come close. Unlike books, there is a limit to land, and it's a limit that can already be seen."

"All right Jason, but I'd guess one not in the business would be surprised what some of those books might be worth...you did say it's a nice collection."

"Sure is. Any collection has some trash. My own collection has some books I thought would accrue impressively. Turns out they were trash. Your mother's collection has very little trash, a number of books worth three figures, and couple of signed, first editions worth four, if you know where to place them."

Bingo's grin was at this point somewhat frozen, with the only movement being the eyebrows, which arched perceptively. This was only momentary, and then his grin was alive again and he was leading me over to the table where he and Sarah had their places. The band was on break and Sarah was there waiting for us. Of course we both knew I might just as well have written the check directly to him, as within months, if not weeks, the money for the books would be his. But he was going to have to wait a bit, and talk to his mother, to find out how much he got.

Meeting Sarah was awfully good. Up close she was even more astonishing. The lean, mean, ache-in-your-loins body was so nicely complimented by the full, loose, natural flow of light red hair -- none of that teased up, bouffant look so many of the country girls affect -- soft, pert face, a nice little pout to the mouth, freckles across the nose and bright blue eyes, and a way of moving -- including her splendid hands when she talked -- that had you noticing every little thing she did. She was obviously a good deal younger than him, or me; just a little bit more than a kid who, outdoors with the right hat, would have been the perfect female counterpart to Huckleberry Finn. The hard body and soft face, bright eyes and pout, yielded a combined willful innocence that would, I thought, capture anyone she wanted and quite a few who, like me, wouldn't be able to help themselves. We were introduced.

"Claire has been talking so much about you," she said. "She says, 'Oh daughter, this Jason Niles is just the nicest, most intelligent man...he's my kind of people.' It's not everyone that makes that kind of an impression on Claire."

I said, "That last part has got to be the best thing anyone has ever said about me, at least from the best source. But I'm not making any claims about the rest of it."

Bingo said, "He's got a head for business, I'll say that right now. That takes some kind of intelligence."

"Or shrewdness," I said.

"Call it what you will, it's the *kind of* intelligence you need in this world and Sarah, he's got it. He's just about to make a bunch of money off my family's books, the deal's done, and he's still close to the vest and not saying how it's all shaking down. I like that. I'd take him as a partner *or* a competitor and think I was dealing with a good man either way. But then he's in books and I'm in land. We might better avoid that mix."

"That would probably be the wisest choice," I said.

"Hah! -- You goddamn right!" he came back, and offered a big slap on my back to boot.

"Yes," Sarah said, smiling wonderfully, "let Jason have a nice business, like rare books. Don't corrupt him with one of your land deals."

We could all smile at that, each from our own perspective, and I had to like the way she said it, too, with a good, not overdone, country drawl of the type that centers in West Texas and that many rural New Mexicans still carry against the urban, homogenizing tide.

The band started up again. This was no uptown, country rock group, but they tended more to the traditional, with a fiddle and acoustic rather than electric guitars, so it struck me as appropriate when they hit up an old Hank Snow classic:

Pardon me if I'm sentimental, when we say good-bye,
Don't be angry with me should I cry,
Though you're gone, yet I'll dream a little dream
as years go by,
Now and then there's a fool such as I.

Bingo said, "You'll excuse us," and took Sarah out on the dance floor. This gave me a chance to eye-ball Sarah as she moved around. Like most men -- if the truth were told -- I am blantantly physical about women. I'm a looker, and with Sarah the look was so good it almost hurt. As any ranch girl would, she knew the two-step well, and the thing was the way she would toss her head and her long red hair as she danced and talked to Bingo or jived with another couple as they passed by; and the way her legs went all the way up to her ass, which was lean in the hips with a soft crease in the center of her jeans where they molded around her tight buns; her ass had that nice swelling in the rear of the rump, like you think of in a Black woman. I didn't want to stare too hard and I made my eyes move around to some to other people, other couples, dancing here and there, and there -- good grief! -- there was a Black woman! She wasn't dancing, but rather was off across the dance floor at a table with another couple, but that didn't lessen the shock. Like most Americans -- if the truth were told -- I am fascinated by race. And races. Including my own. Call it what you will, you don't expect to see a Black at a small town, redneck country club in the Southwest where even an Hispanic who's not waiting tables is an item. In fact I knew this women, or rather knew who she was. I'd seen her around, had never met her, but she was the one referred to as, simply: "the Blackwoman." It wasn't ever said pejoratively or with malice, at least I had not heard it that way; but simply: "the Blackwoman." That's what a rare species she was in Del Cobre. What's a Black woman doing in Del Cobre at the honkey country club dance? And a dark-skinned Black woman at that. A very black, Black woman. Poor thing, she stuck out like a sore thumb. It was probably the only sight that could have taken my eyes off Sarah for any length of time, and then she was gone behind a dancing couple and I went back to Sarah and the savory crease in the jeans folded over her high, tight ass.

The band played on. I got -- or rather someone got me -- another beer. Someone's wife I didn't know got me to dance, and later I returned the favor. Everyone was very friendly and seemed to know who the new man with the new business downtown was. There were lots of friendly exchanges of partners; no one was puckered up about keeping one dance partner. Then I sat out a few until I found an opportunity to dance with Sarah. She danced so very well -- she was as good on her feet as she was graceful talking with her hands -- and I felt like we danced well together. The juxtaposition of willful innocence seemed even more vivid with her in my arms, her lean, hard back under my right hand and her lovely all-American, pretty-girl face looking up to me as we talked. After a bit of inane conversation, I decided to try her out.

"You and Bingo figure to move out to the ranch after Claire dies?"

She dropped her head momentarily, then looked up and said, "that doesn't sound very nice."

"Well, we all know she's going to die, and not far off. I figured you must have made some plans."

"We're not moving out to the ranch. Bingo doesn't like the ranch."

"Do you?"

"I grew up on a ranch. A big ranch, near Las Cruces."

"Do you miss it?"

"Maybe. But Bingo doesn't want to go back to ranching. The Callahan place isn't really a ranch anymore, anyway. It's more of a..."

"Homestead."

"Yes, that's what it is."

"And what's Bingo going to do with the family homestead?"

"You know damn well what he's going to do with it."

"How do you feel about that?"

"It's served it's purpose as a ranch. Now it's going to serve another purpose."

"That sounds like Bingo talk."

"Well, he'll own it -- we'll own it -- and we'll do as we damn well please with it."

The song ended and we turned to go back to the table. I let my hand, quickly yet gently, slide down the crease in the jeans folded over her high, tight ass. It wasn't a grab or a goose, just a surreptitious feel, designed so she wouldn't know if it was an accident or on purpose. I did it right because there was no overt reaction but she flushed visibly and said "thank you" without looking at me as I left her at her chair. Well, I couldn't ask her out, could I? If something was going to happen between us it would have to be something not very nice. I'd served notice that I was willing to be not very nice and I was happy to let Bingo have her for the next dance, confident I had put some new thoughts in her head.

I'd had, by this hour, a few beers -- maybe more -- and was having a pretty good time. So was everyone else, by the look of it, saving that very black, Black woman, who sat without expression, looking on, and who had yet to step on the dance floor. The older couple she was with had been out there, and I rather expected that he would in politeness ask the Blackwoman to dance; surely she was their guest at the Del Cobre Golf and Country Club. Yet there she sat, very black, and having accentuated her prominent Negro features by pulling her hair back tight around to form a bun at the back of her head. With some Black women that works. With her it worked very nicely, it seemed to me; I liked looking at her; but no one, it seems, would touch her, and so after a while I got up and took a circuitous route so she wouldn't see me coming and when I got behind her I tapped her on the shoulder and then in the same motion reached down and took her by the hand. She looked up with big eyes and in great surprise and said automatically, "I don't dance Western."

"I'll show you how," I said, and with some cajoling and literal arm twisting I got her reluctantly out of her chair and a couple of steps towards the dance floor to where it would be more of a scene for her to turn around and go back than to take up the music and dance. So we danced. Her name was Terri Vinson and she was a tall and rather big-boned woman, a substantial woman, well-formed nonetheless, with a more defined figure than Carla, but without the grace and style of Sarah (already I knew I'd never seen anything like Sarah), and with more hips and a bigger bum behind. Of course the two-step is not difficult and we focused on that for half the song till she was getting it and then I said, "What's a nice Black woman like you doing here with all these rednecks?"

She smiled and took that well and said, "I was invited, Whiteman; I'm a guest of the Jensens."

That rang a bell and I said, "Who are the Jensens?"

Signal To Depart

"Dr. Jensen is head of the business school at the college. I'm an instructor at the business school at the college. So he's my boss. And they're friends. They've been very kind."

"How do you happen to be at this college?"

"College teaching jobs are hard to come by. My resume went all over and one opening came in the mail. It's okay till something better comes along."

"So you're not from Del Cobre."

"No one Black is *from* Del Cobre."

"Are you the only one in town?"

"The only one what?"

"You know what I mean."

"No. There's several others...I hear about some guy working out at the mines, and there are a few athletes at the college."

"Athletes, of course."

"Man, do you always take this great interest in racial matters?"

"I'm mostly interested in you. But racial matters are interesting. And a problem. *The* social problem, it seems, in our country. But a problem America might solve if we were to look hard at the truth."

She puzzled momentarily and said, "Are you the man with the new bookstore in town?"

"Yes."

"I friend of mine at the college told me she was in your shop and bought a book. She said you were interesting to talk to."

"You're stroking me just right!"

"And she said you have a *real* bookstore."

"I like that even better."

"Have anything in your shop on Black history?"

"*Black history*, strictly speaking, does not exist in America. Any more than White history. Because, ever since history in this country began to be recorded, each ethnic group has had its time, place and events wound up with the history of one or more other ethnic groups. So it's futile to try and study *Black history* in and of itself, not that some won't try. I mean, imagine a course in a college curriculum called: *White History*. However, I do have books on the Southwest, many of them of a historical nature...Southwest Americana. And as Blacks are a part of Southwest history I have some books that may satisfy your interest, or at least pique your curiosity, in Black history."

"Blacks as part of the whole."

"Yes. Of course, we're all part of the whole. Come by some time. We'll talk and I'll show you my stock of books."

"Maybe I will. If we both look hard at *the truth*, maybe we can solve *the* problem."

"Yes," I said. "And toss around some black history to boot."

"If we can find it, lost in the whole."

"We'll find it," I said.

By the end of the song she had the two-step well in hand; next time someone asked her to dance, I told her, she'd have no excuse to say no. She said, "next time?" like I didn't understand Black life in Del Cobre very well. She had the last word on that but I made sure I held her hand tight till she was back at her table, and I said it was "my pleasure" as I bowed slightly and let her go. She bowed slightly too, and said, "No, no, the pleasure was all mine, Whiteman." The Jensens were smiling and they laughed at our last somewhat affected exchange and it appeared they had enjoyed watching us. We did have fun. And before I went back to Bingo's table I introduced myself to the Jensens. Of course I wanted to ask him if he was the Jensen who was cheated by Bingo Callahan. I was well into blunt questions and direct conversations by this time and I almost did. But his wife was sitting there and I thought better of it. My guess was, this was the man -- how many Jensens can there be in a small town? I'd find out.

Back at Bingo's table and the band was once again on break. I sat, surrounded it seemed by Bingo and his cronies, who were standing and leaning into another anecdote by the big guy, and looked for an opening to get away and have some more conversation with his wife, Sarah. She was having none of it, flitting about the table talking with this or that of the membership, avoiding me expertly; that is, so it didn't seem like it. But she was. And then I heard her behind me telling another woman she was off to the ladies room and as she went by my chair she leaned over and told me in my ear: "Nice move Slim, maybe you'll get to fuck the Blackwoman just like the Aguilar girl."

That gave *me* something to ponder as she took her ass across the dance floor and around the corner to the ladies room to piss. How could she know about Carla? Already? It was possible, of course. In a small town. A local woman leaves her car all night out front of a man's downtown apartment, leaves at a certain hour in the light of day, give it 18 hours, and anybody who's got an interest in that sort of thing is likely to know. Somehow Sarah knew. She was interested. And a little miffed. A very good sign. They don't get miffed if they're not interested. They don't get angry if they don't care. And I liked the nasty way she put it, too.

I liked what I'd done for the evening; I'd had a real good time and felt like I'd stirred things up. I always enjoy that. I sought to quit while well ahead; let Sarah come back to find my empty chair. I got a hold of Bingo, broke into the conversation, and thanked him profusely for the good time, the drinks, for having me as his uninvited guest. He was all good cheer and it was hard to break away. By the time I did, Sarah was back. I started across the floor for the door, waved good-bye to the Jensens and Terri, and I heard Terri say, "see you, Whiteman!" Then I sought the eye of Sarah. Had she offered a look I would have waved good-bye to her, too. But she was nearby with others, pretended not to notice my leaving; I kept my farewell to myself and directly I was out in the cool night air. I looked forward to the walk home and started at a good pace down the road under the stars...

I loved Claire. I loved her in a way that was new to me and that I didn't understand. She was not of my time, and I was wanting a great deal more for us than we could ever have. I loved her, and she was going to die.

I liked Carla so very much. She was lovely and vulnerable and yet still strong in her way; intelligent and creative and good-hearted too, a rare confluence of the good. Ultimately, she would not be right for me, but she was wonderful to me; we would come to mean something to one-another and I would probably hurt her before it was done.

I liked Terri, too. Not so very much as Carla -- not yet -- but I liked her and could like her much more and I hoped she would like me, too. She was very black and very good to look at in her way and I liked the way she sauced me back and she deserved to have more than me asking her to dance.

I wanted Sarah. I wanted her enough that I didn't entirely like it; it had a dangerous feel to it, for it just won't do to fall in love with something you can't have. I knew already that if anything happened with Sarah I was a goner and wouldn't have a chance in the world.

I hated Bingo Callahan. What he did. What he stood for. And what he had. He had some money, my money, coming to him; he had Sarah; and he thought he had the Callahan Ranch. But it was almost certain I would have the ranch. And I almost had myself hoping that in time I would have much more than that.

I had a head full of thoughts of all of them as I walked home in the cool dark of a spring night headed for my new home in Del Cobre, New Mexico.

Chapter 8

On Monday morning I left my shop at five minutes till nine wearing a summer weight sport coat but no tie and walked up the street to the office of lawyer Thomas Wynn. The downtown was peacefully busy by this time and I waved at a couple of colleagues of American free enterprise who were opening up their shops as I walked up the street under a warm cloudless sky. And the old man who for forty years went round and did everyone's windows was at the shop next door to the lawyer's office, working a squigy brush and a sheen of water down a clear pane of glass. I greeted him, too. Then I opened the door and the secretary immediately passed me on into the office of lawyer Wynn.

Claire was there. She was lovely, spiffed up in bright clothes and a colorful scarf for downtown, though with weight loss and fighting the pain you could see she wasn't near the woman she had been just a few weeks before. She was sitting in a chair across the desk from lawyer Wynn who was a white-haired gentleman of florid complexion and a rather worn countenance, looking like a fairly serious after-hours drinker. He was sober and professionally composed this morning though and I could tell they had been talking and were both expecting me. We were introduced and I sat down in the other chair opposite lawyer Wynn.

"Mr. Niles," he began, "Claire has come to me this morning with what I regard as a somewhat extraordinary proposal. Are you in fact prepared to buy the Callahan Ranch?"

"I am," I said. "I'd like to own it."

"She has told me this morning about a cash sale of forty thousand dollars."

"That's what we agreed on."

"Are you prepared for that purchase?"

"I will be, given a few weeks. I made a certain phone call to the right person yesterday."

"Mr. Niles, how about some earnest money?"

"How about ten percent? I can come up with four thousand right now."

"Claire?"

"Oh that's more than enough down. Are you comfortable with that, Jason? You can make it four hundred down and suit me because I know your good for the rest."

"Four thousand is no problem," I said.

We all talked on about this and that of the deal. Claire and I couldn't find anything to argue about and lawyer Wynn asked questions and took notes and toward the end said he'd have it all written up according to specifications. Then Claire said:

"Now Tom, you and I know there's going to be a fuss about this when it's known, and that means it is not to be known outside of this office till I'm gone, which won't be long. And more than that, Bingo and a few others are bound to claim that the old woman had no idea what she was doing and was taken advantage of by a stranger in town. But you and I understand that I know exactly what I'm doing and that I wouldn't be selling to this fine young man if I didn't want to and believe as well that he was the one and the only one to own my place."

"Claire, as I always have, I'll handle this legal work precisely to your wishes. I know why your doing this and I don't disapprove. I'd handle it the same even if I did, but in this case I'll be happy to carry out your wishes in this matter, the papers will not be filed until the appropriate time, and as for anyone else, they can fuss if they like. You own the Callahan Ranch and can sell it to whoever you wish."

Shortly the conversation went from the sale of the land to some changes in Claire's will. It was no place for me and to the surprise of lawyer Wynn -- though I don't think much to Claire -- I reached into a bulging coat pocket and counted out four thousand dollars in cash and then excused myself with a comment to lawyer Wynn that I would be in touch on the matter of the rest of the money, and a promise to Claire that I would visit soon.

I left the lawyer's office, walked back down the street and opened up my shop.

Chapter 9

There came the beginning of the long, slow-passing, warm summer days. Some of them were hot. An inveterate traveler of the great Southwest, I had known hot summers, but as an indoor person, insulated by air-conditioning. Like most people anymore. But all that changed now. Daily I would close up shop at five o'clock, or earlier, and using the route of the creek, hike out to the Callahan Ranch. The days of early June were long and getting longer and hours of daylight and mid-day heat remained as I would come up the slope to Claire, sitting in the shade of those cottonwoods with the dog close by, waiting on me with that ice-cold tea. We would have our talk and then we would do her chores, the actual work of which was now left mostly to me. We would gather eggs and weed the garden and milk the cow and after a lesson or two she would send me off by myself to some portion of the fenceline that needed repair. There were some broken fence posts and some wire down here and there though no place where the fence itself was down to where the cattle could get out. But that would happen soon enough without some work and so I did the work so that, in her words, "you won't have to worry about any of them getting out after it's yours." Where I could reach the fenceline in a truck I used hers, but for much of that fence only a horse would get you there. She showed me how to saddle one, in this case her sorrel mare, and we would pack the horse and me with the staples and a small roll of wire and that handy item known as a fencing tool that can hammer staples and pull staples and cut wire all in one, and an ax to cut new posts from the juniper trees that dotted the hills, and the post hole digger across my lap, and I would ride off, thinking myself quite the hand. It was a taste of a labor and way of life I in a sense knew so well, and yet had never done, and it would seem at times that nearly all my life had been taken up in a choice of dreams over experience. I consoled myself that I was here, now, and that it was not too late.

One of my chores one evening was to repair a gate in the far southeast part of the ranch. Here the large pasture of what remained of the Callahan Ranch had been truncated and through the gate and down the hill was the five acre lease and trap, confined by a connecting fence, of Santos Aguilar. The place had come up in conversation between Claire and me from time to time but the significance of it, and of the man who lived there, had not. I replaced a broken post and fixed the gate with an eye on the old homestead below. It was a small but fine looking white stucco home, more like a cottage, with all the outbuildings, corrals and such you'd expect of a small ranch, everything neat and in place, and a lovely grove of cottonwoods in a notch in the hill just above the house. There was a pickup out front and a couple of horses and some chickens about but no one appeared for observation or a wave.

~ ~ ~ ~ ~

Claire's tractor was an older model Case, real basic, none of that cab-over stuff, about forty horse, and one evening we cranked it up and hooked it up to the two-bottom plow. We worked up that portion of the bottomland, about twenty acres, where they had done their small-scale farming so long ago. Claire assured me that the periodic high water from the creek, laden with silt, had kept the ground fertile, but she said we must work it up and summer fallow the land, so that it would be nitrogen rich and largely weed free the following year when I could put in a grain crop while seeding it down to a legume grass. I was made to know how to plow a field by Claire, what power and gear to use, and what pace to set, how to set out my "lands" and keep the furrows straight, mark out the "headlanding" to turn around on and then plow it down at the end so the whole field was done, an age-old skill that has been almost entirely lost in America in the space of a few generations. With the field plowed there came the disc; straight discing and then on the diagonal, to break down the plowing and fill the deadfurrows, and then the cultivator, with periodic spreadings of manure from the manure spreader; that too was worked down and into the dirt; and as weeds would appear I would give it a going over with the cultivator and rip them up to the surface and the sun where they would dry out and die. Those were long, hot, dusty evenings, or entire days on a Saturday or Sunday, when I came to love the heat and sweat and the dust and the noise of that old machine and the satisfaction when done of a field made rich and clean and ready for planting without bags of store-bought fertilizer having to be spread over the dirt to make it rich, or layers of spray spread over the weeds to make them die. And she made me aware of another type of farming I might try in time.

"If we still had our team I'd show you how to harness and work them," she said. "A tractor has its place but you should have a team to really farm right. They're slow but they do the work well and everything to make them go you raise right here on the place and even what they leave behind you put to use."

I said, "One of those old ag books you sold me tells all I need to know about farming with horses and shows you how to harness them and all of that," I said. "I'm keeping some of those old books to help myself out."

"Child, you will have this place working just like we did back then," she said.

It pained Claire to ride much now and she liked having me do it for her. So I would ride out with the dog loping alongside and check the nine cows and calves and move them around as Claire explained she didn't want them spending all their time eating all the grass in the bottom and along the creek. One day, the horse and the dog and I were instructed to "gather," and bring them in, and I brought them in, and as I drove them up toward the barn I saw the corral door was open and the dog knew what to do as well as the horse and though the cattle got fractious when they saw the corral and the gate we got them into the corral and the gate shut with no animals breaking away. Sarah was there with Claire, ready for work. Bingo was to have come too, to help, but "bigger business," Sarah said, had kept him away. Claire said, "That's all right, we three won't have any trouble with this little bunch."

We were going to brand nine calves and castrate that four of the nine that would have been bulls, only we would make them steers. And we would do it the old way, on the ground with a rope and a horse and some willing hands and without the help of a squeeze shute or branding table. Of course I had no idea what to do. I thought I did, for I had read about this traditional spring ritual of branding and castrating calves; but when Claire, mounted on the mare, smoothly roped the first calf over the head, and Sarah said, "put him on the ground!", I panicked and ran in and tackled the critter like this was some kind of football game, which I had played for a time as a kid. But this was a different game. The calf did not go down but I did and I got kicked good in the balls in the process; the starch was all out of me for a time and of course Claire made a joke about it all and then both women laughed. Then Sarah showed me how. She ran in and got a knee in under the brisket just right and her hands over the top, and though she couldn't have weighed much over 100 pounds she got the calf off its feet and as it landed on its side its air went out and she had a knee across its neck and a front leg in her hands, bent under at the pastern and the whole leg locked up so the calf stiffened and groaned. She held this grip on the calf and had me get both hands on one of the calf's kicking hind legs, and the other hind leg at her instruction I pinned down to the ground with my boot, rendering the calf spread eagle and helpless for the time. Claire had stepped down from the saddle. She was clearly having some pain with the exertion but just as clearly this work enthralled her. The horse set back and dug in and held the rope tight to the saddle horn as Claire came to the fire and got the iron. The brand, a C Bar, had been heating a livid red-hot in an oak coals fire nearby, and Claire brought the iron and deftly burned the C Bar mark into the flank of the calf's flesh. The groan I heard was almost human and the animals tongue lopped out and you could smell the burnt flesh. She took the iron back to the fire then returned and pulled the jackknife from her pocket and bent between the calves legs and cut away the soft pouch of flesh where testicles, left alone, would descend. But they weren't left alone. With the pouch opened and bleeding not too much really, she pushed and probed with her fingers and the testicles popped out and she pulled them out till the cords attached were tight. Then she cut them off at the base of the cords and sprayed the wound with an antiseptic. The calf reacted less violently to this removal than to the burning, yet moped about droopy and acting sick for days afterwards, like a young male animal that had...well...just had its balls cut off.

We were about half done with the nine calves when Claire gave the rope and the horse and the saddle to Sarah. Sarah mounted and with the same grace in movement that always had you noticing every little thing she did, she shook out a loop and cornered a calf and threw a small, tight, circle, just the size and just the throw to fit perfectly over the calf's head. Claire said, "that-a-girl!...Oh child, she's a hand...as good as I was in a younger day!" I had got the hang of putting these calves on the ground and I busted this calf and Sarah stepped down with the mare holding the rope tight and Sarah this time pinned and spread the back legs and Claire again marked the calf. Then, the last one, the women had me work the iron and the knife. I did it -- burnt the mark into the flesh and cut the testicles out -- and something of the reality of meat was brought home to me. I had always liked meat yet, like most people of our time, I had never killed or prepared my own meat. Nor, until recently, had I even seen an animal killed or prepared. The week before I had seen Claire kill and dress a chicken as naturally as, by pulling it out of the ground and scraping it and cutting it up in the kitchen, one would kill and clean a carrot. With blood now on my hands, I knew that I would soon be able to kill too, if not with pleasure, than at least with a modicum of satisfaction and pride.

Our work done, we rested, the three of us, under the cottonwoods, drinking iced tea, and Claire especially was very tired, yet exhilarated by the work. I was too. And I was, without saying so, pleased with myself; even with two women, one quite old and sick and the other slim as a reed, having to show me what to do, and having out-worked me to boot, and Claire still teasing about that calf that kicked me in the balls, and Sarah seated beside me, laughing at what Claire said and yet somehow conspicuously

not noticing me, patches of wet in places on her shirt, and a fine
bead of sweat gracing her upper lip.

~ ~ ~ ~ ~

Some evenings I would just saddle up and take a ride. The
dog always went with me now, jumping and spinning and yapping
at the sky in her excitement, and each time I would find the hills
and little valleys and sharp little canyons and the tree-lined creek
and all held a myriad of beauties and discoveries, even within the
confines of a mere 200 acres. And horseback travel, at a walk,
trot, lope or gallop, gave me a mobility and vision and some
nameless rapport with what I saw and where I went that I could not
have found in any vehicle or even afoot. It was not hard to realize
how a whole economy and mythology and culture, and yes even
literature, had arisen from the experience of Western men and
women horseback. Invariably, at some point in the ride, I would
top out on some hill and look down to the ranch, and my eyes
would find her, and she me, and we would wave and connect and
love each other the only way we could.

In the beginning she would cook us a supper and would feed
me after the evening's work. In time though, I would need to help
her and towards the end I prepared the supper for both of us. We
would eat at the kitchen table and talk about the ranch and the
work, which she enjoyed, and I would ask about everything I could
think of that I would need to know to make the ranch a working
place again when it was mine, and she very much enjoyed that, too.
And so she told me all about the modern ranchers, what she called
"living-room ranchers," who did most of their ranching from the
living room, or the cafe, or the pickup truck, or from some office
far away, and who no longer raised their own food but bought it at
a store like city folks, and who spent all too little of their time on
the land and with their stock. And she told me how she and
Clemson and Santos, back when the ranch was big, would spend
long days horseback moving the cattle around and often sleeping
out on the ground with the cattle to keep them grazing hard for just
the right length of time, and then moving them on to another
portion of range so that no part of the ranch was ever overgrazed.
And she told me all the things I'd need to know to make what had
become a mere 200 acres produce well but also for all time. Then

we would do the dishes together, till I came to do them myself, and then she would take her pills and I would put her to bed. I would read to her the best selections, the ones she liked, from the *Western Ranchman*, till she fell asleep, and then I would use the roads to walk myself home in the dark and the summer air.

It seemed for me there was little else but Claire and the ranch at this time, though there was Carla too. Sometimes, arriving home late at night, I would call her and she would come over. And sometimes she would just be there. Her project was underway, she had been talking with Santos, and wanted to talk to me about it. I would lend my interest and what help I felt I could. We would talk and go over her work. She had the project well in hand from the start, was a good editor by instinct and a good writer by talent, yet I feel I was able to offer possible solutions when the book would stall, without putting anything of myself into the work. And she knew everything about me, about my life with Claire and the ranch, and knew that, with Claire dying, I was hurting too and desperate for life; finally I would allow my mind to come away from the old woman I'd come to love a certain way, and Carla would be there, loving me quite differently. And then we couldn't keep our hands off each other.

And, too, there was Bingo and Sarah and Jill, their little carrot-topped girl. They came out to the ranch once or twice a week, sometimes in the evening when I was there. This was a great joy for Claire. She didn't like Bingo Callahan but she did love her son and it warmed her when he would come, whatever his demeanor or intent. His demeanor showed that he was discomfited, his personable we're-in-this-together grin was largely gone. He couldn't wait for his mother to die but it clearly bothered him to have to watch, and it bothered him as well that someone else had to an extent assumed his role. His intent, I think, was as much to check up on me as Claire. He knew I was there every evening and Claire told him, without his asking, why: "We're fixing up the place," she said, "because it pleases me to see it that way before I'm gone." Who could argue with that? Not even Bingo, though he must have wondered if there wasn't something more. But he was too much man to ask about something he didn't already know. For my part, I complemented myself that I was belittling the man by helping his mother and doing the work on the ranch that was by rights his own. And that pleased me.

Sarah, it seemed, was genuinely kind. She fussed over Claire and helped, as Bingo would not, around the house, gathering up the sheets and other laundry and doing them at their home in town for Claire, then bringing them back next visit to make up a clean bed and put clothes away. Other things she would do around the house for Claire, too, and toward the end she was not above putting her arm around Claire, with Claire's arm over her shoulder, and helping her to get around. This had become my job but Bingo wouldn't have me helping his mother that way when he was around. He would get his wife to do it and Sarah was glad to help. And she knew how much Claire liked talking about the ranch and she would take an interest in that and they would talk about what Claire and I had been doing to fix up the ranch. One day the three of us went out to the barn and Claire showed Sarah how we had been fixing the roof, which had begun to leak, and scabbing in some two-by-fours and four-by-fours in the right places to reinforce the building and make it strong again, and replacing some of the old sheet metal with new. On the way we made a detour to the garden, and the plowed field, passed by some of the cattle, the horse, and some chickens, and I could tell from the conversation between the two women as we went along that Sarah really was a hand just as Claire had said and knew the whole of agriculture in the Southwest from the ground up. And at the barn she looked at the work I had done critically and commented favorably on the work to Claire. It had amounted to a good deal of work before it was all done and I knew I had done it well; nonetheless, I was pleased at the comment from Sarah, although, as usual, the comment was directed to Claire, not to me. For me, Sarah had nothing more than a generic greeting with no name attached when she and Bingo arrived, and a similarly inane farewell or wave with no name attached when she and Bingo left. Between times she would offer nothing more than the occasional, cryptic glance when she thought I wasn't looking, or the occasional, direct, inscrutable look when she knew I was. At first I thought maybe this was just because Bingo was around, but when he wasn't, as when we all went for our walk to the barn, nothing changed. For Sarah, I was hardly there. Or so it seemed. I certainly did not know what was in her mind at that time, in so far as I was concerned, but I did feel certain it was more than what was being presented. I let it lay. I was at that time involved with Claire, a love with a woman in a way I had not known before, and that was enough. I was content to look at Sarah, for she was even more lovely out there at that ranch than when I had first seen her at the country club dance. She belonged there in the out-of-doors, on that ranch, and was most beautiful there and never more so than when she helped and got dirty and worked up a sweat and unconsciously displayed her considerable competence. I really liked that about her. I tried not to look too obviously or too long, or with too much admiration; like her I took to acting like, for me, she was hardly there. My guess is, she knew better.

And the finest thing that Sarah did for Claire was bring along that carrot-topped girl, little Jill. She was too young to understand death and would run and shriek and posture as little girls will do, and she played most of the games she had always played with her grandmother and gave Claire a joy none of the rest of us could provide. Surely it was a joy to watch them together, though there was for me a pinch of discomfort as well, not only seeing Claire passing through her final days; but too, they were all a family, an extended family of grandmother and son and parents and child, and were in a realm a prickly bachelor would never know. I'd been made aware of this juxtapostion before, and never felt like I missed anything. At least anything I wanted. But now I did.

Of course none of this could last. Claire grew weaker. The pain came and went. It did not seem to me that it grew worse and she continued to insist, "It's not so bad." It was largely controllable with those pills, when she took enough of them, though the pills put her in something of another world. Meanwhile she was home, with four people who came by at times with whom she could relate and find some goodness and joy, and of course that little blue-heeler dog who was always by her side, day and night.

But there came that day when Bingo and family drove up and couldn't help but notice as I was helping Claire at her task inside the outhouse door. She had come to be so weak that once on the seat, she had trouble getting herself up. When I wasn't there she took a staff with her and, leaning on it, got herself up when she was done. But it was a struggle for her and it had come to be that I would help when I was there. From a distance Bingo saw this that day and it was much too much for Bingo. He put Sarah to replace me at the job at once, and, once they were in the house and with Claire resting on her bed, an argument began with Bingo announcing that it was time for Claire to go to the hospital where she could have "proper care." The thought of the hospital clearly put the fear of death in the old woman -- she had seemed almost serene about the ultimate result to that point -- and for the first time she broke down. There was panic, and tears, and great remonstrations with what strength she had left, but Bingo wasn't arguing, he was deciding. It seemed a family matter, I waited awkwardly out under those cottonwoods with the little carrot-topped girl while the argument and Bingo's decision came down inside. I could hear Sarah making some attempt at mollifying Claire, to no avail. When Bingo and Sarah came out I accosted him.

"Let her stay, Bingo," I said. "I'll close up shop for a week or two and move out here. She won't be alone for a minute."

"Are you some kind of nurse?" The Bingo grin was entirely gone now but the eye contact was right there.

"Considering what needs to be done, I'm not sure that matters, but I'll take your point. Why don't we hire some in-home care. It won't be long either way, but the idea is, it would mean a lot to Claire to be here."

"We could hire a nurse," Sarah said to Bingo, like she'd thought of it herself. "And I could help. It could be done, Bingo."

"You've got your own to take care of," he said. "My Mother's going to the hospital in the morning; she's going to have the proper care."

Bingo scooped up his little girl and started for the pickup. I tried to catch Sarah's eye before she left, but nothing doing. She was with Bingo, walking away.

I went back into the house to be with Claire. I got her comfortable on the bed and let her lay there and weep as she would. It was a little early for supper but I told her about how I would cook us up some chicken soup with rice and with some bread and butter on the side and then I went into the kitchen and got it started. I took my time and went back and forth between the kitchen and the bedroom as supper was prepared. I brought the supper in finally on a tray and set a small table between us and she sat up on the edge of the bed and ate her supper. It was a good rich soup and made with one of the chickens we had butchered and we talked about that and had a nice supper and it seemed to help.

After supper she said she might like to "rest a bit," meaning sleep, and she took one of her pain pills and I helped her get undressed and into a nightgown and into bed. In spite of her age this had been a fine strapping woman just a few months earlier when I first saw her at the post office, but the sickness had rendered a sad sight of skin and bones in that short time. She knew this even more vividly than I and was embarrassed even in all her weakness and she seemed relieved when she had gotten her gown on and was in the bed and out of sight under the sheet and cover. I did the dishes and checked on her when I was done and she had fallen asleep. It was still early evening with hours of light left and I went outside to do the chores.

I fed the chickens and gathered the eggs and fed the horse and fed and milked the cow and puttered around a while, and then I took a walk. With the dog ahead of me, jumping and spinning in her excitement, I walked south, past the barn and corrals, along and just below the rim of the bluff, for about a half mile to that patch of mesquite and some nameless brush where Claire said "The People," meaning a village of the Mimbres Indians of the Mogollon culture, had lived. In fact there were patches of similar scrub trees and brush all along the foot of the rim and there was nothing notable about this one. In recent weeks I had ridden by here many times and had looked for signs of ancient life. I had never actually entered to look but had looked from a distance for some semblance of an outline of structures in the trees. I could never see what I looked for, but now as I stopped there and looked from a distance of perhaps fifty yards I felt there were indeed some unnatural outlines to the lay of the land. At least I thought that for a while. Then it all seemed a mirage, that I was in fact "seeing things" just because Claire had told me they were there. Certainly no one would see it who hadn't been told and shown the way. Then, for the first time, I approached and went into the trees. The scattered, scrubby, desert arboretum of mesquite, juniper, piñon, cholla, patches of gramma grass, and a bunch of stuff I couldn't name, was maybe five acres in size and lay along the bluff. It was quite a level stretch of land and stopping at the edge of the scrub and looking out it did offer a nice vantage to the creek and bottom land just slightly less elevated below. Still, there were dozens of places on this 200 hundred acres where The People could just as well have made their home. Wandering through it was apparent that if there was anything left here it was long since overgrown with the vegetation that grows in this climate, up against a bluff, at about 16 inches of precipitation per year. Looking closely now, I wandered about. I saw no remnant walls or building blocks or signs of structure of any kind...until I came to that place where an ephemeral stream of water coming off the bluff in heavy rains had worn a small arroyo in the land. I followed the arroyo towards its source at the bluff and suddenly crossed the first wall, visible not above the ground but under the ground where the water had worn the surface away. I scrapped away at the dirt and uncovered that which had first caught my eye, the butt end of an adobe block. It was oblong in shape and the long side ran parallel to the bluff and looking now parallel to the bluff I could see the outline of the wall on the surface of the ground. And then suddenly, now that I could see one wall, it seemed I could see them all, and the irregular outlines of an oblong shaped room came to form before my eyes. I walked about rapidly now, away from the arroyo, and, yes, there were rooms beneath me throughout the area, all equally invisible just moments before but readily visible now. This had been a village of some size with many rooms and structures, all the walls now leveled by time and covered with sifting dirt and vegetation but with no doubt many treasures and the history of their lives remaining underneath. I returned to the arroyo and tracked it through the original room, where nature had done some digging for me. My vision was much better now and I quickly spotted what I had walked by before, a rounded, off-white and odd looking rock that didn't look like a rock anymore. The dog, as always, wagged and showed an intense interest and understanding at whatever I had in mind, and she was digging too, as I dug away the dirt, and I knew I was uncovering pottery, an olla as it turned out, with the rounded bowl narrowing to the small opening at the top and not unlike a flower vase of today. It was too small to be used to haul water but it had no doubt been used to hold water once the water was hauled, the rounded bowl portion formed for quantity, the narrow spout for pouring and to keep out the dirt. But it was not just intact and functional. I held it in my hands and rubbed away a few patches of dry dirt and was delighted to read a story painted black on white on the surface of the olla, as the peculiar decorated stick men of "The People" carried sheaves of grain out of their fields; these two were followed by a child and a dog and a woman with outstretched hands awaited them.

This was an awesome find; great treasure indeed. Here were the lives, the art and culture, of a great and unusual people captured in my hands, and laying here for a thousand years, the final decades with the last quarter of the twentieth century eating up the world all around. I felt as I have before upon finding a truly rare book, another real treasure, at a flea market or bargain bookshop, that long lines of passing people had overlooked for days or even years. In this case however I felt I ought to return the treasure to its proper place, yet not before I would show Claire, for this if anything would please her. I started back to the ranchhouse and carrying it in my hand I heard something rattling inside the bowl. I took it to be bits of dirt and rock and stopped to pour them out and noticed there was congealed dirt, a plug of crude pottery, in the spout. I dug it out with my pocket knife. Then I tipped the olla and out poured a few small bits of dirt and rock and a little handful of red and white, parti-colored beans. In size and shape each was like a pinto bean, with however a mottled pattern of red and white unique to every bean. I had to question now how old this olla might be and indeed I wondered if there was somehow a hoax, for while an olla of well-made pottery could last a thousand years, organic matter would surely rot away in a fraction of the time. Or would it, tucked away as it was and in a dry climate? I now had more to show to Claire, and questions to ask. Claire would know. I returned the beans to the bottom of the olla and hurried back to the ranch like a goofy little kid going home with a frog in his pocket.

She was still asleep. Peaceful as she was in sleep, and out of pain for the time, I hated to wake her, and yet I held her hand until she came awake. It took a few moments but when she finally came awake and saw the olla I was holding beside her she was quite lucid and said: "Oh child, you have been to the village of The People!"

"Yes," I said. "And look what I've found."

I turned on the light beside the bed and held the olla up to show her the painting around the bowl. She waited for her eyes to adjust and then pushed the bowl further away to bring the scene into focus and I turned the bowl to show her the farmers and the family and the crop. She brightened and said: "Oh honey, they were good farmers. They must have been to keep themselves fed without so much as a hoe or an implement or a mule to pull it."

"And what about this?" I said, and I poured the beans out beside her on the cover.

"Why those are their beans, child, and they would bring home a jackrabbit and cook it up with a big bunch of these beans and they would flavor it with whatever wild plants and herbs they knew about and could find and have a good meal."

"But how could these beans last all that time?"

"Oh child, believe me; they're still good. We used to find these beans when we were kids, hidden away in bowls like this, and we planted them and grew these beans for several years. This was our little crop and we brought the beans to the kitchen and we all ate them. They're good beans, better eating than the pintos, but somehow as we got older we lost interest and let the crop go. These are the first I've seen in a great many years but they are the same as what we found as kids and if you plant them you can start a crop. You should plant them in a week or so when the rains come and they will mature and harden in the pod before the frost."

I put the olla on the night stand by the bed where she could see it. I gathered up the beans off the bed and put them in my shirt pocket. Meanwhile, she started to tell me about planting and growing beans, and as I had done before when she would give me these lessons in agriculture, I got a pad and paper and I was asking questions and taking notes. And she told me how people would pay an extra good price for these unusual beans handed down from the

Ancient Ones, and from beans we went on to chickens and goats and she told me how I could expand the chickens to several hundred laying hens and sell the eggs from these free-ranging chickens at a good price to people who want real farm eggs from real farm chickens, and she gave me her recipe for goat cheese which she felt, too, I could make to good advantage and we went through the whole cycle of crops and livestock, and in time it was not "I" but "we," and it was like we were planning our year's labor together on this farm/ranch enterprise and we talked on like none of it would ever end.

She was alive and it seemed almost well till well into the night as we talked and then finally she tired. I set down pages of notes and went and got a glass of water and gave her her pills for the night. I turned off the light, and without really knowing much pain she was asleep.

I sat by her through the night, the blue-heeler dog in her usual night-time place on the space rug at the foot of the bed. I would doze off in the chair and come awake when she would wake with her dreams and some rambling talking in her sleep. She had taken an extra pill and while it deadened the pain she was less coherent and she would appear to be awake, though it was difficult to say for sure, and she would say things from way back in her past I couldn't understand. After midnight her sleep went deep and she didn't wake until just before dawn, with the birds singing outside, and this time she was lucid and alive and she said, "I want to see Santos. Oh child, you must go get him now."

She seemed to assume I knew all about her and Santos Aguilar. I said, "Bingo's coming, Claire."

"Go get Santos now, before Bingo comes. Tell him the truth. Tell him I'm leaving and that I'm going to die."

It was June, with first light about five o'clock, and I considered that Bingo probably would not come before breakfast, and looking at Claire I knew I had to go get Santos Aguilar.

I said, "Where are your keys?" and she said, "Take the horse."

This made sense as it was a long way around by road and I stepped out of the house into first light and headed for the barn. I bridled and saddled the mare quickly, led her out of the barn, stepped on and started at a lope down the slope and across the flat, headed southeast, the blue-heeler dog racing alongside. It was still half dark out and it was a little scary running a horse that way but I knew the horse could see better in the dark than I and would not try anything she couldn't handle. She wasn't a young horse but she could still run and we covered the flat at a gallop and went down the creek, then slowed some as we went into the hills on the east side. It didn't take long and I rode into the yard in front of the house of Santos Aguilar. I didn't fancy waking up a man I didn't know with the message I had but, ranch hand that he was, he was already out and about, feeding his own meager flock and nursing a warm cup of coffee in his hands as he eyed me, riding up. I stepped down and accosted a slim, wizened man of uncertain age and a sharp, brown, Indian face. His expression was incurious, almost like he was expecting me. I said, "Claire is dying; she wants to see you."

There was no apparent hurry to the man, he seemed almost deliberate, and careful like a man who wasn't quite well, but it sure didn't take him long to ready a dark brown -- almost-black -- horse, and away we went. A red sun cast streaks of light across the higher hills; the *vega* was still in deep shadow as we galloped across. At the house we just dropped the reins and he went inside. I followed, as far as the kitchen. I put some coffee on, waited for it to perk, poured some, and left two cups nearby. In the bedroom they talked in Spanish.

I sat outside under the trees with the dog and the horses standing nearby and drank coffee and watched the sun walk across the valley and fill it up. It was warm already and you could tell it was going to get hot. I went back in and refilled my cup and I could tell that Santos Aguilar had found the coffee and the cups. I went out and slowly drank my second cup but by now I was getting nervous and when I finished I went back in and stepped to the doorway of the bedroom and told Santos Aguilar it was time to go. I went back out and worried that I was going to have to go back in and get in an argument with the two of them about it, but within a few minutes he came out. He expression was nothing I could read and he stepped up on his horse. He reined around and nodded my way and started off at a procedural trot and never looked back. I had seen "cowboys" ride in Western movies, but as I watched the rider leave I saw that Santos Aguilar rode easy, natural, as relaxed as sitting in a chair; the horse had a bounce with the trot as he went away, but the rider didn't. Claire rode like that, I had noticed, and, yes, Sarah too. I watched him ride off till he disappeared in the trees along the creek, and I considered that with enough time in the saddle I might one day ride easy and natural too. Then I walked Claire's horse to the barn. I unsaddled the horse and when the dog and I got back to the house Bingo Callahan drove up in his pickup, followed shortly by a county ambulance that inched it's way down the hill and over the ruts and into the yard. Bingo and I gave each other a distant nod as we faced off, then I went in for a quick good-bye while Bingo turned to give directions as the ambulance backed into place.

Claire was bright and full and teary, greatly immersed in the emotions provided by the visit of Santos Aguilar. I told her that I would take good care of everything we had and keep it as it was. She said, "Oh no honey, you're going to make it better." I was teary too, and there she was telling me not to cry, that Santos and I had given her everything she could ever ask to say good-bye. Then I heard them coming in through the kitchen door. I squeezed her hand and gave her a hug and then I left, passing the people dressed in white and the stretcher on the way. I sat on the wall outside but out of the way and Claire never saw me as I watched them bring her out, the dog trotting along bewildered underneath the stretcher and she jumped right in as they slide the stretcher into the back of the hospital wagon. One of the men in the white clothes cursed and grabbed the dog and put her out and the hospital wagon drove off with the dog sitting there, like me, watching it leave.

Bingo Callahan came over. He said, "I suppose I ought to thank you for helping to look after my mother these past weeks and so I'm doing just that, I'm thanking you. I'm also telling you there's no need for you to be around here anymore."

I said, "I figure I'll milk that cow, feed the chickens, and give the horse a flake of hay. Then I'm headed back to town."

"I imagine you've got a lot of work to catch up on back there."

"That's correct."

"Well you don't need to worry about the chores around here. You finish up this morning if you like. Starting this evening, I'll send a man out to take care of what little there is."

I just stared at him and said nothing and he added, "You'll want to remember who's place this is."

"It's Claire's place," I said, "everybody knows that."

My particular conversations with Bingo didn't number the fingers on your hands and I was pleased to note that so far I had an answer to everything he had to say. He just looked at me without his grin for a time, then he turned and started to leave and then he turned back and said, "You tell me something: where did you get that pot?"

"That's Claire's pot."

"I never seen that pot before."

"Claire said it's been here all along."

"Well if it's Claire's pot it belongs to this place."

"If I was fixing to steal it Bingo, I would have hid it away before you came in, 'stead of leaving it by the nightstand."

"I never said you were fixing to steal it."

"You didn't exactly say that."

He offered just a bit of that we're-in-this-together grin but he didn't do a very good job with it. And I wasn't looking so good myself. I had been crying and, facing off now against a grown man, it showed and I didn't like it at all. And it occurred to me that a horseman, somewhere off on a far hill, was probably watching us both.

Bingo Callahan turned and walked away. He didn't look back and he got in his pickup and drove off. I watched him go, till I couldn't see or hear his truck anymore. Then I did my chores and when I was done I started for town. The dog, for the first time ever, started to follow. I turned and said, "Go to the barn!" She turned and started for the barn, then stopped and turned again and looked at me. This time I told her that I'd be back and to just to stay and watch over things; I left her there in the front yard as I turned and walked to town.

Chapter 10

On the last day of June the drought and heat broke with a fine display of thunderclouds, noise, lighting and rain, and Claire Callahan died. I hadn't gone to see her in the hospital. We'd said our good-byes and she hadn't lasted three days there and within hours of her passing it was around town and the evening Del Cobre *Region* had it on the front page above the fold. I didn't read it beyond the headline. I had been getting the paper delivered each afternoon at five at the shop but when it came by and I saw they had the news of the death of one of the county's most prominent citizens, one of the last of those who could still recall an earlier and a different time, I threw it away and pulled on a pair of rubber boots and a coat and hat and headed for the ranch. It was still raining when I left and I dropped off into the creek, flushed and swollen with the rain. With my knee-high boots I made my way with no trouble and at times I would just stand there in the creek and feel the water coming down from the high-lonesome go around my legs and I watched it rush by. In time I crossed the fence onto the property. I didn't go up to the house but climbed into the hills above and stood by a big Piñon tree, where I could see all around and not be seen. By then the rain had stopped but you could smell everything alive the way you always can in that arid land after a rain, and a heartstopping blue sky had come on as proud and sure as the clouds and rain just hours before, as the sun dropped away yellow, then pink, then red, then with colors fading and gone behind me. I stood and looked out over the place till I had just enough light left to come home by, and thought of how good a rain it was, and what good it was going to do, and how important it was that it happen again and again through the remainder of the summer, and what all was ahead of me now, and if only Claire were with me to help and share it all. But I was going to have to manage this by myself.

The next day, right on schedule, lawyer Thomas Wynne filed the papers.

Signal To Depart

PART II

Chapter 11

Of course Bingo came by. I knew there had to be some response and a man like that wasn't going to accost you on the phone and I was only surprised it took him three days to make his appearance. He was human -- I saw that when his mother died -- but now she was gone and when he came in that morning that we're-in-this-together grin was back in place, with scarcely a tremor of the lip or a hint of the untowards. This was business after all, and whatever his feelings about my recent dealings, he was right at home. Still, I was one-up on the bastard already and I looked to throw him off straightaway.

"What took you so long, Bingo? You just find out or you been planning what to say? Coffee?"

I had a chair for customers right by the desk -- I was sitting behind it with my own cup of coffee -- and he didn't look stumped for long. He grabbed that chair and brought it around to the front of the desk and turned it around backwards in one motion so he straddled it as he sat down. He was far and away the biggest human being I'd ever seen in that little shop cramped with books.

"No thanks...and I just found out," he said. "And good thing for you that I did. I was about to take a dozer blade to that barn and corrals. I was fixin' to leave the old house. But I had plans for that place. Still do."

"Tell me about it."

"First you tell me how you talked my mother out of the family ranch."

"You know better than that Bingo. You, and the town, and that country club, and you again, tried to pry that place loose from your mother time and again over the last dozen years. She didn't want you to have it. So time came, and she sold it to me. Not for me. She didn't do it for me. She did it for the land itself. She did it for the Callahan Ranch."

"Don't lecture me about the Callahan Ranch. When did you ride in here anyway? I was born there. I was born in that house. I grew up on that place, when it really was a ranch. You're telling me, I think, that the Callahan Ranch has a great history. All right. I know that. Hell, I'm part of that history. Why else would I want to leave that worthless old house? But it's got a great future too, and the two aren't the same. That ranch was the first really successful settlement along *Gavilán* Creek, between the town and the county line. There were others, before and after...little, hard-scrabble outfits. They all bellied up. But the Callahan Ranch was always there, it held on, and it served this community and helped it grow. Well times change, don't they, Jason. You and I know that ranch isn't helping this town grow any more. It's just a piddly little 200 acres and it's in the way. Christ sake, Niles, look at the truth. You got 200 hundred acres that can't support a dozen cows and all around it you've got a growing community of good people, sound American stock, ready to build them a home, borrow money, start businesses, raise them a family and send their kids to our schools. This town is a sleeping giant ready to gather up and go and that land will be a bigger part, a better part, of this community than it ever was as a ranch. Christ sake, Niles, you can't want to hold all that up for that little piss-ant homestead."

"Actually Bingo, I kind of like the idea of this town having to go around that ranch. It'll forcibly remind everyone of certain values otherwise lost. The value of open space, of the culture in agriculture, of why we need clear creeks and riparian communities as well as people communities. There's a family of Mexican Black Hawks nesting along that creek, right on the ranch. Nesting black hawks north of the border you can count on the fingers of your hands. I think it's kind of nice having them this close to town.

"Christ, Niles. Jesus H. Christ. The way you trade books for profit, and cut deals for land, I never would have believed you were one of them."

"I'm not sure that I am. There's a lot about me that *they* wouldn't like. But what's the problem, Bingo? Look at it this way. You got a good chunk of my life's fortune for that land."

"It's worth five times that. Easy. And there's one thing you don't understand -- I don't do this for money. Not anymore. I don't need money anymore. I believe in what I'm doing, as much as you believe in old books, Mexican Black Hawks, and obstructing progress. And I'd like to tell you about a value that's above all the rest...the principal of highest and best use, and why growth is necessary and good, but my lectures on you aren't going to work any better than yours on me. I came here, really, to present you with an option. The first is offered to your better instincts as a trader. The thing is, I can get you your life's fortune back, and then some. I'll give you double what you paid for that land. I'll give it to you cash and I'll give it to you now."

"Since it's worth five times what I paid for it, why would I take just double. I'd be better off to develop it myself. Milk it to it's highest and best use."

"Have you ever developed land?"

"I have not."

"It's the hardest job in the world. It'll work you twenty-four hours a day. You fight the government, you fight the banks, you fight the goddamn environmentalists. And it'll bankrupt you for life with one bad move. It's a financial high-wire act. You have to have the gut for it. You don't have it, Niles. I do. But you're a trader. All right, you price it."

"I like the place the way it is, Bingo. Simple as that. What's you're other option?"

At that Bingo stood up and, eyeing my coffee momentarily, which I had been drinking right along, he turned and paced off enough time to regroup his thoughts while he looked for the coffee pot he knew must be there. He found it in the back corner of the shop and got a cup and poured himself one. He had a way of doing it like it was his own pot and his own coffee and his own cup and he didn't ask me anything about a refill for my cup. Then he came back and once again straddled that chair.

"All right, Niles, see if you don't like this better. You sell me one hundred sixty of that two hundred acres. You price it. We draw the lines so you get that old house and the barn and corrals and a piece of that bottomland and creek. That's forty acres. That's plenty for any little ol' homestead operation you want to play around with. I'd like to have it all. I feel I ought to have it all. That's Callahan land. But I'll settle for one-sixty, a quarter section. I can do most of what I want to do with that."

"And what do you want to do with it."

"I won't shit you about that. I'm not shittin' you about any of this. I'll sell a big chunk to the country club, which is really the city, for the other nine holes we need, and I'll keep the rest for development, for homes, for those good folks I told you about. We both get what we want. And the town benefits. The whole community benefits. You and I can work together on this. You get yours, and I get mine. You like that better?"

"I like that better. But maybe not good enough."

"You can't do better than that, Niles. You get the old homestead, and a place to play, plus the development price for most of the land. We can work together on this, Niles. And while we're working together, we can make some arrangement for those *underground* developments only you and I know about."

"How's that?"

"I didn't shit you. Now don't you shit me. You didn't pick that pot up at the antique store down at the corner."

"As far as the world's concerned, there's no telling where I picked that pot up. I can't help you, Bingo. The way I see it, I'm kind of holding the place in trust. Strictly speaking, forty acres is more than enough for me. But I feel like I'm attached here to a higher calling. Claire and I made a deal, and that wasn't it."

Bingo'd had that engaging crooked grin most of the way, but he lost it now. Or let it go. He finished his coffee, got up, and returned the chair to its place. He went to the door. He turned back to me and said, "Niles, when this is all done I want you to remember that I gave you a chance. I gave you a choice and you turned it down. That's Callahan land. The sign by the cattle guard coming in says so. And by Jesus I'll have it back."

Bingo started to step out the door. But he stepped back.

"And I'm going to find out where you got that pot, too," he said.

Chapter 12

For most of the ranch, there really wasn't a whole lot to do. The fencing was sound now and with only nine head, and the rains coming on, the cattle were feeding themselves. I might have to provide some hay and cake and other supplemental feed come winter, but for now I just rode out there once a day and watched the ignorant yet somehow engaging brutes at their business of eating and excreting, enjoyed their place in the scheme of things, and occasionally moved them around so they didn't eat too much down along the creek. The twenty acres we'd plowed up was fallow until next spring and there was nothing more to be done with that except rip up the weeds a time or two more with the cultivator so it would be clean for planting next year. I milked the cow and gathered the eggs. In the barn, the little blue-heeler had a fifty-pound sack of feed for dogs with a hole in the bottom she could eat out of whenever she wanted and so she could feed herself. The whole business didn't take me an hour a day. Of course I had a pile of big plans derived from my talks with Claire about making use of some of the water rights that came with the land to make the whole valley bloom -- crops and hay and fruit trees and vegetables. And the livestock options. Nine cows with calves was all this land would ever need but some milk goats had appeal and more free range chickens would come in time and a few hogs, too. But I wasn't in a hurry about any of that. I had a lifetime to learn how to work this land so it would produce for all time and I wasn't going to get it all the first summer. I still had my novel in progress to work on and a full-time book business to work and my 200 acres was a hobby that would evolve into a business and a way of life over time. The one thing that did give me a job of work was those beans.

My first walk out to the ranch, after I owned it, I went into the bedroom, looking for that olla on the nightstand. Of course it wasn't there. This didn't surprise me. I had bought the place but Claire's will, I knew, left most of the named items of a personal nature to Bingo -- pictures on the wall, guns, the furniture, stuff like that, and that was fair enough. The olla wasn't one of the named items but of course Bingo had picked it up. Whether he'd picked it up before or after Claire died, before or after I officially owned the place, and how that would all boil down legally, I couldn't say and didn't have any interest in finding out. I had the land and that's what counted, although it did eat on me a little knowing the mistake I'd made in ever letting Bingo see that pot, and wondering what he would get in dollars for it. He probably had the money already and I knew it was plenty; there's a ready market of serious money for that old Mimbres pottery. Still, better than that olla, I had those beans. To have found a work of art a thousand years old was monumental in my collector's mind. But there were doubtless a great many other pots on the place, some perhaps even more fine, and they could stay right where they were. Where they belonged. It was enough to know that they were there. But those beans were something else. In those beans The People had left me something that was, in a sense, still alive. At least that's what Claire said.

I had been carrying them around in a shirt pocket, closed by a flap, ever since I found them. I liked knowing they were there. I liked feeling them there, and now and then I would take one out and hold it in my hand and imagine that it would grow for me pods and pods of living seeds. But now, owning the place, I took them down to the creek and rinsed them carefully, one by one, letting clear water run over each as it lay in my hands. The dust, ages old, came off and the white and deep red parti-color patterns came on vividly as the gentle current washed them clean and the sun dried them on a rock. They were little jewels and there were twenty-seven of them.

Down near the creek, within Claire's last vegetable garden, there was a large plot of unused ground. Her garden was not ambitious her last year and there was plenty of space for expansion; within the good fence that kept out the cows there were three acres the family had had as a good corn, bean and vegetable garden in years past. By Claire's last year, less than half an acre was growing mostly lettuce and carrots and squash. Even that is a lot of garden as anyone who's tried it knows and she had not been able to keep up with what she had. She hadn't put any beans in but I would and I couldn't help but recall from my reading and re-reading of Thoreau that his first year at Walden Pond he had put in a bean crop about two-and-a-half acres in size. I was happy to attempt the same.

With my Mimbres beans, clean and dry in my pocket, I got the tractor and plowed up the remaining two-and-a-half acres inside the fence. I disced it down, again and again, and then ran the cultivator over it time over time to break it down to good soil I could work with a hoe. With mechanization on that small plot that didn't take very long. Then, hoe in hand, over the long weekend of the Fourth of July, I worked like a hungry Indian, like the survivalists in ancient times must have worked, and backed down the plot, row after row, cutting the furrows with canted hoe, each about three feet apart. I found that two and a half acres is a mighty project with hand tools. But I was tough from many days of work on the ranch with Claire and almost frantic in my will to see the beans planted early on in the rainy season, that they might fill and ripen and mature in the pods before mid-October, the expected time for the first frost. We had had the first rains so the soil was moist and ready, yet I was blessed with constant sun for my weekends' work. I planted the beans six to eight inches apart, dropping them in by hand as I walked the rows, as The People must have done, that silly dog following along and watching my every move; her head and eye dropped with each bean that fell in line from my hand into the furrow. Of course my meager supply of twenty-seven Mimbres beans took up but a small portion of one corner of the field. I planted black turtle beans and blue corn I got from the feed store in the remainder of the plot. By late Monday evening I was backing down the last of the rows once more, gently guiding a two inch covering of loose dirt into the furrows and over the seeds with my hoe. Then I leaned on my hoe in the finality of the dusk and felt the evening breeze dry the sweat on my shirt. I'd sweat so much from my non-stop, all-day effort my shirt was stiff with salt from perspiring and drying in the sun and breeze. Now the breeze in the evening drying my shirt felt almost cool, and that was good. It was all good. I still had books to read and books to buy and sell. I had a book on the shelf and another in the works. And I still had my dreams, more than ever before. I was full of dreams. But now, it seemed, I was doing something too.

Chapter 13

The benevolent monsoon rains came sometimes every day, but at the least every few days, and the arid lands of southwest New

Mexico were now green. I made my evening hike to the ranch to watch my crop, and ride around, shuffling my little herd here and there, and of course I had to feed those silly chickens and milk the cow. Mostly I watched my crop, since it was my first ever, and I wanted to see what would come up and I was all but saying prayers for those twenty seven Mimbres beans. Within a week after planting the first of the green corn sprouts began to show and then the black beans shortly thereafter. There was nothing green showing in the little parcel of ancient beans except the first of the morning glories and pig weed and other growth of weeds I didn't want which was coming on strong and these I got at right away, throughout the garden, with a hoe. Claire had told me how they would get to be too much to handle if they ever got a good start and I was committed not to let them. But after a week of daily work at hoeing, and watching my blue corn and black beans sprout and grow, and with no signs of life in ancient beans, I quit going down there. It made me sad, to tell the truth. It wasn't just that those supposedly living ancient beans were dead after all. It was that Claire had been wrong. We had placed great faith in each other. But her mind could not have been clear those last weeks, her memory could not have been strong. Facing death, she wanted those beans to have life. And so did I. So I stayed away from my 2 1/2 acres and tended my cows and chickens and horse, and did a little work around the adobe house until, even looking from the front yard of the house down to the flat I could see that the morning glories and pig weed, *et al*, had come back anew and were about to overcome my crop. The next day, a Saturday, I faced a full day with hoe in hand to recover my garden before it was lost to the weeds. Oh those weeds! Those goddamn weeds. They were as appreciative of the benevolent rains as was my now-beleaguered blue corn and black beans, and had achieved such a burst of growth that with all the hoeing I didn't until late morning notice that amongst the weeds, in one small corner of the garden, was a line of new growth, nineteen sprouts of Mimbres beans, all in a row! Or rather several rows. I worked my hoe furiously, I made its blade a blur, as I chopped out the weeds down each row of blue corn and black beans and toward supper time I finished with that, and set my hoe down, and went to my precious, ancient sprouts on

"You wrote this book?" she said.

"Yes," I said.

"Can I read it?"

"Maybe some day."

"Let me read it, Jason."

"Some day. When we know each other better."

She left me, a little huffy acting but mostly bemused, and went back to the bookshelf in the middle of the room. She would pull a volume off and using both hands hold its cover out to me, showing me the book; I would look at it from across the room and she would say, "What's this one?" or "Tell me about this one." I would recognize the book and I would provide a short comment... "*Roping Lions in the Grand Canyon* by Zane Grey. Rather scarce in the first edition you have there. It was written for young adults, that they might thrill to the hunt and the great outdoors and protect the wild, but, unfortunately, almost no kid today is given it to read. Lion hunting is no longer politically correct. Buffalo Jones and Uncle Jimmy Owens are in it, along with Dr. Grey. Hunters and houndmen still value the book and it provides a unique look at what the canyon was like before the goddamn Park Service and mechanized American tourists ruined it...*The Plumed Serpent*, D.H. Lawrence's Mexico book, much reprinted lately but, again, quite scarce in the first edition you're holding. It's artistically flawed but a significant creation nonetheless. It's dense and uneven but, like most of Lawrence, provides something new every time you read it...*Sky Determines*, Ross Calvin, a New Mexico classic which is out of print and out of favor now due to some of the author's sociological observations. But really the best book of its time about New Mexico and a seminal interpretation of the Southwest...literate and poetic of prose, unflinching of opinion, and perceptive of the singular qualities of a region, and its people, past and present..."

She was enjoying this game she was creating, smiling and even laughing a little, and was evidently pleased that I was going along. Now and again she would disappear behind the shelf in the middle of the room, and then she would pop out one end or the other with another book in hand and "How about this one?" or words to that effect, and I would offer my critique. Then she was behind the shelf again and I didn't hear from her for a moment and, when I did, she was still hidden behind the shelf and I heard her say: "Is this one any good?" She did not reappear so I got up from behind the desk and in a few steps I was around the corner of the shelf.....Sarah was naked, almost, -- her back to me and her jeans and boots and socks and blouse and all else on the floor -- save for her pale blue panties which, knowing now that I was standing there and watching, she slowly peeled down over her high, full-and-tight, and awesome ass. She did it with a certain style. Of course, I had been with white women before; they are not essentially different -- how could they be? -- but still, there's nothing quite like it. And never one quite like Sarah, with her great shock of red curls to her shoulders and the homespun freckles down her back, as she bent over taking those pale blue panties slowly down, down, as she got them, finally, to her knees, and stepped out. Carla was brown, soft, a pliant female form you had to know and touch to love; Sarah was creamy-white, chiseled, curved and firm, and her muscles shown through her skin. Then she turned and held pale blue panties as she approached, dropping them finally to the floor, and then I could look only at her. Where she was haired she was pale-red -- another great shock of it -- yet you could see it; she got me looking at it, I went to my knees for her, she arched, and held my head in her hands and told me how and why and all about it; and when I finally stopped she was so close she said: "Oh you bastard!" But I wasn't being mean. I stood and let her strip me; cloth was torn and some buttons were lost forever as she got me ready.

"If you won't let me read your book, at least let me fuck you. And now Jason, I don't have much time."

She wouldn't have it any other way. Both naked now and the room only lit by the muted light of the street outside, she had to climb me; she rode me as I walked her around the room, midst all those books and manuscripts, my life's work passing by, and finally, right in front of the door, the town of Del Cobre just a step away, I held her up, and down, hard: a woman, grunting obscenities as I urged her on, while I almost thought I saw a shadow come and go, outside, just a step away.....

She insisted on cleansing herself, "so Bingo will never know." In the bathroom she squatted, shameless, in the tub, over an inch or two of warm water; she splashed it between her legs, and used some soap too. I pulled the lid of the seat down and sat nearby; she had that great flair with any body movement and I watched...she was without shame, beautiful, perfectly and gorgeously obscene. It seemed an unspeakable intimacy to me, even more so than what had happened midst all those books, and I told her so.

"You have some way of saying things, Slim. We'll do lots of *unspeakable* things before we're done."

"Will we?"

"Sure."

"Let's."

"We will."

She was elegant and all naked lurid grace, even at a squat, and I said, "How's Bingo taking it?"

"Your real estate deal?" She stood now in the tub and without getting up I tossed her a towel.

"Yes."

"He's not happy about it," she said, lifting a leg to the lip of the tub and starting to towel dry. "But he's already hard at work on that new development over east...he bought the McKinnon Ranch you know."

"I didn't know that," I said.

"We'll, he's got it, and that helps him take his mind off that deal of yours. And there's a part of Bingo that can appreciate a land scam, even if it's not his own. How are you taking it?"

"My real estate deal?"

"Yes."

"I'm trying to do right by the land."

"Need some help?"

"I could use the right kind of help. Claire told me a lot but I'm new to it and some things you just have to learn as you go along. I think it would take a family to really do right by that place."

"So do I. You be patient, Jason. We'll do right by that place."

"It's going to be hard to be patient with you."

"You be patient, Slim. This will take some time. There are some things in my life that you don't have. In the end we'll do right by that place. What are you going to do with the old Aguilar homestead?"

"Let old Santos stay there, so long as he lasts."

"Sure. That's good. Just don't do anything stupid. That's a nice place. And there's a real good spring up the hill behind the house."

"Yeah, I saw those nice cottonwoods."

"That's a nice place. We wouldn't want to lose it. So don't do anything stupid. Be patient. We'll do right by all of that place."

"You think we're going to get away with this?"

"Sure, Slim; don't worry. Men are easy to fool, and the husband is always the last to know. And Bingo has so much else on his mind. My friend Karen lives just around the corner from you. The story goes like this: I get away one night a week to be with friend Karen. And Karen holds the story while I'm here. She's helped me before."

She was vigorous with the towel, until even the pale red feathering between her legs was dry. And then she was dressed and then almost as quickly she was gone. There was none of the lingering, childlike hugging of Carla as she left, an affectation I found myself wanting now. She merely stepped to the door, opened it, then turned and said, "I still want to read your book some day."

"Yes," I said, "when we know each other better."

"We will."

I watched her leave, wanting the sight of her as long as I could have it. I hated to see her go; she had a way of moving that had you noticing every little thing she did as she was down the street and around the corner and gone. Back to friend Karen. And then...home. I hated for that to happen. But I couldn't stop her. I knew I couldn't stop anything that might happen from here on in.

Chapter 15

The next night Carla came in late. Late enough that I would be through writing, or nearly so, and she sat by the desk, as she always did, and asked me how my story was going this evening.

"Not so good...not much progress tonight."

"You've been getting a lot done, night after night. Maybe you need to leave your story for a night or two, and collect your thoughts. That's what you suggest for me, and it works."

"I'm seldom amenable to my own advice."

"You've probably got a lot on your mind."

I just looked at her when she said this, thinking it was some kind of a provocation, but if it was, I couldn't read it.

We went to bed. It was easy; it's never been a problem for me. More than one is good; I've always liked it. Of course I wanted to be with Sarah. But more than that I didn't want to be alone, Sarah with someone else. I was with Carla now, it was my joy to please her, and not have to think about Sarah all night, as I had all the night before, after she had left, and as I had all day; and what I most liked was taking the hurt out of her back. I could feel the tension in her back, it was always there at the end of a day, the muscles hard and unyielding, and of course this is what kinked and compressed her spine and pinched nerves there and made her careful of movement and aware of pain. A day of life would simply do that to her. Erotic tension, followed by yield and release loosened everything up. And then I would roll her on her stomach and work into her backside, from her neck down into her buttocks, focusing finally on the small of the back, in and around that scar, until the most stubborn muscle went to jelly in my hands. I couldn't imagine Sarah needing, or having time for, or even wanting any of this but especially this night I wanted to do this for Carla. And I did, and with her backside finally like pudding in my hands she said, "Were you this good to her last night?"

"No, it was nothing like this last night...I guess that means it was you?"

"Yes, I guess it does. It was probably more than me. Anyone who walked by would have known. But I stopped at the door."

"Have I hurt you terribly?"

"Not so terribly. At first, yes...at the moment. I could have come through the door and you two would not have enjoyed this mad *Mexicana* at that moment. I almost did. But I was more hurt than mad and by the time I was more mad than hurt I had left. And then I wasn't either one very much. I have never expected you to be faithful in that way. Net yet. You're not the type. You'll either be doing it here, and there, or wishing you were and thinking about it, so what's the difference? I have considered it's probably not the first time since I've known you, just the first time I know of."

"Actually, it is the first"

"Well it won't be the last."

"Probably not."

"Well, you won't want to live this way all your life. In the end I think you'll like me best and want me most. You'll see what's right, and then we'll see what I decide."

I did not respond and I was still rubbing her back.

In time she said: "How is it going...are you a farmer and a rancher now?"

"I don't have any illusions about that. I'm still a loopy book dealer, only now I've got some dirt under my nails. And my beans and corn are growing. My Indian beans are growing real well. I've got several broods of chicks coming on, buyers for real eggs, and I'm keeping the cattle moved around so they don't overgraze along the creek or anywhere else and the black hawks have their family and the young ones will soon be ready to fly."

"Do you really mean to make it a life's work?"

"Yes. I'm going to make it produce, all of it, but in a way that's easy on the land. I'm going to farm it, and I'm going to raise livestock. But I'll only take on one new thing each year, so I can learn as I go along. The riparian will be retained for wildlife, otherwise the rest of the bottomland will produce a crop. The hills will have grass and deer and just enough cows, there will be goats and pigs and poultry -- just enough of each -- and the grain crops will rotate with the stock and the legume feed crops so there will always be enough plow down and manure to retain fertility without having to buy it at the feed store, and the rotations and cultivations will keep down the weeds and bugs. In time I plan to learn to do most of it with harness and team. It's going to be a showplace one day, showing how it can be done."

"You have a dream, Jason. More than a dream; a cause. A fine cause I think. Even a noble one, perhaps. The kind that is so very hard to maintain."

"I think it is a noble cause."

"It could be. It could be a noble cause. No one I have known has had such a chance to do such a good thing. Or a more difficult one."

"I don't see how it's so difficult. It'll just take time, I have so much to learn."

"You have an uncommon dream, and a lot of people will see it as a problem. A threat. An obstruction. Especially folks around here. They will see a stubborn, useless iconoclast, standing in the way. Only they won't put it that way. They'll just say, 'He's one of them *em-virum-enolists*, trying to save that...er...*ripareum* habitat.'"

I smiled in response in the dark, at her good imitation of Anglo redneck accent and cultural thought, and said, "I suppose. But I own it; nobody can stop me. I'm going to do it. And they can just sit there and watch, and stew in it if they like."

"I hope you can do it. And I'm wondering if you might have a place for me in this."

"I would want someone who could live it."

"I have never lived that way. I missed that way of life by a generation or two."

"Well, so did I."

"And I'm not strong for that kind of work."

I kept rubbing her. Every muscle had come loose. Her back was free now. But of course it would never be strong. She said, "Jason, what will you do with the five acres that is leased to Santos."

"Well, the lease will run out the end of this year, so we can renew it."

"I have been talking to him. He would like to buy it."

"He can renew it, every year."

"He would like to own it."

"He can have it for a dollar a year. He can do whatever he wants with it."

"You can understand that he would rather buy it, and own it."

"And then he dies some day and what happens to it? Or he goes off on a toot and looses it, like he did before."

"That wouldn't happen now. He would never do the wrong thing with that land. He grew up there, and he owned it once. Now he would like now to own it again."

"That's not part of the plan."

She rolled over on her back then and pulled up the covers like it was time to sleep. "That hurts me more than whoever you were doing it with last night," she said.

Chapter 16

In the heart of the great Southwest, the Callahan Ranch bloomed through the summer heat and sun and rain. In the hot time of late afternoon I would make my way there. I would invariably take the creek now; it was cooler along the creek in the shade of cottonwoods and hackberry and sycamore and willow. And I was drawn again and again to the art work The People had left on the canyon wall that ran off the creek just inside my property line. So before going on up to the ranch and my chores I would go up the canyon, time and again. I was drawn principally to the strange figures about to have each other, the tumescent man, and the woman, at once yielding, urgent, her reaching arms and spread legs expectant and almost demanding. The day did not come when I could pass it by, or fail to stay, staring, far longer than I would ever plan. Carla and I were there; we were like that I thought. She came by more often now, more urgent and yielding than ever, though not expectant, but hopeful, and certainly not demanding, but holding on more dearly, and yet still saying confidently, "You won't want to live this way all your life," proclaiming that in the end she would decide. But not on Wednesday nights, the night each week when Sarah, so the story went, could "get away" to visit friend Karen, and then come by for me. I'd had to tell Carla that Wednesday "is not a good night for us." She understood implicitly, and complied, often then coming by Thursday nights, more yielding and urgent than ever. Yet Sarah was indeed expectant and demanding; where I was seemingly in command with Carla, Sarah was surely in command with me, expectant and demanding of satisfaction, much like the woman of an ancient art. And too, we never had much time, or needed much. Yes, Sarah and I were there too, portrayed in bold, ancient, everlasting strokes. But that wasn't all I saw. For if Sarah was with me on Wednesday nights, she, a married woman, must be with someone else the other six nights of the week, and on one or more of those nights -- though one couldn't surely say which -- they must surely fuck. I liked having them both. I needed them both. And I didn't care what else Carla did. With Sarah, I was surely starting to care...there he was on the wall in ancient paint, pressing his ineluctable organ upon her, and how yielding and urgent, expectant and demanding, was she with him?

Chapter 17

And so The People were very much with me. More and more I wanted to know them, to know their lives and art, and to live something of their lives myself. And so from time to time I would leave my beans and cows and such and visit the secret place where they had centered their lives in this valley. The little blue-heeler dog would go with me, as she went with me everywhere on the land, and as I would walk about the acreage in the trees and brush where The People had lived she would flush and chase cottontail rabbits, dig for ground squirrels in the hillside cliffs that skirted the grove to the west, occasionally in fact catching one or the other of them, and sniff the myriad scents offered only to a dog in the scrubby semi-arid patch of trees and shrubs. She was oblivious to the human heritage that we stood upon in our walks over the village of The People, but no more oblivious than I to the interests in her life that she found over the same terrain. And indeed, as to heritage, there wasn't much to see. Nothing, in fact, if you didn't know it was there. I did, and the outlines of their architecture and their lives were vaguely visible to me as I walked over their homes, courtyards and meeting places. Or at least I imagined they were. In fact, only along the arroyo, where running water had cut into this architecture, was there solid evidence that people had lived here. And I had made sure the most obvious of that evidence was no longer visible. The fine jar with the agricultural scene that had revealed itself in the dirt I had removed and lost through carelessness. Elsewhere along the cut in the earth I had found several other artifacts peeking through. It was tempting to dig them out, examine them, have them. I had resisted that temptation and had used my hands and a trowel to cover them up entirely to make them invisible to any other wandering eyes. Claire had been right of course, and I had learned from her as she had learned before me: "The Ancient Ones have earned their peace." They were safe now, especially with the vegetation of a wet summer filling along the arroyo, and yet knowing they were there midst the vague outlines that stretched this way and that for acres, I could wander about, or sit under a tree, for hours, and picture their lives. Then, on summer days such as I knew, the dirt walls would go up all around me and near naked people would come and go through their doors. Smoke and good smells would come from the cook fires. The commerce of a small village would take place between peoples before my eyes. Men, women, and children of sufficient age, would make their way from the village down to the valley floor for their day's work in the fields where, among other things, they would tend to the health of marvelously colored beans. In the evenings they would return to the village as tired and hungry and sated with work as farmers of any life, race, or generation. At about that time of evening a few others, all male, would return from farther afield, home from the hunt, carrying a bow and arrows or a throwing stick, followed by a dog, burdened lightly with a hare or a couple of birds or, if uncommonly lucky, burdened heavily with a carcass of venison, any and all meat for the pot. At night they would live in a darkened world, lacking, in all probability, even the crude lamps of later races and more modern times. So only the muted light from the flames and flickers of the cook fires would aid night vision. I guessed that for them that was enough. They would see better at night, be more competent there, than us. Perhaps in the hour or two before their laying down for the night was some leisure provided for some woman of talent and imagination to sit by the muted light of a cook fire and decorate a bowl with art that would one day startle the modern world. And later at night, when all had lain down, lovemaking was common, and openly done. Near naked communal peoples would not hide it, nor fear it, nor coat it with shame. Judging from the art they left behind, they adored it. Indeed, lacking the myriad diversions of our times, and living life in a primordial world, they may well have made more of it than even we in our sex-sodden times, when sexual adventure is the only part of the primordial left to us. But we have cloaked our acts in shame. They were shameless; things went on that we would not believe. Yet they would not have known any of it as abnormal, and would have been comfortable with all acts -- going naked, living communally, raising their own food and killing their own meat, eating round a cook fire, making art in near dark, nursing a child until it was two or even three years old, thereby delaying the next conception, accepting the commonality of death, pissing and shitting upon urge and need, and fucking for life and pleasure. My musings here were fueled by my readings. At times I would take a book to the village and sit in the scrubby grove and read of the legends and lore of The People, passed along in the oral tradition from a civilization that had broken down and descended to the Pueblo peoples of more recent times, and so in time into print. In one of these legends I read of one of Kokopelli's most astonishing adventures. In a village where the trader had stopped to visit, the story goes, he noted a particularly beautiful nubile who made a daily visit at a regular hour to a certain spot in the bushes where she would squat to relieve herself. Kokopelli, lurid, earthy rogue, prepared his hiding place there and waited. The nubile came at the appointed time, squatted, and no sooner was she done than she felt the extraordinary organ of Kokopelli moving inside her. The pleasures of this event brought both back to the spot again and again, the true source of the pleasure always a secret to the girl, until she found herself with child, a child she could not explain. But the fertile nature and earthy pleasures of Kokopelli had been served, the story itself satisfied. I knew it all -- I could see it -- in my secret visits to the remnants of an ancient life. And I was content to simply know it was there, and let my imagination do it all. But it was not hard to understand how others, in well intended sacrilege, could want to uncover this heritage, dig it out with precision and archeological skill that all might know more of it and understand it better. I could even almost understand how others yet, in a sacrilege of greed, could want to dig it out in a brutal, commercial rape, finding money in the treasures. That temptation was perhaps natural too, at least in our time. But only I knew and I would not allow any of it.

Chapter 18

Early in August there came a great rain. It was not the short, intense afternoon thundershower, the typical monsoon rain of the Southwest, which is followed closely by the bluest of skies and bright sun. It started that way -- a brief, pounding rain with great claps of thunder and wild lightning skittering across the skies -- but it never cleared, and as the thunder and wild light receded the rain evolved into a slow drizzle that went on through the night. The next day it continued unabated, a gentle rain but seemingly without end, and in the afternoon I sloshed down the brown, rising creek in my rain gear and rubber boots, bypassing the ancient canyon art this time, to stand by my crop with the dog in the rain. Water lay in puddles midst the beans and corn, flecked continually by the small steady drops pelting the surface of the standing wet. Rain, I thought, can never really be overdone in the arid Southwest -- one should bless whatever one can get -- for while rising waters may inconvenience or even occasionally endanger an urban human population, the overall health of the land, which is all that really matters, can always use it beneficially. I looked at my crop and determined that it was benefiting, albeit rains had already been good through the summer. Yet days later I felt some alarm. There had been no letup in the steady drizzly and when I got to the creek that evening the swollen waters were too high to cross and filled the canyon wall to wall. I made my way out there by the roads and the final two-track trail that led to the ranch and there in the valley the creek had overflowed its banks, had come out from the trees and was moving in a brown wet rise up into the valley floor. The desert lands and mountains of the entire drainage were now saturated, nothing was soaking in anymore, and all that fell from the sky was running off and spilling out wherever it could find room. I stood in the pelting rain by my crop with the dog and saw that the east edge of my crop was but yards from the rising flood. The dog stood beside me and watched too, seemingly in sympathy with my concern, though I could not believe she could understand it, and threw off big drops and a shower of wet with a shake of her ample coat.

That night the rain intensified, still a steady drizzle but heavier now. I couldn't sleep and didn't want any company and was relieved that no women came by and I got up from time to time in the night and stood at the sole window high on the wall of my bedroom and heard the rain on the roof and watched it roll down the glass in sheets. The next morning at breakfast at the cafe all the talk was of what the rain was doing to all manner of human commerce, enterprise and living. I shared the concern now and when the afternoon Del Cobre *Region* came out there was news of record rains -- at least by our short historical reckonings -- and there were photos taken from around Arthur County of bridges that had gone out along the Willow River to the east, and the *Rio Jalisco* to the west, stranded livestock and hikers in the mountains, and one car that had been swept away at a crossing, its luckless driver still not found anywhere downstream. I walked out to the ranch late afternoon, the rain unabated. At the crest of the hill overlooking the ranch I looked down at the lake that covered the valley floor. The house and barns and outbuildings and all the livestock and that silly blue-heeler dog were all okay but as I waded out to my crop in knee-deep water only the corn plants were visible, their tops wavering above the slow, brown flow. I stopped a ways away, fearing I would walk in on my underwater beans. My crop could not take much of this, perhaps could not take any of this. The slope of the valley downstream was very gentle so that the flow of water was very gentle too and it did not appear that my beans and corn would be uprooted and carried away by the waters. But after a time -- and how much time? -- they would die under water as surely as the creek moss would die should the waters of the creek ever recede entirely away. The dog came swimming out and circled my legs in a dog-paddle, till she grew tired or bored and went back to land behind me and shook off to instant comfort and sat and watched me as I stood in the flow till my legs cramped and ached in the chilly flow, the victim of nature's extremes.

That night I needed sleep and rest from sleepless nights of worry about the rain. But there was always that rain on the roof to hear and a wet pane of glass to watch as the drops inching on down moved and distorted the view up into a dark starless sky. I let the radio music play to drown the rain on the roof and went under the covers and, finally, did sleep for a time. I awoke at an early hour in the morning and when I turned the radio music off I realized I couldn't hear the rain on the roof anymore. And when I went to the glass only a few wet streaks marred the outside of the pane and above, way above, I could see the stars in the night sky. The rain had gone on east to others who probably didn't need that much of it either.

The sun held and by early evening the waters of the creek had receded as rapidly as they had come up once saturation was reached, and my beans and corn and the entire valley were revealed again, covered now by a layer of silt. The dog and I stood in the evening sun, still warm, and looked over my crop. A few of the corn plants had gone over in the flow but most of them had not. The bean plants, their stringers of tiny vines and delicate leaves and growing pods, were all there, layered with the sifting brown top-soil the waters had left behind. The dirt they grew in was mud now but even most of the standing pools of water were gone and each plant was thirstier now for the sun that had saved them than they had ever been for rain in their short lives. I knelt by the rows of my nineteen ancient plants. I could count them all. They had fared as well, perhaps better, than the rest. A hardy race of beans to be sure. And now they would really grow. It was then that, for the first time in over a week, I thought to see how the remnant village of an ancient tribe had weathered the storm.

The mix of desert scrub and piñon, juniper and stunted oak and arid grasses, had held the acres of land that held the village intact, still secret wherever it had been hidden before. But where an arroyo had begun to cut into the first layer of village life the latest flush of water had cut away layers of primitive life and

-116-

generations of a time gone by and exposed it to the views and possible machinations of a modern age. Before the cut was no more than a foot deep. Now it was twice as deep, though not much wider than before the flood. Before you had to look carefully, even anticipate, to see the first layer of shaped dirt that formed the remnant of an adobe wall. Now a child could see at a glance how a crude architecture had laid block upon dirt block, forming the same wall nearly hidden before, and other places where cobblestones with a dirt mortar formed other walls that were now revealed. And along the length of the washout lay a treasure chest of shards, arrowheads, metate grinding stones, scraping tools, shell bracelets and half a dozen intact pots and bowls. One of the bowls covered the head of what we call a Mimbres Indian, long dead and preserved in skeletal form. He lay at a right angle with the course of the newly deepened arroyo; only the head and shoulders were exposed, sticking out of the bank and awash in mud and silt. I lifted the bowl, revealing briefly the face of the dead. What showed through the silty visage revealed sound, strong teeth in the usual macabre skeletal grin, and a substantial head and shoulders I took to be a male in the prime of life. It was the one thing uncovered wherein the dog would not share my interest. There was no apparent reason why he had died.

I had been gathering up the pots, bowls and artifacts as I walked out the arroyo and I put them up on the bank above where I found them. I did not take the time to clean and examine any of them -- not yet -- though I meant to before I was through, and I placed the death bowl on the bank above the dead.

The arroyo essentially ended in the grove, just this side of where it would have cut through and out of the grove and down the slope toward the valley floor and the creek. But near the edge of the grove, rocks, brush and debris from the run-off had piled up behind a huge boulder, a natural dam had been formed, and behind it mud and silt had built up and backed up the arroyo, filling it, and spilling the water as it rose over the top in sheets and rivulets which ran harmlessly out into the grove here and there and down the slope towards the creek. I saw in the tons of soil backed up behind the dam the material with which I would refill the arroyo to its former form and rebury its treasures for all time.

Signal To Depart

The next day I didn't open my shop but came out to the ranch at first light. I got the wheelbarrow and a long-handled spade and walked it in front of me the half mile from the barn to the grove and the revealing arroyo and all its treasures. It was grunt labor and I was in shape for it and I worked with passion and sweated through another sunny day as I filled the wheelbarrow time and again from the silt and mud at the end of the arroyo and, starting at the head underneath the bluff, dumped load after load of the silt back into the cut so that most everything that had washed down was now back up the arroyo where it belonged. It wasn't a long stretch of wash and I worked without any significant break through the day. As I refilled the arroyo, I contoured the silt as I dumped it in so it lay up against the banks as well, and where the wall of a room was revealed by the cut I landscaped silt to cover it up so that less was readily visible than before. And of course I would have to fix it so that the next rain would not give it away all over again.

Toward supper time, still three hours of light left, I rolled the wheelbarrow back to the barn and saddled the horse. There were several great long railroad ties behind the barn, meant for some construction project on the ranch that never occurred, and I put a rope around the biggest of them and took the other end to the saddle horn where I made couple of wraps and then I stepped up and pointed the mare to the grove of past life and touched her flanks with my heals. She lowered her hind quarters and dug in and once she got it moving walked off with that railroad tie with no great strain and the power you'd expect of a thousand-pound animal at work. She dragged it at my direction and left it right where the water came off the bluff to start the wash-out cut in the earth. There her work was done. I got down and took the rope off the tie and while I couldn't lift it I found I could roll one end of it and I did that, so that the water coming off the bluff would be turned away from the arroyo by the tie and angled off into the grove. To be sure I got a flat rock I could barely move and dragged it in under the bluff and just behind the big lumber so that the falling water from the bluff would splatter and dissipate on the rock and spread out into the grove and would not undercut the tie and wash out the arroyo again.

There was still a small stream of water coming off the bluff. It was clear and cool to the touch and nice to look at and good to hear as it came off the bluff and fell maybe ten feet and splattered on the rock. I wanted to have a look at the best of what I had found before I buried it forever. I went along the bank of the arroyo and gathered the bowls and pots and shards and ancient implements and brought them up to the stream of water coming off the bluff. It was the arrowheads and scraping tools and pots and bowls that interested me most and one by one I held the seven arrowheads in my hand and let the falling water clean them and examined each with great pleasure. They were of an off-white or black color and while two were crude and misshapen and two appeared to have been broken by time, three others -- two of a black obsidian and one of a white stone I could not name -- were near-perfect and were works of art that could kill. I had my reasons and put three arrowheads in my pocket. I put the best of the scraping tools in my pocket too. Then, one by one, I washed off the pots and bowls. The pots, every one, were strictly utilitarian, made for use and without decoration. Of the five bowls, three held geometric designs which told not stories -- at least none that I could read -- but which used a positive, black, to set off the design in negative, white. The other two bowls held me for some time. Under the gentle falls, the first one showed as the mud washed away a simple yet captivating scene from the hunt, as one lone hunter walked round the center of the bowl with a hare in one hand, a bow and several arrows in the other, and a middling-sized dog that almost looked familiar in company behind. His face was expressionless but the artist had somehow captured both fatigue and the pride of a trophy taken in pursuit in the stoop of his walk and the carriage of his head. It was a great and timeless scene from past life and created within me new dreams and I wanted to keep it so much I knew it would take a great personal effort to put it safely away in the ground. The second bowl, that which had covered the face of the dead, also came away clean in falling water. And here The People, once again in perceptive touch with the human condition, had left for me to see a humpbacked man in great stress, who stood straining to control a penis, a cock, his own, out of all proportion to reality that emerged above swollen testicles and curved out and away and up and back in upon him and yet nowhere within reach of his frantic outstretched hands. The strain was in his body and the fright upon his face as in vain he reached to control his unbounded, suddenly consequential lust. Or was it greed that one could read in the outstretched arms and struggling form? Or was some boundless hubris represented here in that errant cock that had come back to haunt him? Was that a loss of wisdom suddenly realized in the frightened face? Whatever, clearly my man's luck had here run out. And nearby, one could only speculate as to what unbounded, consequential lust, or greed, or boundless hubris, or loss of wisdom, had contributed to the fate of the luckless human form I had recently returned to the mud. Something had happened to The People.

In the last hour of the day I dug a deep hole in the side of the bank near where running water had cut into the first room of the village. Therein I reburied all bowls, shards, and various implements, save the telling bowl which I returned, reburied, to cover the face of the dead, and saving three perfections of arrowheads and a scraping tool which I held in my pocket. Some evidence of my day's work remained, but with running water now diverted from the arroyo I could believe that my work, and time, and some new growth of vegetation would leave the secrets of The People safer than they had ever been in modern times.

In near dark I rode the horse back, followed by the dog. I unsaddled the horse and gave her some grain and left her on pasture and when the dog tried to follow me on my walk home -- a hopeless gesture she'd try from time to time -- I hollered at her: "Go to the barn!" She had shelter there, and that open sack of feed for dogs, and water, and had no business trying to follow me off the place. She understood everything I said, it seemed, and to the barn she went. We would share other pursuits though, she and I. I would not come to know The People by digging them up and laying them out here and there for all to see. I would come to know them by sharing something of the way they lived their lives and I walked home in the summer dark dreaming and planning a hunt.

Chapter 19

One of the things you can learn from books is how to make a bow and arrow. From my own books I had any number of volumes on the Indians of the Southwest. These were not how-to books but books of history, and life and culture, yet more than one of them told a lot about how various tribes hunted. I supplemented this reading with a couple of library books which held information written by hunters of today who had studied the Indian way and attempted to duplicate their pursuits of game and fish.

Throwing sticks of a non-returning boomerang design had an ancient heritage and I read that a few of the Hopi of Arizona could still make and use them. Various traps, usually in the form of deadfalls and snares, were used, and the ancient atlatl had a vogue among some tribes. The Mimbres in particular were not featured in any of this reading -- though a great deal has been written on their art -- and it appeared that their hunting techniques had not been studied to any extent. Yet the art they left behind told a lot. It indicated that the bow and arrow was for their tribes and relations, as for most other of the Native American groups across the continent, the weapon of choice, for war and hunting. Their art further indicated that while deer, bear, antelope and bighorn sheep were highly valued and occasionally taken, small game was much more common and a likelier kill. In particular rabbits and hares. This was borne out further by what I read: the bone piles of ancient tribes of the Southwest indicated that rabbits and hares were the most prevalent form of protein consumed. And the bowl I had examined told me that the hare, or jackrabbit, was the prize. It would have been as common as the cottontail rabbit -- in open country more so -- yet three times the size. A grown hare was still three to five pounds of meat dressed out. Mixed in a stew with ample supplies of beans or corn and a single hare could feed a family for several meals. I determined that I would make a bow from native materials that might take a deer or other large animal one day but that would be used first in an attempt to kill a jackrabbit.

Historians wrote that they had learned that certain types of wood were considered prime by ancient tribes and modern enthusiasts of primitive weapons had confirmed the knowledge and preferences of the Ancients. These woods included Yew, Osage Orange, Black Locust, and Mountain Mahogany, with varieties of the common cedar or juniper a fair substitute for the above, especially if one was making the bow from a sapling or limb. I figured that the Mimbres would have made use of readily available saplings and limbs so they could make a bow in a relatively short time and readily replace it when it was broken, damaged, or no longer a good weapon. There was Mountain Mahogany in the higher hills of the *Mondragón* Range to the north but a wealth of juniper in the hills of my own 200 acres. I liked the idea of finding material for a bow and arrow weapon on my own land. The day after I finished my work at the ancient village and retrieved my treasures from there, I closed shop at 5 P.M. and headed for the hills to find a bow.

The dry weather had held as steadily as the clouds and rain that had dominated the week before. Even the usual afternoon clouds of the Southwestern monsoons had ceased for the time, and as I stood on the hill overlooking the homestead, the sun dropping in the west, the sky to the east was a deep and electric blue over the hills, now verdant and green with the recent rains. I came on down and the dog picked me up and ran circles around me and jumped and spun and barked as I walked to the barn to get a hatchet.

On my homestead just a smattering of juniper, piñon, yucca, oak and other vegetation warted the ridgelines and the south slopes -- it was mostly grass -- but the north slopes, especially where they were steep, held trees of some size, especially over on the east side where the hills were higher. We walked that way, stopping to look at the crop. All my corn and beans were burgeoning, and it seemed that they had benefited from the flood. I walked into the garden and wrapped my hands around an ear of corn and felt its good size. And the pods of my beans were filling as rapidly and some were as long as the span of my hand. I could feel six, seven, even nine or ten beans forming in each pod and this included my rarified crop of Mimbres beans that had now caught up with the rest. They were a drought resistant crop yet clearly they benefited from and appreciated rain when they could get it. The pods were still green and the beans would be tender and I was tempted to pick a few and put them in my pocket and take them home and boil them up with some meat to make a hearty soup for supper. But I didn't because I had only nineteen plants -- though a number of pods per plant -- and wanted dry beans that would keep and could be eaten at any time and some of which could be saved for a much expanded planting next year. I held a pod that I could not yet pick gently in my hand and the dog, as usual, wagged and wiggled her hind end and showed enthusiasm and good feeling whenever she sensed it in me.

We crossed the creek and walked toward ascending hills. There was good bottom land for farming on this side of the creek too and it was apparent it had not been farmed in a long time. One day, when I had learned to farm and not abuse the land, I would expand my farm to the east side of the creek. In the swale before we ascended very high I marked very lush stands of now green tobosa grass, intermingled with the exotic yucca and an odd looking plant one of my books had identified as, by common name, Mormon Tea. There was history there no doubt and I examined the plant that looked from a distance like a cactus but which up close held no spines but rather a rash of closely cropped, odd, green stems. I would read further, when I got the chance, to find out if indeed Mormon pioneers or others used the plant for tea. If they did, I would, too.

Up in the hills, almost as much as in the bottom and along the creek, the grass was longish and green and my nine cows and calves worked a portion of range that had never been overgrazed. Recent readings of mine, mostly in the newspapers, told me of the great controversy over allowing any domesticated animals to graze the rangelands of the Southwest. It was, as usual, an increasingly polarized issue, with extremists capturing the debate on either side -- with room in the middle I felt for not too many animals moved around properly on enough range. I would just have to learn how Claire had done it. And I had hopes now -- even a promise -- that Sarah would help.

On a high slope I admired three Mule Deer in a coulee below, my good grama grass coming on all over now with the rains, much as my beans and corn, and I flushed a red-and-white cow and her similar calf from some shade. They were hardly scared and they leisurely came out from under the trees to look at me much as I was curious to look at them. They were fat and handsome in their way, utterly dumb and degenerate in the wild sense, yet they could take grass that a person otherwise couldn't eat and turn it into something very good to eat. I owned some now myself and I liked my cows.

My reading had told me to look for an appropriate limb or sapling, straight as a string, as free as possible from knots and branches, about an inch, or slightly less, in diameter, and by the traditions of the longbow, of a length to match the height of the archer, in this case a little over six feet. On the north slope of the highest hill on the place I found a surfeit of right-sized juniper trees; and though good looking saplings and branches on larger trees were scarce, there were so many trees to choose from I soon had a dozen six-foot staves hacked off and laid out before me in the grass. From there I weaned down to four that offered the best combination of straightness, a lack of imperfections (though none was perfect), and a certain springiness when I bent them over my knee. That silly dog sniffed each one as it lay there in the grass and then sat by one and looked up at me as if to say, "This is the one." I noted the one she seemed to prefer, as at this point she probably knew as much about bowmaking as me.

With staves in hand, or rather in hand and resting over my shoulder, we topped out on the highest hill, drawn by a certain known industrial noise I'd been hearing since I crossed the creek. From the high spot I could see that it was, indeed, Bingo Callahan, in force. That is, he was by himself save for his irresistible D-8 Cat tracking noisily beneath him and his expert, deft, movement of hands on levers. He was perhaps a quarter mile off, just beyond the boundary fence, and despite the distance and the size of the machine he sat, he was a big guy in a dirty white T-shirt and a summer-style, air-mesh, tractor cap. Bingo had bought the McKinnon Ranch -- it was all over town -- just recently, just as Sarah had said, and he was already at work, contouring roadways into the hills in preparation for the homes demanded by an expanding population Bingo was proud to serve. The dog could see him too -- she seemed to have good eyes -- and of course she knew that sound. She knew the particular sound of Bingo's machine just like she could recognize every vehicle that came to the ranch before it ever came into sight. Here, by sight or sound or both, she recognized Bingo, and, clearly upset, she wiggled, stared, listened and jumped and spun a couple of times, looking at him and looking at me for signs of my response, that she would be knowing of hers. I was upset too, though I could not see how a dog could know, but it seemed she did. I waited and watched the husband of the woman it seemed I could never get out of my mind until the machine had jerked around, with one track braking and the other grinding the hill, until his back was to us, so he wouldn't see any movement of me as we stepped away, out of sight downhill. The McKinnon Ranch was the final link to surrounding what I owned; it would fill in with houses and trailers and bound the east, as the golf course bounded the south, the dump and more houses bounded the west, and the town bounded the north. I could hardly applaud the sale and development, but the new owner of the McKinnon ranch had by purchase and intent both rounded things out and squared things off, making my remnant rural preserve with its hidden, ancient treasures that much more valuable for its own sake, and important to me and, I felt sure, the world. The sound of the machine trailed away as we descended the hills of my surrounded sanctuary. It seemed that things were coming to a head. And I felt sure I was at least holding my own. After all, I owned the Callahan Ranch. And, I was fucking his wife, and he didn't know it. But then again, so was he...and I did.

On the way back we stopped at the creek for a drink and to cut some arrows from willow saplings. The dog drank and I cut the saplings. And then she walked with me through the lush riparian garden along the creek. Fish darted in and out of the shadows beneath giant cottonwoods and lesser white-barked sycamores, and new young galleries of each, all of which as trees dwarfed the young willows that grew midst the tall slough grass. I cut a dozen small, arrowy willow saplings while the dog wagged approval and consent all around. And cutting the last of them we came in under the nesting Mexican Black Hawks. They rolled off their family home and circled, appearing now and again filtered through the branches above as they soared and dipped without flapping a wing, a good middling size as hawks go and looking black as crows in the sky, and they offered us their screeching scold until we had gone on. Away from underneath their tree I could see they had successfully raised at least two fledglings; they stood on the edge of the nest looking like they were perhaps ready to fly, hunt, and scold intruders themselves. Here at the northern fringe of their sub-tropical range, the Mexican Black Hawk family were doubly rare for their presence, here on a riparian refuge surrounded by the growth of town and urban life.

I left the pathetic, obedient and finally forlorn looking dog at the barn, and walked home alone, facing west, trapped by the magic of a brilliant Southwestern sun going down. I had time to dream and plan. In the morning I'd strip the bark off the staves of juniper and willow, then leave them for weeks in a cool dark place to cure and season with the finality of preparing the wood being the working in of animal fat to preserve and temper a bow and arrows that would work and last. Then there would be a couple of day's work -- perhaps more with a beginner's likely mistakes -- to shape, string and prepare a finished, ready bow, and fletched arrows with ancient, killing points, and then a good deal of practice on targets before I would risk dealing death on the worthy hare. This rural living took time; one couldn't rush the processes of nature. And, like The People, I felt I had plenty.

PART III

Chapter 20

The Blackwoman came into my shop one Monday afternoon in October. I had changed into my work clothes and was preparing to close the shop and walk out to the ranch. My corn and beans, and especially my Mimbres beans, were nearing a point of harvest, and Sarah was all over my feelings and my thoughts, and it did me good every day to hike out to my crop and nurture it this last little bit and look at what I had done. So it was Sarah I was missing. But there was Terri Vinson stepping into the door of my shop. We hadn't seen each other since our country club dance, months before. But we remembered each other all right.

"I heard you bought a farm," she said. "You look like you're going to do some work out there."

"I was."

"Well don't let me keep you."

"It's okay," I said. "It'll be there tomorrow...and we need to talk."

"Do we?"

"Yes."

"Well I like the sound of that. And we'd better do it now, because I'm leaving in the morning."

"Oh?" I said, and I motioned her to the chair by my desk and went to put on a fresh pot. On the way I stopped to lower the blinds and I flipped the OPEN sign to CLOSED at the window. I got the hot water started and she waited until I was back, seated in my own chair behind my desk.

"I'm going home," she said. "I have a job waiting."

"Teaching business?"

"Yes. I have several courses lined up at a junior college for next semester."

"How do you take up a whole semester with something so simple as business?"

"Simple? Well, there are the different aspects of buying or selling a business, and accounting, shipping and receiving, inventory management, labor management, anticipating trends in sales, tax management, managing cash flow, business law, so you stay out of trouble, lots of stuff. Any of it can be a whole course of study. You're in business, man; you think it's simple?"

"It is simple. You buy low and sell high. And don't let the government know what you're doing, or especially how much money passes through your hands in a year."

"That's good advice -- buy low and sell high -- but I'm much too paranoid to try and trick the tax man, or to teach others to do it. Anyway, if it was all that simple I'd be out of a job, teaching business."

"Why teach it? Go into business for yourself."

"I have thought of that. I have some ideas, and I'm going to work into them, without cutting the salary cord all at once."

"Okay. That's reasonable. And it's understandable that you'd want to leave. But I wish you wouldn't."

"Why would you say that, Jason?"

"I don't know. It's just good to see you right now."

"Is it?"

"Yes."

"Well, I feel the same."

"Do you?"

"Yes, I do. But we don't have much time. It seems we'll have to get acquainted at the end instead of the beginning."

"Well, maybe that will be best after all," I said.

"Yes, sometimes that is best," she said.

"Tell me where you're going."

"I'm going back to Houston. That's my home town. I've known it for a while, but I stayed on to help Dr. Jensen with some things at the college."

"Oh yeah, Jensen. Is he the guy Bingo Callahan cheated in a land deal?"

"Yeah, one of them. They had some sort of partnership for a while, on a particular development. I don't know too much. But Dr. Jensen told me that some of what Callahan Construction was doing there was not ethical...*dirty development* is what he called it. Something about talking prospective buyers out of down payments for land he didn't yet own, then using the down payments to go out and buy the land with money that wasn't really his, then selling it at a profit to the people who provided the seed money to start with. And never telling anyone involved what was going on. Something like that. And I guess a lot more besides. Anyway, Dr. Jensen just wanted out, and the money back that he'd put up at the start. Bingo Callahan wasn't going to give it to him. So yes, he tried to cheat him. But Dr. Jensen did pry it out of him eventually. He told me once that doing business with Bingo Callahan had him re-thinking the whole idea of land development, and how it should be done. Dr. Jensen and his wife have been my only real friends here, throughout. So I was glad to help him out. But that obligation is paid, and I'm packed, and tomorrow I'm gone, gone. It's going to be so wonderful, Jason, driving out of here. I've been planning it ever since I got here, and I don't plan to hurry. I'm going to enjoy every mile I leave behind. I'll make it to Ft. Stockton the first night, and I'm going to get a nice room, if there is one in that town, and treat myself to the best restaurant and most expensive meal in town."

"I've been there. Anything you find in Ft. Stockton will still be pretty cheap, and their best will be none too fancy."

"I know. But that's the halfway point and I'm going to be as nice to myself as I can. And then with a long drive Wednesday I'll be home for supper with my folks Wednesday night. And living where I'm not the only black face in town. I almost feel like celebrating."

"Almost? Hell, let's. I'll be nice to you."

"Will you?"

"Yes."

"Oh I like the sound of that, too."

I was looking at her closely as we talked; indeed I was looking her over, and I was already feeling better, for Sarah was always with me now it seemed, though I only saw her once a week, and much of that time it hurt and I couldn't stop it; but now here was Terri Vinson, and she was a fine, tall, big-boned woman in faded jeans and bright green blouse seated with good form in a chair close by, and a fine, a truly fine black African-American face accentuated by her tight hair drawn back straight into a bun behind her head, and I was starting to feel better already.

"How do you celebrate in Del Cobre?" she said.

"We'll think of something," I said. "For starters, I'll take you out to dinner."

"Will you?"

"Yes."

"Oh Whiteman, that sounds good."

I got up and went around her and said, "Coffee or tea?"

"Tea please."

"You want regular black tea or something New Age and herbal."

"Oh something herbal, and you pick it. And no sweets."

I made her a plain cup of Rose Hips tea and poured myself a cup of coffee and brought it all back and sat down.

"What brings you to the Roadrunner Bookshop?"

"You mostly. I wanted to see how a man makes a living by himself with a bunch of old books. And I wanted to see what you've got on you're shelves. Have any interesting books on business, or Black history?...pardon the expression."

"Oh yes, Black history...I almost forgot. Now business books, in the sense of corporate climbing and middle-management and get-rich-quick and all of that, we don't have. I do have a few books on book collecting -- that can be a business of a sort. And I have lately been collecting and stocking in more old timey agriculture books and books on homesteading and sustainable agriculture and the like. That's business of a sort, too, but probably not the sort your interested in."

"Probably not. I've always been a city girl, a big-city girl, until my stop in Del Cobre."

"Well, we can talk about business here, even if we can't read much about it. As for Black history, we do have books. Not many -- there isn't much on Blacks in the West -- but they were here along with all the rest and what I have is good, and pertinent, too."

"Blacks as part of the whole...I almost forgot."

"Yes, of course. Fact is, Blacks -- as part of the whole -- were more common and more notable and of more consequence in the Old West than is generally recognized. Even by historians of the period. Especially by historians of the period. And especially by Black historians, who have little interest in any Blacks in history who weren't obviously put-upon, or somehow connected to the civil rights movement. All of which is why there are a dearth of books. But for example..."

And I got up and went to the shelves and knowing my books well it didn't take me long to find three of interest and I brought them back to her. She picked the first one up and perused the title and contents. And she said, "Buffalo Soldiers?"

"In our prickly, oversensitive times some folks are inclined to pussy-foot around the derivation of that name, but the guy who wrote this book is not so inclined and has the facts; that the Black cavalry that pursued the Apaches around here back in the 1870s and 80s were called *buffalo soldiers* by those Indians because their dark kinky hair resembled the curly shag on a buffalo's head. There was no disrespect intended by the name then and none should be taken now. In fact, the Apaches were much impressed by the Black cavalry as soldiers; they respected them as great warriors. They also took pride in killing some of them off whenever they got the chance, along with a number of White soldiers who were hot on their trail."

"Were the Black and White cavalry units integrated?"

"In the 1880s?...certainly not. The Apache spent several centuries defending their homeland from Spaniards, then Mexicans, then Americans, Black and White, so they were over time threatened and at war with every race available. On the other hand -- and those prickly, oversensitive people avoid this -- they regularly killed and raided such peaceful agrarian tribes as the Pima and Papago and Pueblo over an even longer span of time so as victims the Apache are less than ideal. They were warlike, their economy was based on raiding and pillage, and they were essentially predators, which is probably why it took Black and White American soldiers ten years longer to subdue Geronimo and the rest of those equine buccaneers than any other Western tribe."

Terri turned pages and came to a section where some historical photographs of the Black cavalry of the Southwest were collected and there she paused.

"Do they look odd to you? I asked.

"They do," she said. "I've never seen a cavalryman of the Old West standing there in his uniform and all the regalia and holding his horse, and he's Black."

"I've always felt the same way myself. Shows you how we get stuck on misconceptions."

"Stereotypes."

"Ah yes, stereotypes. Anyway, whichever side you want to take, the buffalo soldiers were a significant part of the Apache wars in the Southwest and this book properly places them in the historical record and perspective. Of course, being a university press book it was way overpriced and not promoted and after a few years they remaindered them off. I picked a bunch up for a song. And now they're getting scarce and there's a price on them."

"Buy low and sell high!"

"Goddamn right. I still sell them pretty reasonable though."

She had noted my price penciled in and said, "Yes, I'd like to buy this book."

She picked up the second book to view a dust jacket that featured a remarkably clear historical photo of a handsome Black man of stern face and looming countenance dressed in the formal frock of the period -- about mid-nineteenth century.

"Jim Beckwith," I said. "Sometimes written Beckwourth. He was a Mulatto freeman who went West during the mountain man era well before the Civil War. My guess is, trapping beaver up high in the Rockies in that realm of perfect primitiveness he found more freedom than any Black man has known in this country, before or since. He was a significant explorer and mountain man. He survived, and only the best survived that lifestyle. He lived on into the era of the buffalo hunters and came to make his home and life with the Blackfeet up north. So he became something of a Black Redman, you might say, picking up their language, lore, and who knows how many of their squaws. And then he was half White, too. An interesting sociological and psychological study, to my mind, and a hell of a man. The definitive biography of him has yet to be written, but this one's not bad and the best available to date."

"That is a tough looking dude."

"Yeah, I'll bet everyone who knew him tried to get along with him. That title is reasonably priced, too."

"And I'm going to buy it, too," she said.

She looked at the third book I had given her, thumbed through some pages, and said, "What was a Black Moor doing in the Southwest?"

"Estevan! Probably the most extravagant, fanciful, intrepid and incredible of all the explorers of the West, black, white, or otherwise. His time was so long ago that much of his history is clouded in myth. What remains of the Spanish history coincides well with the Indian legends that come down to the present time. He was with Cabeza de Vaca and three other Spaniards, stranded on the coast of Florida in 1528, long before Jamestown or Plymouth Rock or any of that Anglo history stuff. He alone was Black. Somehow, over the next eight years, they made their way across the South and the Southwest, to arrive in *northern Sonora* for Christ sake in 1536. *Eight years* of travel. Five, six, eight thousand miles! Who knows? And no motel, no Dairy Queen, no Quick-Stop along the way. Several times they were enslaved by Indians, and every time they saved themselves with their powers of healing, or at least they convinced the Indians of that power. Their medical knowledge couldn't have been much but it was more than the Indians had, or at least they made the Indians believe it was. Estevan it seems was particularly good at this salesmanship and apparent quackery, and in 1539 he led the Spanish expedition of Marcos de Niza north from Sonora into the territory of what is now New Mexico. He was sent ahead in an advance party and commenced a conquest of that land by fraud and deceit. He dressed himself in extravagant feathers, rattled gourds and bells and spoke in tongues -- at least it was tongues to the Indians -- and convinced tribe after tribe that he was a God. In return for the blessings he claimed he could bequeath and disasters he claimed he could avert, he demanded tribute in turquoise and women; the best they had. By the time he got to the Zuni lands a hundred miles north of here, he had acquired quite a stash and an impressive harem. Of course, this charade could not last. At a certain village the Indians called him onto the carpet one day and when he failed to produce some of his God-like claims they saw him as more man than God, and angry at being the butt of a hood-wink they killed him on the spot and cut him up into numerous black pieces and displayed the remnants of the hoax all over the territory. Even today, black Kachina dolls of the tribes of the region keep something of the man and the legend alive. But the point I'd make is that one could say that the principal European discoverer of the Southwest was a rogue, a rake, a charlatan, and, as it happens, a Negro. Unfortunately, there is a great dearth of books and information about this man; that volume you have is truly hard to find, plus it's signed, and the price reflects it."

She noted the price and said, "That's a month's wages where I've been teaching school. Now I see how a man can make a living with a bunch of old books. There must be some money out there in the rare book market."

"Yeah, and that one's not even rare; it's scarce."

"What's the difference?"

"Well, the rule of thumb is: a scarce book is hard to find; a rare book is hardly ever found. That title's just scarce. If it was rare, I'd jack up the price considerably."

"Well it's too rare, or scarce, for me. But what a wonderful story."

"Check the Houston library when you get home. Somewhere in that vast system they may have a copy."

She put the book down on my desk and wrote out a check for the other two.

"My check good with you?" she said.

"Of course," I said.

"I'm leaving tomorrow. You'll have a quite a time collecting if it bounces."

"I have great confidence in you," I said.

She smiled and handed me her check and said, "So how come a grumpy White guy has developed a special interest in Blacks in history?"

"I don't have a special interest in Blacks in history. I do have a special interest in the history of the West, and Blacks are a part of that history, so why ignore them? But here's the thing -- you can't understand America today without an intelligent reading of the Western expansion. You have to understand the frontier. The eastern frontier was just as real to those who first saw it, but it was way back there and didn't last as long and less has been written about it. But out here, it lasted to about 1910 and there are people alive today who can recall remnants of it -- a big wild country, largely empty of people, but full of physical challenges and moral dilemmas. The Big Horizon. And it was all new, to all but the natives, and so there was little precedent available, either for actions or behavior. The country was extraordinary, and it demanded character. And so the characters, extraordinary characters, emerged. Men of vision. And men of spirit. And women too. I'm not blind to the fact that some of those characters brought some God-awful abuses of people and the land that we're still contending with. The Western expansion inspired our best imaginations, and some of our worst acts. But this awesome country created those awesome characters, and the characters created the history and the stories we'll tell and retell till the nation is lost to our times. And maybe beyond that. The way we're going, I think those stories will outlive the nation. Western Americana is a gold mine. People can't get enough of the stuff. They like those stories. They want the frontier spirit. They're looking for that vision. They want those characters. The books you have there tell of people who were masters of fate -- they collared it, throttled it, and kicked it down the road. Or at the least they tried. And when fate won, they took it with scarcely a wince. People today can see the difference. They want characters equal to their best imaginations, not the whining, simpering, angst-ridden heroes of our time, awash in their ambiguities. I think the frontier spirit is needed even now. Especially now. Only not in conquest. The conquest is done. It had to be done. The challenge today is restraint. A measured, intelligent yet determined restraint against the boomer mentality that afflicts us. That takes vision too, and a certain spirit. Just because some is good, doesn't mean a whole lot is necessarily better. Our republic has never understood this. That's the quintessential problem. And it's still a Big Horizon. In a way it's even bigger. But it's a new horizon, with different challenges, and a new vision is needed to find the balance. And the literary heritage left to us -- those stories -- they provide us with the history we need to know to understand ourselves today. And the spirit and vision we need for the future. Conquerers like Estevàn and defenders like Geronimo -- they had that spirit. And John Wesley Powell, the first man to run the Colorado, he had that spirit too. But he came a little later and he could see what was coming. He was a man of vision, a personal vision, and running the Colorado he committed a remarkable act. And then he wrote the first warnings that there are limits to this land we've conquered and put under our thumb. And Aldo Leopold was a 20th century adventurer. By his time the West was pretty tame, and it's even tamer now, but he saw the challenge ahead, and found his own adventure there. He hunted, and studied the lands and waters and wildlife, in the mountains of New Mexico, just north of here, and in the mountains of Old Mexico, just south of here, and he articulated the very ethic we need for a sustainable future. He knew the spirit of the Old West, and he respected that culture. That's why he tried to preserve wild lands, and he loved to hunt, in the old way. And somehow, writer that he was, he could capture that spirit, and retain it, within a conservation ethic. He showed us that we can still be pioneers, and without killing off the things we love. Of course Leopold's writings are widely admired today, and still largely ignored. And the wildness and the heritage and the nature and culture of the West is being ground out over time by bad behavior and unmitigated growth. The Big Horizon is being taken up by strip mines, subdivisions and people parks, and if we don't begin to care then pretty soon that's all there will be to see. But all the lessons we need, all the greats of history that we need to know, are in the pages of the books in this room. And as it happens, some of those greats were Black. Like Beckwith, and Estevàn, and the Black cavalry...dinner?"

We left the shop and went down the street in the slanted evening sun and long shadows, and in the shade the air was the cool air of early fall, and then we went into the cafe. Of course people in a cafe will look up when someone walks in, and if they see a White man with a Black women they will keep looking longer than otherwise, especially if they sense the couple is romantically involved. Terri Vinson and I weren't romantically involved, yet, but we may have had that feel about us as that's what we got; a look, and longer than was usual, or seemly. We were followed by some curious eyes to our table, and then as we absently looked about a bit those glances went away. Terri noticed, too, and said, "You and I are going to be all over town."

"Good," I said.

We each ordered a beer and plates of Mexican food and the beer came first. We raised our glasses a couple of times in good cheer and best wishes and spoken regrets that we hadn't got to know each other sooner, and spoken pleasure that it was better late than never, and some real anticipation over making the most of the short time we had. We were into our second round as food came -- hot plates of enchiladas curled around chicken and swarmed over with cheese and green chile. It was good. And Terri was looking good and I was feeling good and as we talked I came into one of my moods to provoke.

"So how does it feel," I said, "to be an enterprising, educated, successful Negro, a nice, midddle class, upscale Black woman with a good job and no accent or jive vernacular, and watch TV every evening as your race-concious Black counterparts carry signs and march in the streets and piss and moan the world's against them and collect food stamps and welfare checks and have children they can't take care of and burn their own neighborhoods and burn out on drugs and commit crimes and go to jail?"

I would periodically still try something like this on Carla, and no matter how many times I did, she would stiffen and steam and respond defensively, but Terri, eating heartily, just turned her head to politely hide her smile and when she could smile up front she said, "It makes me especially glad and proud that I'm enterprising, educated, moderately successful and, yes, Black."

"You don't feel tainted by all that?"

"Well, here's the thing, *pardner*...I'm not responsible for problem Black people any more than you're responsible for problem White people. Lord knows you folks have got your share of assholes. And anyway, the majority of Black people in America are not unemployed, do not collect welfare checks, are not in jail, do not have children they can't take care of, or piss and moan the world's against them, and are not even particularly race-conscious...less so than you, Whiteman."

This set me back, and made me smile, because of course she had me all the way. But I recovered.

"You'll agree there's a problem."

"Oh certainly there's a problem."

"I mean, why is the Black family more broken and unworkable today than it was just a couple of generations ago? The incidence of single parent Black families, the incidence of illegitimacy, is much higher today, in the last quarter of the 20th century, then in the '30s or '40s, or even '50s, and in those days Blacks really were put-upon, and were much more poor relative to the rest of society."

"I don't know. I've never thought about it that way. But I'll bet you know, or at least you think you do, or you wouldn't have brought it up."

"Damn right! I think it's economics. The way our economic system works -- what it rewards and what it destroys. Because there's lots more single parent families now, and broken homes, illegitimacy, troublesome youth, crime and all the rest, regardless of race. But here it is...for the last I don't how many thousands of years it was normal for people to farm their own land -- that was the most prevalent occupation even until a couple of generations ago -- or to have shops or stores or businesses of their own, home businesses, and as they had children, the children were a part of these occupations, outside of schooling, from the time they were old enough to help to the time they went out and started farms or shops or other enterprises of their own. So from time immemorial it was the natural thing in the human species for a family to be an economic as well as domestic unit, and the wife and the husband and the kids, all in a sense stayed home. This was true even up to the '20s and '30s. And where everything went wrong was when we left the rural agrarian life and small town life and went to the cities. Urban growth did it. Blacks got hit first...leaving the rural, agricultural, small town life in the South to congregate in the cities up north where the farm and the family business has no place and everybody works for somebody else...that's when the Black family came apart and the result is ghettos, poverty, no pride and victimization, illegitimacy, crime and all the rest. And, belatedly, we're seeing the same failure in White folk's families, and other families, and for the same reason. Then along came this little blip in our history that followed World War II and that lasted but a generation or two when the wife stayed home and the husband went off to work...our parents' generation. Even that is currently considered hopelessly old fashioned. And now, of course, nobody stays home, not even the kids, because they are farmed out to preschool as soon as possible so the woman can resume her career outside the home where papa has been all along. And so this considerable mess we find ourselves in comes right out of an economic system that has fostered an unnatural, unworkable family life, an aberration in family history where the family is no longer an economic unit and is thereby much less of a domestic unit, or family unit, as well."

"Very nice, Jason, but we can't all go back to the farm."

"We can't all go back to the farm but many more of us could live that kind of life than do now. I'm finding that out on my own little spread. On a few acres, with just me and all my ignorance of agriculture, I'm about to harvest more food than a family of four could consume in a year. We'd have stuff left over to sell. I've been reading this little homestead book that shows how a family could grow and raise most of what they need on a city lot! This is the yoeman farmer ideal that this country was founded on. I've been reading about this sort of thing...wouldn't you know...and I was astounded when I found that perhaps the wisest of all Americans once wrote: *The greatest fine art of the future will be the making of a comfortable living from a small plot of land.*"

"Let's see...that would be Thomas Jefferson."

"That's what I would have said. Turns out it was Abraham Lincoln."

"My he got around! I thought he was busy freeing the slaves."

"Well, he took time off from freeing the slaves to establish the Department of Agriculture in 1862. He was an old farm boy himself and he said something much needed and almost totally ignored in our time. And now the slaves are long-since freed, and we're all of us, of every race, strapped by the economic hydra and boomer mentality that's captured the times and destroyed the American family. If we would only pay attention to what Lincoln and others wrote...I'm telling you Terri, the answers are all in the books."

"Perhaps. I like the idea. Not the farm part; not for me. But if we could add the small business owner to Lincoln's ideal, I'd sign up for the course. I had a little business myself for a while...typing and editing and word processing services."

"How'd it go?"

"I had too much business. I still had classes to teach and I didn't have time for both. And I was afraid, to tell the truth, to go in with both feet. I was afraid to cut the salary cord. And I don't know enough...about that kind of business."

"But you're a teacher of business."

"Not home business. Not family enterprise. I've never seen a course in that. In my field, a small business is a company with less than one hundred employees."

"Well, there you are."

"What do you mean?"

"There's your opening, your opportunity. They ought to have a whole field of study at business schools...call it...*Cottage Industry*. And you will write the lead text for it...call it *Home Business 101*...and that will be your small business. And at the ag schools, they ought to have a whole other whole field of study called...*Homestead Agriculture*."

"Good idea, Whiteman. And beginners' course 101 in Homestead Ag would be...*Forty Acres and a Mule*, and you will write the text for it."

"Goddamn...yes!"

"And in my text on Cottage Industry, I'll use you're buy-low-and-sell-high book business as one of the profiles. Only I'll leave out the part about cheating the government."

"That would probably be best."

"And you're going to have to do something about your *book*keeping."

"What's wrong with my *book*keeping."

"Unless I missed something in your shop, your keeping records with notes on scraps of paper and your own faulty memory."

"Actually, I have great stacks and files of three by five cards, and actual notebooks, plus those scraps of paper and my own faulty memory."

"I could save you time and money with a simple-enough word processor and some not very expensive software. You could have your whole inventory, book wants, income and expenses, everything you would ever need and want to know on the tips of your fingers. You could learn it."

"Maybeso. But mine is a personal, one on one, business, even if most of it is mail order, with each book a special item, not just an item of stock, wanted by a special person."

"A good system wouldn't keep you from inscribing books, signing letters or invoices in ink, adding notes when you want, doing book searches to find special books for special people, or anything of a personal touch you do now. In fact, you'd have more time for that because it wouldn't take you an hour and a half to see who's on the want list for *Buffalo Soldiers!*"

I smiled at that, because once again she had me, and I said, "I guess you're telling me we're going to have to somehow blend the old with the new."

"I think so. If you weren't so *antiquarian* you'd know it's computers and word processors and fax machines and all of that technology that makes home businesses so feasible nowdays. And more and more, people are catching on -- even if the business schools still don't get it -- and they're starting their own cottage industries."

"So what do we do, Terri?"

"We lead by example, Whiteman."

"Yes?"

"You do your little farm and make it work and let the world see and I'll do my little home business course called *Cottage Industry* and make it work. Then we'll *integrate*, if you'll excuse the expression, our families -- when we have them -- into what we do and we'll let the world see that too."

"Goddamn Terri, you're brilliant."

"We're brilliant."

"Are we?"

"Yes."

"You know, Thoreau is always quoted as a nature writer. But the first chapter in his book -- and by far the longest -- is called *Economy*. That's where he tells us how we might live our lives.

Where he explains that less is often more, or at least better. And somewhere in there he said, *Be sure that you give the poor the aid they most need, though it be your example which leaves them far behind.*"

"That's good. We'll do it, Jason, each in our own small way."

"Well," I said, "I'm glad we got all that solved. Now what, Terri?"

"You tell me, Whiteman. We don't have much time."

~ ~ ~ ~ ~

Outside it was past evening, dark had come, when I missed her most, when she would be with him; and inside it was just light enough that we could help each other undress, and we kissed, and I was frantic to be with Terri Vinson for the night. Of course, I had been with Black women before; they are not essentially different -- how could they be? -- and yet, there is nothing quite like it. And never one quite like Terri; who said: "Just go slow and do me, Jason...it's been forever since I've been laid." She was wonderful to be with me this night and I would do exactly as she liked; and in time I went down, further down, to the great length of dark, supple thighs. At the confluence she was purple-black, all around where she spread and yielded a pink, fluid, swollen and savory slit; long dark fingers came down from the supine form to the ample, shocking blue-black and smoothly-kinky fur and around the opening to -- incredible! -- pull the slit even further apart for me; an open, gathering feast. I started in and wouldn't stop until she couldn't stop; her legs came up in a groan and closed around me and she flexed and trembled until she was done. Then it was all for me, she said, and as much as I was wanting it I was already losing it; for what was Sarah doing here now, all over me and very much with me even now, with what she did with him; and what we were doing they were doing and I was surely losing it now. Yet Terri was with me somehow and gathered me in and she called for me to let it go and with her all around me and my hands underneath holding dearly to the seat of her urgent form, I lost it -- I shook and sobbed white and naked and helpless, on and on...

"...Let it all come out, Jason, let it all come out."

Signal To Depart

In time she had me laying like a child in her arms, and her fingers were stroking my head, and when my crying was gone she said, "Tell me what's wrong, Whiteman."

"I don't know where that came from."

"I'll bet you do."

"It wasn't supposed to happen this way."

"You had me fooled. But then I could tell I was making it with a desperate man."

"Yes, I'm really not up to my heroes. Here I am -- whining, simpering, angst-ridden...next thing I'll be joining a support group."

"That I would have to see. But don't be too hard on yourself. Even your frontier heroes wept, and felt things go bump in the night. Anyway, I wouldn't be in bed with you if all you had to offer were your sour opinions. I knew there was more. You're more interesting this way. Now, what is it?"

It's sleazy, mundane, tawdry, deceitful...reads like a cheap novel. And I'm in way over my head. I thought I could handle it."

"Trying to love two women is seldom a good idea. And it's never easy. Especially when one of the them is surely a scamp."

"It sounds almost like you know something you shouldn't."

"Why shouldn't I?"

"Nobody's supposed to know."

"It's pretty well known around town that you've been seeing Carla Aguilar for some time. And more recently Sarah Callahan."

"Nobody's supposed to know that."

"Good luck."

"I suppose I shouldn't be surprised."

"No, you shouldn't."

"How do you know it?"

"Oh you just hear things in this town. On this I've heard it enough I figured there might be some truth to it. I'll admit I was a little worried who might show up. They say it's strictly take-a-number around your place."

"She wouldn't show up this late."

"Which one?"

"Carla. Sarah only comes on Wednesdays."

"I wouldn't want to hurt Carla. She's a sweet girl."

"You know her?"

"Not really. Just in passing. But women size each other up real quick. Carla's a sweet girl."

"And Sarah's a scamp?"

"And that's being nice. I sized her up from across a room."

"Well, me and that scamp, we're making plans."

"Tell me."

"She's going to leave him, to be with me. And we're going to take what's left of that ranch, that 200 acres, and bring it back to what it was, or even better, while Del Cobre and the sunbelt boom all around us. I've got the ideas, and she knows more than me how to make it work."

"Word around town is she's up to something."

"Well, she is. But the town doesn't know what. And neither does Bingo Callahan."

"Good luck on that one, too."

"The husband is always the last to know. And I've told Sarah everything I've ever dreamed. With just me, it's hardly more than a fantasy. With her and me the whole dream comes round and forms and it's real. Like something out of a great book. It's all so close now it seems I can hardly fail to have it."

"So what's the problem, Whiteman?"

"She says, *be patient; we'll be together soon.* But soon is not now. Now, she's with him. She's with him right now. It's late at night. They're in bed. Everyone is in bed now, and she's with him. They're in bed together, naked, right now, just like us. I know it. She says, *it doesn't happen very often.* But what the fuck does that mean? I know it happens. I don't know when, so I know it could be anytime. It could be right now. I can see them...he could be fucking her right now..."

"You make it so all of it is in the physical act."

"Yes, of course."

"Men do that."

"I do it. I can't help myself. And it's killing me."

"Well, you picked a married woman."

"I know it."

"And a married woman having an affair is doing it with two different men."

"Don't I know it."

"And a married woman having an affair, especially one with a family, usually leaves the affair and keeps the family when it's all over."

"Not this time. We've made too many plans."

"Good luck, Jason. Does keeping Carla on make it better?"

"It's never better. But without Carla it would be worse. She's doing it; I can do it too."

"That's a cheap defense, and hardly fair to Carla."

"I think it's clear I'm not doing any of this to be fair to Carla. Carla's wonderful; a rare confluence of the good. But the hell of it is, that's not what I want. I want Sarah. She's lean and curved and firm and tough and competent. She's willful, and nasty in bed. And yet I see her all innocent and open when all that red hair comes down over me when she can't control herself anymore."

"You've got it bad, man."

"Don't I know it. It's a disease."

"Well, for what it's worth to you, I vote for Carla. But I can see you're going to have to get this thing done with Sarah first."

"That's the thing...get it done. I can see it -- it's all right there -- but I can't make it happen."

"You'd better make it happen. You're frying you're brain with that woman."

"Tell me, Terri."

"Put her on the spot. Make her shit or get off the pot. And I don't mean next week. What have you got to lose? -- you're not getting it done this way. If she's what you say, she'll be there for you."

I lay there for a time, and the sense of it, and the inevitable, came down, and I said, "Well, you'd think I would have thought of that."

"You haven't been thinking...not with the love life you've got yourself into."

"Ah well...yes!" I said. And then I was reaching for her, touching her face with my hand. "I should have told you, Terri. Before all this happened."

"If all this hadn't happened, you wouldn't have told me anything."

"It's true. And what do they say... 'was it good for you too?'"

"I've been lonely. Not the same as you. But I've been so lonely sometimes it hurt. No one here has ever been mean to me. But White folks aren't quite themselves when there's a Black person around. And all those white faces all day, every day, everywhere I'd be, and then I'd see my own black face in the mirror at night, and I'd start to look different, odd, strange, even to myself. That's lonely. You're an awful grouch sometimes. And you're being a real prick with Carla. And you're a troubled man. But you've got your own thoughts, and that's unusual enough. And some of them are good. You asked me to dance, too. And made me do it, and took me through it. Taught me the two-step! That was the sweetest thing...! Anyway, somehow I don't feel lonely with you. I'm glad my number came up."

~ ~ ~ ~ ~

In the morning I was able to lure her into the shower so we could wash together. Women are funny that way, especially when it's a one and only night, how they will get naked in the night and do the most incredible, unspeakable things, and then hide their bodies in the morning like none of that ever happened at all. To shower and wash together then becomes much more intimate and fearful to them. But I got Terri Vinson into the shower and we stood under the hot flow and clouded in all the steam, and she was a fine, tall, big-boned woman with great curves, and she let me watch her wash her hair. I told her how lovely that was. And then I got the soap and washed her all over and especially her breasts and stomach and down her back with the cloth which feels so good when someone will do that for you, and then her legs and gently where her great thighs came together and the great swell and crease of her fine black rump; for she was quite wonderful and a credit to any race and she had given so much more to me than I could ever give to her; I could only lavish the warm soap and water over her to let her know how I felt.

And then we were dry and dressed and we stood together in the shop with the morning sun outside and it was time to say good-bye. I reminded her, for she had forgotten, and she went to the desk to pick up the two books that she had bought the evening before, and as she did I went to the desk, too, and got the volume on Estevan that she could not afford, and I gave it to her. Of course she said she couldn't take it but I was emphatic and told her there would be no denying me this. And so she took it and then I took her by the hand and we carefully leaned to each other and we kissed like siblings and then she was gone.

Chapter 21

Later in the morning I went down the street to the cafe and had breakfast. It was already quite warm after a cool night and the sun was out without any clouds in a blue sky and you could see it was going to be a very lovely Indian summer day. I had a good breakfast and read the paper and I felt good.

I got back to the shop and opened up and someone had leaned a brown manila envelope against the door. I picked it up and went in and put the OPEN sign on the door and sat down behind my desk and took a manuscript out of the brown manila envelope. It was the first draft of Carla's book and it captured my interest from the first strong sentence. It was the story of her uncle, a flawed man who had led a fascinating life, "a life from another time," as Carla put it early on, and such as no one of my generation or later could ever know again. He was not an educated man or of a bent that he could have written this story himself, but he had a strong oral narrative voice that Carla had recognized and captured on the page and she had woven that voice in with her own writing and the editing and translating and she had done it all to good effect. In between the occasional customers who came by through the day I read the entire story, of an errant young man who had run away to be a New Mexico cowboy in an era of range life in American that was about to end. Then, as agri-business and the mechanized fall from grace had taken the range, he had gone off to Mexico where the Western Myth lived on. There were, too, his days working in appalling primitiveness in underground mines in both countries, and a history of joyous loves, failed loves, hard living and hard drinking, and bad business, all of it frank, honest, at times humorous, sometimes sad, always moving, and through it all he never looked back. I read on and on and admired the work of Carla

Aguilar and envied the man she wrote of so well. A portion of it told, in a delicate way, of his life with a woman I had come to know. And then the final anticlimax of living out his final years on the family homestead -- five acres he no longer owned. On the dedication page she had dedicated the work to her uncle, Santos Aguilar, and to the passing of the way of life that person had lived. And under acknowledgments she mentioned, among several others, myself. There were I thought a few gaps and weaknesses in the text, easily corrected in a second draft. I made a few notes and suggestions in the margins along the way but there was nothing of a serious nature I could fault and in sum it was a very strong work, a literate and honest work, from beginning to end, and of infinitely more substance and value than the holistic nature-faking, New Age claptrap, self-centered ethnicity, and phony Native American spiritualism that passes for Southwest literature today, and it was all but ready to be enclosed in the covers of a book. I finished it mid-afternoon. I could honestly praise her for what she had done and I looked forward to it.

Late in the evening, just past dark, Carla came by to see me. She had on a bright print pullover dress that hung loose such as a heavy-set woman will wear. She had worn it to see me before and she knew I liked it. She looked very pretty and more Indian than Hispanic with her long dark hair hanging straight and natural over her shoulders and down her back.

"You look good," I said.

"That's nice to hear."

"It's been awhile."

"Yes. I've been working."

"I know."

"I wanted to get it done especially so you could read it. I want you to like it. And I want you to love me."

"You are lovely," I said. "Last time you wore that dress you pulled it up and over to show yourself off and you weren't wearing anything underneath, at all."

"Yes, nothing," she said.

Of course, I knew this would be our last time; but she had come to me dressed for it, and so I undressed her for it; and it was a measure of how good it had been to be with Terri that throughout

I hardly thought of Sarah at all. Afterwards, we were quiet for some time and then we could talk.

"Are you still farming well?" she asked.

"Yes," I said, "in spite of myself. My beans and corn could be harvested any day, I haven't lost a cow or calf, my chicken flock is raising their own chicks and people keep buying my eggs. I've got grass to spare on 200 acres and the young Mexican Black Hawks down along the river are flying around with their folks. There are deer in the hills and jackrabbits all around, and I like watching the roadrunners catch the lizards around the barn. And in the evening, just at dusk, the coyotes howl up their courage and take to the hills and hunt. I like my place. I think it looks pretty good considering how much I still don't know."

"It's been a good summer."

"Lots of rains. Almost too much for a while there. But lots of rains and good sun and that has more to do with it than anything I've done."

"I wish I could help you gather your crop. My back would never take the bending and lifting. But Santos would be glad to help."

"That's okay," I said. "I'll have someone to help."

"I can hardly imagine Sarah Callahan at stoop labor, picking beans and corn like some *mojada*."

I was had again, though not much surprised this time, and I shifted in her arms till I was on my back and looking up in the dark to the ceiling and she lay her head on my chest and out-waited me for a response.

"So it's all over town," I said.

"It hasn't been news for some time, my friend."

"Well, so what does it matter who knows?"

"It might matter if Bingo Callahan knows."

"Do you think he knows?"

"I think you could bet your farm on it, *Señor*."

"Sometimes the husband is the last to know. And if he does know, too fucking bad. It's too late for him now anyway."

"Think so?"

"Yes. It's going to be me and Sarah now."

"Well, not to shake your confidence my friend, but one rumor around town says that if she's seeing you, Bingo not only knows, he's part of it, because you've got something he wants."

"Something's up all right, but Bingo doesn't know what. This is something Sarah and I are doing. If she's been slow to choose it's because I've given her a difficult choice. But it won't be long now."

"*Quizas*. But I can still say to you that I want you to be with me. I will forgive you your time with her. But I don't want you to lose that land because there is another man in my life as important to me as you. Maybe more important. You must allow Santos to buy his home and you must do something to protect the rest of the acreage or you're going to lose it for all of us. They're going to take it away from you."

"They can't take it away from me because I own it."

"Santos knows this town. He knows how power in this town works. He says you are going to lose the land and I asked him how you could lose it and he doesn't articulate that because he doesn't know the law or the procedures but he says, 'They won't let him keep it; he's in the way.' And he knows these things Jason; he knows how the power works."

"Well they can't do it. I suppose they could condemn it if there was a highway going through or something, but there isn't anything like that going on and they can't just take it away because they want to build nine holes and a trailer park."

"Santos knows how the power in this town works. There is another way. And now you listen to me and think about this and then I hope you will let me and Santos and some other people help you save that land...

"I have a friend in Santa Fe. He is a lawyer and he works for this trust. They work with people who want to save open space and wildlife areas and agricultural land and cultural resources -- land like yours my friend. So they buy the land and then contract with the state or federal government to acquire the land and protect it, because local powers and developers might be able to take the land from you but they can't take it from the state or the federal government."

"You know what I think about having anything to do with any goddamn government."

"Just listen, Jason. My friend asked me if you owned the land free and clear and I said you did and he said that would make it easier and it could be done quicker. I told him it was about 200 acres and that the old ranch house was at the northwest corner of the property and Santos' house was at the southeast corner of the property and he said that at the purchase the boundary could be drawn to provide you and Santos with the original homesteads and some acreage to go with it. Then you would sell the rest of it, around 160 acres or so to the trust, and they would make the arrangements for the sale to the right government people. He wanted to know whether there was anything on the property that would make it valuable as something to protect for the public. I told him it was just what was left over of a large farm and ranch but that it had always been treated well and was not overgrazed. He said it would be more difficult to protect it simply as open space. Then I told him about how the creek ran through and all the fine cottonwoods and sycamores and the Mexican Black Hawks you had told me about. Well that seemed to interest him more, but he really got interested when I told him about the petroglyphs and pictographs of the Mimbres People on the cliff walls and in some of the canyons. He said that there was a great interest in the Mimbres culture now and a great demand to protect any remnants of that culture from vandals and pot hunters. He wondered if there were any Mimbres sites or ruins left on the land. I told him that there had been a rumor around for a long time that there was a major site on the land that had never been dug but that if anyone was still alive that knew where it was they were keeping silent. You know, *Señor*, that I was being disingenuous with this lawyer. But he told me that a major Mimbres ruin that had not been dug would be of enormous interest to both state and federal agencies. And to a great many people. And of great value to preserve for the community. And that it was very important to protected it because there is no law to protect the remnants of the Ancient Ones on private land. So now you can see my friend where all this leads. If we let them know what's there then there is still a chance we could save the land."

"What do you mean let them know what's there?"

"Well I know what's there, though I don't know where."

"And what's there?"

"A major Mimbres site. A ruin that's never been discovered except by a few people who had no desire to disturb it."

"I have a whole shelf full of books about lost treasures in the West. Lost treasure stories are part of the Western Myth."

"Now you are being disingenuous my friend. The site is there and Claire knew it and if Claire knew it then Santos knew it and that's how you and I know it. Only I don't know where it is."

"Ask Santos."

"I have. He says it's best if no one knows but him and that when he dies then the secret will die with him. I didn't say anything to him but unlike him I think Claire told you all about it, including where it is."

"Well whatever I know I'm not telling anyone and especially not some Santa Fe lawyer and the goddmamn government agents he brings down here. I mean what could be worse than to turn that place into a people park with public tourists driving all over and a bunch of pointy-headed archeologists digging up the sanctity of a great culture."

"You are as stubborn as Santos. He wants everything a secret and he doesn't like my government idea either. But it's the only way to protect that land. They won't let you keep it, Jason. And as for *public tourists*, the lawyer said there would be conservation easements and other protections to keep it like it should be. And the excavation of the ruin would be done with great care and sympathy. It would help us to understand how they lived and what happened to them and people could come and see their art and works and it would be a lesson to us all. And I believe that unless you do this you will watch most of that place fill in with the second half of a golf course, and a house and a septic tank on every acre left over."

"Well I'm not buying it...or selling it. This all comes out of you thinking Sarah's setting me up. We've got our own plans and they look lots better to me than that goddamn government deal. Meanwhile, Santos can stay as long as he wants."

"Just remember, my friend, you have a choice. You have a choice with me and you have a choice of what to do with that land. I can't work the fields with you but a member of my family can and I can have children by you and we can pass what we have and know and believe on to them, and I can help you with your books and your writing just as you have helped me. And I'll forgive you your time with Sarah. But I won't forgive you if you lose that land for yourself and for Santos and for all of us, because you do have a choice and if you let it go it will be your own fucking fault and that will be the end of it."

"Then let it be my own fucking fault."

"I wish you knew how much like them you really are."

"Sarah and I have got this all figured out."

"It's not Sarah. You'll find out about Sarah soon enough. It's Santos. Because you won't do what's right by him. Because you want it all for yourself."

"Sounds like this comes as much from you as him."

"Probably more."

"Well I have it happening another way."

"I can't be with you like this ever again."

"It's just as well. You're talking good sense. If I was you, I'd have put myself aside long ago. I know what I want. I've dreamed it all my life."

We lay there, apart now, for some time. Carla was crying. But quietly; I could barely hear. In time I said, "I've given you every reason to hate me."

"I had my warning. I did it anyway. And you've had plenty of warning. And now you're going to do it anyway. And now it's over."

"We still have your book."

"Do we?"

"Yes."

"Did you even read it?"

"Of course."

"Tell me then. I know you'll be brutally honest."

"It's a fine work. It shows all of enterprise, authenticity, honesty, and talent. The way you worked his narrative in with your own voice is very creative. It's well organized and coherent and it's real strong with the beginning and there's a fine poignancy with the final chapter. There's a few places I think need work. I made some notes about that which you can respond to or not...you must be the final editor."

"Is it worthy of a book?"

"It's absolutely worthy of a book. It's head and shoulders above most of the stuff-and-feathers that's coming out these days."

"Will it be difficult to find a publisher?"

"It's always difficult to find a publisher for something like that. The book's too honest. The Santos that you've put into print is too human, his flaws are too raw and open, and he refuses to blame anyone for his loses and failures but himself. He won't wear his ethnicity as a scapegoat. A lot of publishers won't like that. Send it off, but don't be surprised at the rejection slips."

"I am going to send it off, after I look at your suggestions and polish it and make it better. And if nobody wants it, I will publish it myself."

"That's tough, Carla. That's real tough for this kind of book. You'd be lucky to get your money back."

"I can come up with the money for a small printing. I'm not going to worry about getting it back. It's Santos' story, and I think it should be told. But first I have to know that what I've done is good. I value your opinion on that."

"It's good; it's damn good."

"So I'll publish it, one way or another."

"I believe you'll do it."

"Yes," she said. "I will make it a book."

~ ~ ~ ~ ~

In the morning we did not make love. She meant it. It was just as well. At the door I would lean to kiss her good-bye and she with great dignity declined. She left with a manuscript held against her with both hands.

Chapter 22

It was Wednesday. Terri was gone, Carla was gone, and I could hardly wait for Sarah to come. That evening, just past dark, she arrived. Being with Terri and Carla had made me want her more; Sarah came last and best and I knew it must be forever for now the other two women were gone and would not come back. Carla had been right of course -- I wouldn't want to live this way all my life. All other women were gone for me now and I could finally see...when you've found the one, there's nothing quite like it.

And I had it bad all right, just like Terri said. And why not?...for she could not move without grace, and all that primal, unattended, pale-red and lengthy curl in all good places; a great shock of it came down over me and she was all open and innocent and sputtering her nasty words as she came to where she couldn't control herself anymore. And then we lay quiet and close and from time to time I would stroke a barely perceptible down, a pale lambent fuzz, in the small of her back; and I imagined that for all of it to be like this, the love must be real.

"It can be like this with only one," I said.

"Yes Jason, only one."

"It couldn't be like this with anyone else."

"No, it never could; it has never been like this with anyone else."

"I knew it."

"You should never have doubted it."

"I know. But I have."

"You shouldn't have. You shouldn't have doubted me."

"But I have. I'm not the only man in your life."

"You shouldn't think about that. You know how it is with married people."

"Actually I don't."

"Well, it becomes a routine sort of thing."

"Does it?"

"Yes."

"But we'll be married one day soon."

"We'll be different."

"We'll be special, yes?"

"Sure."

"We won't let it get that way."

"No, of course not."

"Does he notice this fuzzy stuff right here that you can barely see?"

"No, not at all."

"Sure?"

"He doesn't even know it's there."

"It's so fine; it's barely there. But I can see it and feel it now. It's perfect right there, the way I want it, and all of it the color of you."

"That's just like you, Jason. You make such a thing of it. You make such a thing of me when we're together."

"I can't get enough of you. Doesn't he..."

"Jason?"

"Yes."

"Don't ask me any more questions."

"I want to know. It makes me feel better to know."

"No it doesn't. It's a frenzy and you just feed on it. But you're never full and you can't stop. I'm not going to talk about it anymore. I'll just say that I'm not the same with him as I am with you."

"I wish I could believe that."

"If you can't believe that, then I can't help you."

"I want to believe it."

"No, you don't trust me."

"I do. I believe in you. I believe in us. People know about us, and they're saying bad things about you. They know, and it must be that he knows, too."

"They think they know. People in this town have had me with everyone and anyone at one time or another. For a small town I guess I'm pretty spectacular, and women are jealous, and so they'll talk. But they don't know what's really going on. And he doesn't know. Men are so easy to fool; they'll believe anything forever if you play it right."

"I defended you."

"Well, great. But you don't trust me because when I ask you about the ranch and try to talk to you about it you keep things from me. I don't care what it is; it probably wouldn't mean anything to me. But the thing is, you keep things from me. There is more to your story than those precious little Indian beans you keep talking about."

"Maybeso. But then it's one thing to tell you, another to tell Bingo Callahan's wife."

"I've told you I need the right time."

"Time's a-wasting. It happens that I've been approached by some environmental types about the place. Seems they're worried about developers getting hold of it. And that old man wants his share. And your not the only one who thinks there's more than Indian beans on that property."

"You were supposed to save that all for us."

"That's the plan. Meanwhile, it seems like everyone wants some of what I've got."

She lay there, silent for a while, and I could feel her tension; I could sense a momentary lack of balance, control, and grace. It was unlike her. It seemed that I had in fact put her on the spot. She must now, as Terri said, "shit or get off the pot."

"All right, Jason," she said. "Maybe the time has come. But you know you wander along in your own little world, responsible to no one but yourself, and I have a home and a child and a family and all of that to think of. So it's not so easy for me."

"I believe that," I said. "But it's time."

"Okay, Slim, it's time. See what you think of this. Bingo goes to Denver Friday evening. He's got some business thing up there and won't be back until Sunday night. That gives me the weekend to get together some things I need, and get Jill and me out of the house and over to Karen's before he comes back. And it will gives us some time together. We can have Friday night. And on Saturday we'll go out to the ranch and just walk around and talk about things and you need to show me what you've been doing and whatever it is you're dying for me to know and we can make our plans."

"All that is what I've been saying."

"I know what you've been saying. And I've been saying that it would be soon and that you need to be patient because you can't understand the position I'm in. I said it would happen when the time is right. I needed an opportunity and this weekend I've got it."

"And when the weekend is over it will be just us."

"Sure. You'll have to let me go Saturday some time, so I can get everything done and be over at Karen's before he's home Sunday night."

"You can come here. You and Jill can come and be with me."

"I don't think so, Slim. I'm not getting myself or my child in-between a couple of jealous men. A jealous man hasn't a lick of sense. I'll need to be at Karen's for a while and not let on the real reason I'm leaving till this blows over and he settles down."

"I'll be desperate to see you."

"Monday night sometime, probably real late, I'll slip over to see you. I can go out the back of her house just in case, and down the alley and you leave the back door here open."

"And we'll never love anyone else but each other."

"Sure. Just a little more patience. After a while he'll settle down with what's happened. Just like he's taken it that you have the ranch. He'll go on to his next deal."

"Then we'll be family, yes?"

"Sure we will."

"And we'll have the land and we'll make it work and the town can just goddamn well go around us and it will do them good."

"We'll do it, Jason."

"And we'll make a baby too, for us to love and Jill to play with as they grow up on the land."

"I'd love to make a baby with you," she said. And then she rolled over and it was the front of her all open and revealed to me.

"Sarah, will you do those things anymore with Bingo?"

"I told you not to worry about that."

"It would mean a lot to me if it's just us, starting now."

"You shouldn't worry. It doesn't mean anything to me."

"It means a lot to me."

"I don't want to make him suspicious. I want him to leave for Denver thinking he still owns the world."

"It would mean a lot to me. You can make a man believe anything if you play it right."

"Yes, I suppose I can."

"So I'll see you Friday evening."

"Yes."

"I'll make a supper here for us."

"I'd like that, Jason."

"I have a surprise supper planned for us."

"If any man ever does a supper for me it will be a surprise."

"So is it just us now?"

"Sure it is."

Chapter 23

More and more there were days when I didn't have time for the business of books. I wanted to be out at the ranch; I wanted to be there early and spend the day, inspecting my crop, collecting the eggs and watching the new chicks come along, moving my cows around, watching the little whitetail deer feed along the creek in the evening, and the bigger mule deer graze the hills, and the jackrabbits frolic on the flat, and the roadrunners catch lizards around the barn. And the Mexican Black Hawks hunt and soar and be a family. There were lots of things I wanted to do out there. The morning after Sarah I was up very early, well before dawn, and I knew I had no time for books because I had a hunt planned.

Over the preceding weeks, in the evenings when I had little to do and to get my mind off things, I had prepared my tools for the hunt much as I imagined that the Ancient Ones had done. Using the scraping tool I had found at the village on my land I had scraped the bark off the staves, both the bow and the arrows. I had further scraped the fat end of my bow stave down, to equal the diameter of the thin end, to provide for a bow of equal balance and strength along its length. This scraping of bark and wood took a great deal of time as I was instructed from books written by those who knew that I must scrape at right angles and not whittle else I would cut too deeply at some point and weaken the stave. The Ancient Ones by necessity took the time to do it right and I felt I must do the same. After scraping the bow and arrow staves I had left them in the dark natural air of the barn to cure out. In the dry climate of the Southwest the curing process was relatively short, I read, and after a couple of weeks I had greased my hands with bacon fat and rubbed it endlessly into the juniper wood of the bow and the willow wood of my arrows to replace the natural drying of the wood with oils that would keep the wood supple and springy and preclude brittleness that could cause the bow to snap upon drawing or the arrows to split upon impact. Then I notched the bow at either end and obtained tough, thin, sinewy lengths of leather from the saddle shop in town and cut one to fit as the draw string of the bow and tied it into the notches on either end. Before drawing the bow I wrapped more of the tough sinew around each end of the bow, covering the notches, and wetted the sinew so that it would shrink and tighten and gummed some pitch from a Piñon Pine tree into the sinew, all for the strength of the bow and to reinforce the bow and the notches on each end. I had cut and honed my willow shaft arrows to fit the draw of this six-foot longbow. I had five arrows and I notched three of them to take the three Mimbres arrowheads I had collected, leaving the other two with blunt heads to use as practice arrows. I fit the arrow heads into the notches on one end of each arrow and again with wet sinew I wrapped each arrow head on the arrow shaft for strength and further gummed it up for strength with the pitch from the Piñon Pine. I notched the other end of each arrow, too, to fit the string sinew of my bow. There was no lack of chicken feathers available at the ranch and, per instructions in the book, I cut sections of each feather to fit and I split the quills of each down the middle, leaving some of the spine of each quill intact on either end beyond the feathers. I placed three sections of feather near the end of the stave, near the notch that would fit on the draw string, and using lengths of wet sinew again, I wrapped the sinew around the spine left intact on each end of each quill, thus drawing each feather down to the stave, and I glued it all on for further strength with more of the pitch from the Piñon Pine. I let all dry and had a longbow some six feet long with five arrows, three for hunting and two for practice, and two of the hunting arrows sported small, fine black obsidian points, and one of a white stone I couldn't name. Given the propulsion of the bow at relatively short range, each arrow could surely kill a small or even a large animal. Over a number of evenings at the ranch I had notched the practice arrows onto the string and I drew and released the bow again and again and found it springy and supple and able to propel any of my arrows a good fifty yards. With accuracy and good force however my range was down to about twenty yards and I practiced at that range and closer, firing my blunt arrows at hay bales placed here and there to mimic opportunities on the hunt. I found it best to shoot with both eyes open, to shoot by instinct rather than to try to precisely aim, and within the limits of twenty yards or less I could in time hit with an accuracy that surprised me with my handmade primitive bow. I did not want to break or nick any of my arrowheads but, just once, because I had to try it, I let fly at full draw with the white-stoned arrow at a stout green Piñon Pine some twenty yards away. It took a pair of pliers and considerable strength and some careful work to withdraw the arrow, still intact, from the tree. I had made a weapon.

~ ~ ~ ~ ~

I left the shop in the dark with my bow and three hunting arrows in hand and walked underneath the lights through empty and quiet streets and then out onto the darkened highway heading south of town. A couple of cars went by as I walked along the narrow road and each time I stood off to the side of the road and let the lights go on. I turned east and headed down the access road to the ranch. Most of the houses along the road were dark but there was the hint of dawn in the east and several early risers had lights on in their houses and in one I could see an old boy in a T-shirt and tractor cap at the kitchen table smoking and perched silently over a cup of coffee, watching an early morning TV show on a tiny set, contemplating the day ahead. Such as that was going on all over as the nation woke up all around me, but I had my own plans and continued to walk rapidly and crossed the cattle guard and dropped off on the winding road down into the valley and there was not a light or any signs of human life to be seen. I knew that few if any in our nation would be employed this morning as I; and I stood for a time alone and watched the beginnings of a clear dawn creep over the valley and illuminate the hills and I could not believe that this all was mine. I was still a quarter mile from headquarters but I could hear several of my roosters sounding off like they were just next door in the still air, and then I saw that little blue-heeler dog coming up the road from the barn where she slept and somehow she had determined already that I had come. She didn't bark, knowing all along that it was me. She sniffed me a couple of times and wagged her tail appreciatively, but in deference to the early morning hour and the quiet and stillness there was none of her jump and spin and barking. Then she went off a ways to squat and urinate and then she came back and sat silently, looking east like me at the coming dawn and the morning and the emerging shapes of our hunting grounds.

Of course I knew nothing about hunting. It was as foreign to me as branding calves, raising chickens. plowing fields or saddling a horse had been just months ago. I had never killed a wild animal in my life. But there are many great books of the West written about hunters and as many others written by hunters. Their works, written from their time, leave the hunting of today with roads and pickup trucks and bright orange clothing and scoped rifles and hired men to butcher the game you killed as a slander to traditional pursuit. And among the great hunters of the past were the Ancient Ones who wrote no books but who left their scenes of the hunt and the cycle of pursuit and death and life and regeneration again in artful timeless circle on the surface of pots and the walls of caves and cliffs. And while I knew nothing about hunting I felt I was ready now to hunt and kill as they had done. I wanted the sacrament of it. And I wanted the meat.

Jackrabbits are hares and hares are nocturnal; and on the ranch the hares would feed and frolic during the night on the *vega* along the creek. They would continue feeding into the early morning hours -- I had seen them doing this -- and I presumed this morning to hunt them as they fed, quite visible, out on the grassy flats along the stream. The dog stayed, obedient and expectant, at my side as we descended the slight, gentle slope to the *vega* along the creek and we could see several hares with their peculiar long-legged shuffle and stoop as they moved about, feeding and seemingly unawares. In places the grass was so tall they disappeared, but they were large, long hares who stood on long front legs with head and ears nearly two feet off the ground and they would reappear again, appearing rather stilted and awkward moving, with even longer hind legs meant to push them along at forty miles per hour rather than shuffle around and feed. I knew my twenty yard range well and I sought to walked up to them and shoot them as they fed. They were feeding but they were certainly not unawares and I could not get closer than forty yards to any hare before she would flee. My bow could shoot that far but with uncertain accuracy. I finally loosed three long range shots at sitting hares, as close as I felt I could get to any of them before they would bolt, and was never close; at that range my arrows still could kill but I could hit one only by chance and as the arrows flew uncertainly and the hares bolted I knew the chances were slim. It seemed at that range they had time to see the arrow in flight, or perhaps here the "thwang" of the string, and they were bounding before any arrow could reach them. Each time it took time after the failed shot to find the arrow I had cast. I found the arrows from the second and third shots quicker because the dog caught on to what I was looking for and she could smell my scent on the arrows and she found them for me as they lay hidden in the grass. Sunlight came on and filled the valley and the blacktailed jackrabbits of New Mexico settled in for their day-long hiding and I could see nothing more to hunt. We walked over to the grove of fruit trees by the barn and I picked two apples from one of the trees and I sat down under the trees and ate the apples. The sun was now well up and felt good after the morning cold and I sat there and soaked it up and ate the apples and noted a rider moving easily with an almost-black horse on a far hill, over east. I knew by the horse it was Santos; I would see him from time to time over there in those hills, riding out the early part of each morning on horseback. I thought: He would know how to get a jackrabbit, before or after sunup. But I wanted to do it myself and the ancient way, and I considered how difficult life must have been for the Ancient Ones with no livestock and having to get their meat by hunting. Yet they had done so. The bones of myriad rabbits and hares and other game showed up in their middens and dumping grounds and the art on the bowls showed the hunters returning successful from the hunt. The apples were crisp and sweet and the air cool and crisp and clear but warming. I considered that I knew something about jackrabbits from reading about them in books and from what I had come to know of them on the ranch. And from reading and experience I had come to know that though they apparently disappear during the day they do not go down holes or crawl in under logs or brush piles and out of sight like rabbits. Because they aren't rabbits they are hares and they merely hood up in a self-made form in the grass and dissolve into a carefully evolved camouflage. But they are still there. They would be harder to find and see certainly, but conceivably I could approach more closely. I could no longer see Santos and the almost-black horse, and I tossed my second apple core aside and the dog and I once again descended the gentle slope to the *vega* along the creek, walking slowly, trying to see a hare before she would bound. The first jack bolted up almost from under my feet; I let fly with a quick draw and release and was shooting within my twenty-yard range but shooting at a moving target. I was surprisingly close as the arrow skipped off the ground just behind the running hare. But I was not close enough. Perhaps the Ancient Ones, well practiced in the art, could hit a running hare. I concluded I would need the same luck to hit a running hare at close range that I would need to hit a standing hare at forty yards. With my mediocre skills my only chance would be to spot a hidden hare, within range, and shoot it as it lay. With the help of the dog I found the arrow promptly and notched it and went on; and then the dog this time was trotting out in front of me, not far, and I let her go. She would trot, then slow to a walk, then crouch and test the air with her nose, then move on at a trot; and in time she crouched and held her form. I approached as if I should not even touch the ground and just behind the dog I stopped. The dog was trying the air with her nose, the only thing of her that moved, and I looked and looked and looked to see what she could smell. When I saw the hare finally she was right there and had been all along, hooded up in shallow grass and yet all but invisible by camouflage, her ears folded down over her back, not ten yards away. What I saw first was the bright animal eye, unnatural and alive in the dull grass, and then the lengthy form of a large New Mexico blacktailed jackrabbit could be seen. I had to act. In one motion I drew to full draw, sighted and released by instinct. I felt I had unaccountably missed as the arrow skipped off the ground on past the hare but it had in fact passed through; the hare leaped skyward and flopped, as good as dead though still kicking the air on its side and then the dog was there and grabbed it and held its dying form under her paws. I used my knife and opened the throat and let the carcass bleed. I used my knife and opened the belly and drew the gut and let the carcass cool. The fresh offal steamed into the air as it cooled in the grass. Then, carrying my hare, I went to my 2 1/2 acre garden patch. I walked in amongst my ancient beans and stooped and picked off the long slender pods, one by one, each now brown and crisp with maturity. I split the pods in my hands, one by one, and let the brightly colored, deep-red and white, parti-colored beans roll out into my palm. The dog was there, watching this human act, as she watched all my human acts, with great curiosity. There were six to nine healthy beans in each pod, each about the size of a good pinto bean, and I split the pods and collected beans and put them in my coat pocket until I had about a half-pound of beans in my possession. The blood was still on my hands as I left the field with hare in hand, beans in my pocket and, leaving the reluctant dog at the barn, I started home picking up a few sprouts of the Wild Blue Grama Grass on the way. Through town, before I could reach my door, people took note of an odd hunter, armed with tradition and successful with game. I considered that some might not be pleased with what they saw, for hunting is viewed as cruel in our time, and bow hunting especially so, and indeed it seemed some did look unhappily upon me and my weapon and trophy and meat. But I would not acknowledge that anything was out of sorts and did not tell them of the other treasures I carried in my pocket.

~ ~ ~ ~ ~

The following morning I took small chunks of boneless wild hare out of the red wine marinade I had made for them. The hare provided several pounds of deep red meat when removed from the bone and the marinade had made it even richer even while most of the blood in the meat had drained away. I placed several strips of bacon in the bottom of a cast iron skillet and fried them slowly and made some grease. I removed the bacon then cut up a fresh onion and scrambled the onion and the fresh scent in the grease and browned the onion. Then I placed the fresh meat in the skillet and browned the chunks of hare in with the onion. Then I added water to fill the skillet and added the ancient Mimbreño beans to the water and the meat and the onion and added various spices and let the entirety settle into a slow simmer. Then I thawed some fresh-

Signal To Depart

frozen green chili, peeled the blackened skins, and added the chili in strips to the stew. I had a long day of filling orders for books and kept the store closed and tended my green chili jackrabbit stew at the same slow simmer, and seven o'clock that evening Sarah came in through the back door.

"What's cooking, Slim?"

"Well, I've got this chili thing going."

"It smells like you've got it going good. I thought you were kidding."

"I put it all together myself. From scratch, you might say. Something special for us."

"That's just like you, Jason," she said, and then I set her down at my little kitchen table which I set as best I could with my meager utensils and a few sprouts of the wild Blue Grama grass all headed out and placed in a vase in the center of the table. I poured a good red wine in glasses that were not really wine glasses. She didn't seem to mind my improvised decor and she examined the bottle and could tell I had a good wine and she smiled over all I had done. Then I brought our dish in a large bowl and placed it hot and steaming on the table and I got some hot bread with butter and garlic from the oven and placed it on the table, too.

"So what have you made for us?"

"Just a New Mexico chili stew I put together."

"Smells damn good," she said, and then I sat down across from her and doled out this chili to her bowl and mine and then I reached across the table and took her hand in mine and we raised our glasses to one another and I said, "To the first of many nights together."

"You do have a romantic side," she said. "And about time after all that raunchy sex."

"The romance comes harder for me," I said. "But I feel both with you."

"Well, keep it up; you're getting me in the mood."

We ate with relish and I could tell she liked it and I could tell she was curious, too.

"All right, Slim," she said, "I know you killed something wild to make this. Out with it."

"Jackrabbit," I said.

"That's just like you, Jason."

"I got her myself, with a bow and arrow I made."

"Nobody but you would do it this way. And I suppose these are those Indian beans you've been talking about."

"Of course."

"Oh you're different all right," she said. "Nobody but you would think cooking up a bowl of beans with a damn jackrabbit was romantic."

"I'm pleased with it myself." I said. "Jackrabbit chili. I was worried; it's a first for me."

"Don't worry; it's good. And it's good you didn't tell me till you did...a damn jackrabbit! This is all just like you, Jason."

We ate good, till full, and I thought of how well I had chosen. A woman who could enjoy what was natural and good to me. And there was the inevitable juxtaposition with Carla, who had convinced herself of an unnatural diet, "free of meat," and with Terri who in her urban life would never know the pleasure and sacrament of raising her own crop and killing her own meat and gathering and preparing a meal straight from the land. We ate well and I could sense her happiness with me and it seemed to me then that Sarah must feel about me much as I did about her, and I could see it all coming true for me.

And then, later, during the night, it came so hard for her she was for the first time something I hadn't seen before -- soft and trembling and vulnerable as she wept in my arms.

"What is it?" I said.

"I think I can cry a little now, knowing it won't be much longer."

"Nothing can stop it now."

"I know. It's all coming down. Jason, will you meet me at the ranch tomorrow?"

"Yes, just like we planned. Tomorrow is our day, too."

"And will you show me your life there, show me all your secrets and share everything with me?"

"Yes, we can't have any more secrets now."

At that moment I held her close and with my best strength and this was the happiest I've been.

In the morning she still slept soundly. I got up and covered her with the blanket as the room had grown cool and she didn't move or know I had left the bed. I went into the bathroom and drew a bath and got into the deep tub and soaked and lounged in hot soapy water and every muscle was loose and I was at peace and I thought, if everything could just stop here and stay like this.

In time she got up and came in. She was naked and lovely and perfect and she sat on the lid of the seat and rubbed her eyes and shook some of the sleep out of her head and her long red hair tosseled around her face and then she yawned and stretched her arms and legs out while sitting, like a tawny awakening cat.

"Come in," I said. "I'll hold you and wash you and hold you some more."

"Ummmm," she said nicely, "I've never taken a bath with a man before."

"That's not done in your household?"

"Oh no...that would be unthinkable and forbidden."

"Well it's not unthinkable for us."

"Ummm...only I need to do something first."

"Later."

"No. Can't wait. Give a girl a moment of privacy."

"No. Can't move. It's too good right here. You can wait."

"No. Can't wait."

"Then do it."

"Under the circumstances, that would be unthinkable and forbidden."

"Not with us."

"Do I have a choice?"

"You can wait."

"Can't wait," she said, and she stood and lifted the lid with the perfect form she had for every move she ever made, and she sat and, placing her hands like a little girl who thinks if she covers her eyes she can't be seen, she relieved herself, quite beautifully.

Done, she came to me, and of course when she lowered herself upon me I was ready; I watched her from behind, moving, as the water began to climb in waves in the tub, and she was groaning as it was reaching up the sides and just before it was up and over she was coming down again and again, making her noises and slapping against me and the water slopping in waves over the top.

I washed her, and then she lay back in my arms.

"That's just like you, Jason."

"Is it?'

"Yes. You make me do unspeakable things."

"Yes. Unspeakable and unthinkable and forbidden. Things we couldn't do with anyone else."

"I wouldn't want to be like this with anyone but you."

~ ~ ~ ~ ~

Later that morning I walked out to the ranch to meet her. I dropped of into the creek by the post office and followed the old horse trail that Claire had made over the years out to the ranch. I came up off the creek to the ranch house and sat in the morning sun under the yellowing leaves of the two big cottonwoods there and some of those yellow leaves were already coming down in the fall breeze, one by one. The dog came out of the barn to join me in waiting and I knew she would be there to follow us around. And I wasn't there a half an hour and I could hear the sound of a vehicle and soon Sarah came down the winding round in a new four x four power wagon, "Callahan Construction" on the doors. She pulled up to the parking area just north of the house, and got out and walked over to me; a few of those scattered golden leaves fell around her red hair and white blouse and her jeans wrapped her legs and form like exercise pants and yet she moved elegantly and easily and without a slip in her boots. Then she stopped and lifted a leg and placed one boot up on the low adobe wall that surrounded the *placita*.

"This your new place, Slim?"

"This is it."

"Where do we start?"

"We'll look at the house."

"Doesn't look like you've done much with it."

"I was waiting to see what you would want."

"That's just like you, Jason."

And we went into the house. Of course I hadn't touched it since Claire had died and Bingo had removed all the furniture and we went room to room and told each other what we would like to see on the walls and what furniture we would like and what needed painting and what would stay the same, and I told her how I would plumb the house and add one and then two bathrooms with hot and cold running water all around.

"You do that first; that's a necessity," she said.

"We'll keep the old backhouse intact for old time sake," I said.

"As long as we don't have to use it."

Then we walked over to the barn and the corrals. We looked at the milk cow and decided easily that we'd keep her. She was starting to dry up for the season but she was bred and would calf and freshen again. And I told of how I had a plans for getting some milk goats, for milk and cheese for our own use and to sell some too, and *cabritos* for the meat, and I showed her how I planned to build farrowing rooms for the hogs we would have and of course we would have a second horse, at least, and I showed where we had room for lots more chickens with more roosts and laying boxes I could easily build and instead of two dozen laying hens we would build up to three hundred good game hen crosses for hybrid vigor and because they could raise their own chicks, the old natural incubation, and we would get a special good price for the eggs.

And then I took her hand as we walked down along the *vega*. I showed her my plans for what I would leave as the natural permanent pasture along the creek and what I would plow and plant to corn and beans and wheat and oats with regular rotations of legume clovers and alfalfa hay, for feed hay and then plowdown, and applications of manure, so that the soil would not erode and would remain fertile without throwing anything on it bought at a store. I told her too off my plans to buy a team and learn to work it to farm the land as Claire had done years ago.

"All the tack and harness is in the barn, and the implements are still here," I said, " up behind the barn, and we can make them work again."

"You go ahead and do that, Jason," she said, smiling. "That's just like you."

On the hills around us a half dozen of my meager herd of nine cows could be seen, with their calves who were almost ready for sale, and here I stopped talking and she told me that with grass-feed available in the sub-irrigated flat lands along the creek plus the hay we could raise, we could run a good deal more than nine cows. I told her how Claire had explained to me that it was best to run too few than too many and let them grow better on extra feed rather than to push and abuse the range, but I didn't push that view too hard as it was good to hear Sarah get involved and tell how she thought it ought to be, and she did have some interesting ideas about some cross fencing and grazing a pasture hard for a short time and then moving the cows around.

"We can do much better, you'll see," she said.

I took her over to my little 2 1/2 acre patch of beans and corn, the one thing of my agricultural unit that was more than a plan and that I had done myself. The crop of blue Indian corn was magnificent, I thought, with large, full ears and not a week away from harvest. And all my beans lay in neat rows with the crisp brown pods flush and thick on each bush and some of them could even be picked right now.

"I dream sometimes," I said, "of you and me and little Jill and our own little one all out here picking our ancient beans and Indian corn and putting up our own food for the winter on sunny fall days just like this."

"That's just like you," she said. "Mama had a nice garden when we were little, but when the ranch started to do well for some reason she let it go."

We walked into the garden and I shucked a couple of ears and showed her the deep blue of the Indian corn I had planted and nurtured to harvest. And then, at the bean patch, I lay a pod of the ancient beans in my palm and, cracking the dry husk, the seven bright beans rolled out in my hand for her to see. She took one and held it in her own palm and rolled it there with a finger from her other hand so all sides of the colors and pattern came round and I told her that, of course, no two are the same. She looked at this little treasure bean for some time. And then she looked at me.

"Show me where they come from, Jason. Show me where you found them."

"That would be unthinkable and forbidden."

"Not for us."

"There are some things you know that it's best the world never knows."

"They won't know. We have our own secrets. But after last night, we can't have any secrets from each other."

Of course she was right; we had come just recently from great and unspeakable intimacies and could have no secrets from each other now; and we walked together away from the bean patch and back up toward the house and down along the rim of the cliffs south through open areas there and patches of the dry scrubby woodlands and in the midst of one of them near where a dry wash arroyo cut through I stopped and said, "Look around you now, Sarah, and tell me what you see."

She stepped away from me. She moved so nicely as she always did as she walked here and there and turned this way and that and I could see that she was looking very hard because she sensed that we were there but when she turned back to me she said, "I don't see anything." And then I went to the edge of the arroyo. My work after the great summer rains had been good and the erosion had been stopped and grass and shrubs and brush had grown up along the arroyo; but kneeling by the arroyo I brushed away some loose dirt from the side of the draw and it fell away into the arroyo and then even she could see the ancient adobe block where erosion had revealed it to me months before. And then it was interesting to watch as she came over and kneeled by the ancient wall and stood and turned and looked around as I had done months before, and now that she knew that it was there, the outlines of the walls and rooms and the form of the village came to her as it had to me.

"It goes on as far as you can see," she said.

"It sure does," I said. "It was a good-sized little village once, all along the front of this cliff to the south, under this scrubby little patch of woods."

Moving beautifully, she cleared the arroyo in a long-legged leap and wandered off to the south and disappeared into the woods, and when I found her she was to the south and east edge of the woods, looking out over the *vega* and the creek to the east; and I came up behind her as she turned to me and she tried to hide the tears on her face as she put her arms around me and lay her head into my chest.

"Now we've shared everything," I said.

"Yes," she said. "And what does it mean, Jason?"

"It means that the love is real," I said.

And she said, "I'd like to believe that, too."

~ ~ ~ ~ ~

I sat under the two cottonwoods with a few golden leaves still falling in the breeze and watched her leave as I had watched her arrive. She walked to the truck and turned there and looked at me, shading her eyes in the sun. She got in and turned the key and put the floor shift in reverse and backed the truck most competently around. I saw her shift again and then she was driving away, and before she made the first bend I raised my hand in parting. And of course she was watching me in the mirror and she matched my gesture, raising her hand in a way that was quite her own.

Chapter 24

Sarah was right of course -- it was much easier for me than it was for her. I had no other commitments, my relationships were easily broken, indeed had already been broken away. I could only imagine what Sarah was going through as Saturday night went by, and Sunday, and Sunday night. She was faced with the task of securing herself and her child and their affects in a temporary new home, and contending with Clemson "Bingo" Callahan's discovery of another loss in his singularly greedy life. And by our agreement there was nothing I could do to help. And then Monday came and it was night and I was expectant of her arrival any minute and when she didn't come I contented myself with the thought that the worst for her must be over. And then Monday night passed and then Tuesday and then especially Tuesday night I expected her surreptitious arrival at my back door to tell me all of how she had done it and that she was free of him and we were free to be together. But there was no arrival on Monday night or Tuesday or even Tuesday night and there was no sleep for me Tuesday night for as the night got late I knew that something was wrong. Then on

Signal To Depart

Wednesday morning, an hour before noon as I opened my box at the post office, I got the registered letter that told me that the town of Del Cobre was serving notice to purchase by condemnation the Callahan Ranch.

I proceeded to the office of lawyer Thomas Wynne. He was able to see me without an appointment and in fact didn't seem to have much to do that morning as he sat behind his desk reading a newspaper, as I was ushered in. He looked up over the top of the paper and recognized me and said, "Mr. Niles."

"Mr. Wynne."

"Sit down, Mr. Niles."

I remained standing and handed him the letter. He set his paper down and read the letter without apparent emotion and then he said again, "Sit down Mr. Niles." And this time I did take a seat across from his desk.

"What can you do for me?" I said. "I have the money if you'll take the case."

"What did you pay for the ranch?...two hundred an acre if I recall."

"That's right."

"Well it says here they're offering you four hundred an acre which would double your money in a few months time. On the other hand, I think we could make the case they're still assessing this land as agricultural land while they say themselves right here that the land is being condemned for, quote, "the expansion of the Del Cobre Municipal Golf Course, the Del Cobre Picnic Park, the Tobosa Highway cutoff, and needed water rights, and new housing, and other suitable developments to provide for the orderly growth of the community." So, yes, I think we can make a good case that you ought to receive more than four hundred an acre. That much I can do for you."

"I don't have any interest in debating money with the town. I want to keep my land and I need some help."

"I'll be blunt, Mr. Niles. You can't fight the sale of the land. Not successfully. Municipal and county as well as state governments have the authority to condemn open space or agricultural land whenever they can demonstrate a need. And in this case they can demonstrate that the town needs the water and the land for the other half of the Municipal Golf Course because there's no place else they can put it. And they need it for all the new people coming in. And they think they need to build that shortcut to Tobosa, though I can't imagine why anyone would be in a hurry to go there."

"This is the first I've heard about that highway cutoff."

"Haven't you seen the *Region* lately?"

"It seems I haven't been keeping up with the news."

"Well this condemnation looks clear cut to me. You're already in the city limits, and since Claire died there's no one living on the land except old Santos. And he's a renter. So it's not like they're uprooting families. They have to pay you fair market value for the land. There's certainly room for debate there. You're of course welcome to apply to other counsel. But in my opinion any lawyer who tells you you've got any chance at all of beating the condemnation is stealing your money."

"It says I can present any comments or objections verbally or in writing at the next council meeting."

"They have to say that. They have to let you or any member of the public say their peace. Go on in to the meeting next week and let them have it. You may feel better having done so. It won't change anything. The vote was unanimous it says here and they'll just rubber stamp their earlier decision and make it final after you're done. I know those boys; they're that way, and they're in Bingo's back pocket. But give them a piece of your mind, and if you want, I'll see to it they pay more than four hundred an acre."

"Four hundred an acre is quick turnover for me, strictly speaking. I won't object to four hundred an acre. That land has other values for me. How about if I quick sell my land to some government entity or conservancy or some other outfit that won't develop it?"

"It's a little late for that I'm afraid...look, Mr. Niles, this probably had to happen. I didn't say anything at the time because it meant so much to Claire for you to have the land and I figured it was worth a try. But you're sitting there on two hundred acres with a sunbelt town growing up all around you. The town wasn't going to move as long as Claire was alive and living on the land. Now Claire's dead and it was probably too much to expect that

Bingo and the town would lay down and let this pass. The only thing that surprises me is, it didn't happen sooner. Give it all some thought, Mr. Niles. Go tell them what you have to say next Tuesday night. If you change your mind about wanting more money, let me know. And by all means get another legal opinion if you like."

"I believe that everything you've told me is quite true," I said.

Chapter 25

And when Sarah did not come Wednesday night even I knew what had happened to me. It was the night when, for weeks, for months, she had come to see me. But this time she did not come. And it had come to be I didn't know what to think about Sarah. Anymore, I didn't know what to think but I had to think that the love was real. Terri Vinson had been right of course. A woman with husband, home and family who is having an affair will choose husband, home and family when all is done. Whatever she really wants. I had fallen in love with something I couldn't have. As it happened, I had fallen in love with more than Sarah that I couldn't have. Of course, in my mind it all went together anyway. I had fallen in love with all of it, and it was turning out I couldn't have any of it. Bingo Callahan had it all. He had it all to himself now, and could do whatever he wanted with it. I didn't want to think about that, but just try to stop it sometime. Just try to stop it if you can. See if you can stop thinking about it after it's all gone to Hell. I waited, fed by helpless delusions, far into the night for her, and when even I knew for sure that she would not come I swung around in the swivel chair behind my desk and began to type on my book in progress. I felt I could see the end of that long story and finishing it became important to me now. I worked, typing, far into the night and when I would finally stop to break I would look to my first book, my only book to date, just above me on the shelf. I could see it there and that was important to me, and a couple of times I took it down from the shelf to have it for a time in my hands, before putting it back on the shelf. I had to have something and now my work was all I had. Toward morning, feeling I could not go on much longer, I took my first book down off the shelf and handled it again and placed it on the desk beside my work. That's one thing about a book you have written yourself. Once you've done it no one can ever take it away. Good book or bad book it's your book and no one's book will ever be the same. It will live as long as you; if it's well done and well made it may even outlive you to mean something to someone else in times to come. I had my first book at least, and it was right there beside me now, and I went back to my work, my next book, and typed on until I could see first light through the curtain on the street outside. Then, achieving finally the total exhaustion I sought, I went to my bed and tried to sleep.

Chapter 26

Of course there was nothing in Del Cobre so far away you couldn't walk to it, and that included the town hall, just down the street, north from the post office. I was very tired from many days of sleeping little or not at all. I didn't feel good and I was unshaven and disheveled and didn't look good, and I knew I didn't even smell very good as I'd worked hard and almost non-stop and had neglected myself for days; but I had finished the first draft of my work, my second novel and what would be my second book, just hours before. That was something. That was something good and something new to hold on to. My book, my work; that was all I had anymore. I suppose I still had the ranch but apparently not for long. And I couldn't bear seeing the land. I hadn't been out there since it all went to hell. I couldn't bear to go out there and see it. And I'd neglected myself for nearly a week. I'd spent the time behind a desk at a typewriter and I missed the work out there at the place but I couldn't stand to go out there and see it. I'd stayed in the shop and worked on the book during the day and until late at night and then I would try to sleep in my clothes, till I would realize I couldn't, and I would get up and write some more. And I had finished the first draft of the book. And walking to the meeting it was almost dark and the early fall air was cool and bracing and the walk felt good.

It turned out to be not a large meeting room with chairs for perhaps fifty members of the public to sit and look at and listen to the four councilmen and the mayor and respond as they saw fit when their time arrived. And this particular meeting was a little more than half full. I saw faces I recognized and a few people I casually knew. It was no one's business but my own, the way I saw it, and I sat down in the back with no one nearby and without conversation with anyone; and rather early in the meeting it was suddenly the issue of the condemnation by the city of the Callahan Ranch that was before the council and the citizens in attendance. I heard something about the unanimous vote of the intent to condemn at the previous meeting a week ago, and expansion of the golf course and necessity of acquiring the water rights, and the need for new housing, and for growth, and then the mayor was asking if anyone present had any "questions, comments or objections to this proposed action taken by the council." I waited, hoping that some unknown friend would do this for me. But I, in my life of self, had in fact made only acquaintances in this town, excepting Terri Vinson perhaps, who was gone, and Carla Aguilar, who was gone from me, and Claire, who couldn't help me now. I had made no friends or allies or colleagues in Del Cobre who could help me now. And I had come to the meeting to say something but I had no idea what to say. I considered that this was the perfect chance to stand up at a public forum and raise my voice and tell the world just how the cow eats the cabbage, the opportunity every citizen dreams. In fact I was just scared shitless. There was no response from other citizens. The mayor said, "If there are no comments then I'll ask for a vote that we confirm..." when I stood finally and said: "Mr. Mayor, my name is Jason Niles and I ask that the council reconsider their vote to condemn the Callahan Ranch."

The Mayor said, "Mr. Niles, we understand that you are the present owner of the Callahan Ranch. Your objections are therefore understandable. This condemnation by the town was carefully considered and I can assure you was not taken upon lightly. We have offered what we believe is a fair price based on a market value appraisal. I see no reason for the council to change their vote and I doubt any of us will. But you are welcome to state your case here and now."

"Mr. Mayor," I said, "members of the council, citizens...America is doomed. Unless we act soon this country as we know it is finished..."

"Mr. Niles. I don't think this is the place for your personal editorial on what is wrong with America. We are concerned with the needs of this town and among them is room for growth, public recreation, and a safer highway, all of which is why we must buy the Callahan Ranch. That's the issue here before the council now."

"Mr. Mayor, you said yourself I could state my case. This town needs that land all right. America needs that land. But for something far more important and sensible than growth. I need a chance to explain why this is so."

"Very well, Mr. Niles. But please get to the point."

"My point, Mr. Mayor, is that America is doomed. Unless we act soon, this country as we know it is finished. Now the registered letter you-all sent me the other day said you needed to buy the Callahan Ranch to serve...*the orderly growth of the community.* Well, we've heard that one before. And in this case it looks like this *orderly growth* will involve the expansion of the golf course and country club, housing projects, an RV park, a highway cutoff that'll save maybe five minutes getting to Tobosa, and, as a sop to aesthetics, some sort of a damn drive-up park with picnic tables and cook-out stands where folks can roast burgers and drink beer on Sunday afternoons. Truth is, none of this development is designed to serve the growth of the community, or even to provide for it; it's designed to create it. Once the money is committed to that land and water, the subsequent development of that land becomes more than a goal, it becomes a necessity. That's how the West was won.

"Now I'll admit right here that one reason I bought the Callahan Ranch was to in my own small way put the skids on sunbelt booster projects like this one. Because it's growth, in all its greedy, grabby, insidious economic and biological forms that is killing this country -- its cultures, its traditions, its farms and ranches, its traditional economies and long term prosperity, and the natural world we all depend on. There was a place for it once. When European settlement came here to the Southwest this was a rich, diverse land mostly empty of people. The sparse Native

American population that was here was kept sparse by the difficult geography, a lack of rain and technology, famine, pestilence and disease, and the fact that they tended to war and kill each other off. We Europeans were a mixed blessing to these people. We abused and largely destroyed their culture, while bringing them things they wouldn't willingly do without -- the wheel for example, a written language, longer lives and a declining death rate, little niceties like prenatal care. In an honest moment they can't regret progress, technology, and the creature comforts we take for granted in these times. And neither can I. But sometime between the turn of the century and today this country got full, and we passed a point of sustainability. Here in the Southwest we began to cut our forests faster than they could regrow trees of equal value and heritage; we began to draw down our underground water supplies, so that the recharge of our aquifers is no longer equal to our use of those aquifers; we began to alter our rivers and streams till today they're mostly all dammed and channelized and the riparian habitats cut and grazed and otherwise denuded to where for miles at a stretch you can scarcely find shade or birds or a good fishing hole. And on our farms and ranches we farmed and ranched badly, overgrazing the range and driving out native grasses and watching our limited topsoil and cultivated acres decline in value and ability to produce. But the boomers among us -- and it seems every politician, civic leader, and *prominent* citizen is a boomer -- have convinced us we must continue to boost our populations and pour on the coals to maintain prosperity. We don't need growth -- population growth or otherwise -- for prosperity. There are entire nations, in Europe, that give the lie to that notion. Here in the Southwest, the only people who benefit from this growth and continual influx of population are the boomers themselves, who use it to fuel unsavory developments like the condemnation and urbanization of the Callahan Ranch.

"Now there's not much in the short term you or I can do about the nation's population growth. I've got a diatribe on that too, but it's beyond my crabbiness here. But there is something we can do to preserve our own long term prosperity and the better aspects of our traditions. And snub our noses at mindless boosterism while we're at it. And that's where something wonderful can be done with the Callahan Ranch. It's only 200 acres, but it's typically Southwestern, it's variegated, and it's never been overgrazed or farmed badly. And it's right on the edge of town. Some think that makes it perfect for development. I'm thinking it's perfect, right where it is, as an antidote to development. It was my idea to learn how to farm it and graze it and make a living off it and satisfy my own interests as to how a life should be lived on the land. But I was naive. Fact is, I was stupid. I didn't believe the town would or could take it away from me. And I was selfish. Hell, I was greedy. I didn't think to offer to work with the community at large that the Callahan Ranch might serve a larger purpose. I want to make that offer tonight. I see the Callahan Ranch as community property, a kind of agricultural reserve within the city limits, that can show anyone whose interested how we might produce meat and crops, year by year, for all time, even on the smallest parcels of land. I see that 200 acres as a wildlife reserve and natural area. With its dry rolling hills, bottomland, and riparian stream course running through, it's a prototype of Southwestern life before we came in and mucked it up. I can see hiking trails provided for the walkers, and horses provided for those who don't get around so well anymore. And in the spirit of compromise I can even see setting aside a small portion of the 200 acres for that damn Sunday afternoon barbecue/picnic table setup you've got planned. As for the golf course, the RV park, the highway, the subdivisions, and the rest of that barfy urban plan, that schlock is going up and spreading out and eating up rural American anywhere you look right now. This community has a chance to do something different.

"And another thing. Some one thousand years ago there lived in this valley a remarkable race. We call them *The Mimbres*. It's imagined that they referred to themselves as, simply, The People. By our standards they were primitive folks. For their time they were a prosperous and socially complex and culturally advanced society. They began from ragged bands and stragglers. They progressed by way of a blessed, yet fragile, environment, agricultural competence, and hunting skills, to a measure of relative success, leisure and ease. They became a culturally advanced and superior society and within that society a strange and wonderful art flourished for a time. It's so strange and wonderful it continually astonishes the modern world of art, and the artists of our time. And even some of the boomers and boosters have noticed it; its discovery and sale brings big bucks, and its display in books and the public arena has brought the world's notice, and the beginnings of a tourist trade, to our community. This race did not survive as a people or as a culture. They disappeared and left these valleys empty long before any Europeans got a look at them. A lot has been made of the great mystery of their disappearance. But in the last fifty years archaeology and biology, and the painted pots and bowls and cliff markings they left behind, have given us the general outline of their decline, and the information can now be found in books. It's known that at their height their culture featured a population of at least 5,000 people in the Willow Valley alone. Other nearby valleys, like along our own *Gavilán* Creek, showed a similar rate of increase in population over time. There's evidence that they gradually killed off the game, having to go further and further afield to get meat, until the hunts were no longer practical. There's evidence that they cut down all readily available timber for housing and fuel wood, having to go further and further afield to find suitable trees, until the search was no longer practical. There is plenty of evidence that their growing population forced them into an increasingly intensive agricultural along available streams. They pushed the land too hard, and ended up with salinity, and a loss of topsoil and fertility and production. The evidence finally tells us that somewhere in the glory of their rising population and culture, they overpopulated their range and past that point of sustainability. At the very height of their success, when their most priceless art would flourish, they were already to the brink of their fall. Only they couldn't see it. Or by the time they did it was too late. They lost it. Take it all though, and they didn't do too badly. Their culture grew and flourished and gradually prospered for a thousand years. And they left us their art. As for us, we've been in their same locale for little more than a hundred years; and the way were gathering up the countryside, what are the chances that we'll last nine hundred more? Even one hundred more? The stuff we're doing would astonish those folks. Imagine the pictures the Ancients would leave behind, after they'd had a look at the way we live today? Hell, I'd love to see their take on that goofy golf game some of you want to build in place of the natural world along *Gavilán* Creek. The Southwest was not designed by nature to accommodate the life all the boosters are telling us we ought to live. And in the end it won't.

"So I've got this idea. It's coming to me even as I ramble on here. It won't change the world, or give all the boomers a new religion, but it could make one small change in one small town. Think about this: I propose that the town purchase from me the Callahan Ranch, within the outline of use I've talked about here, not for $400 per acre as proposed, but rather for $1 per acre. I'll gladly accept the sum total of $200 for 200 acres, and thereby save the community $79,800, which can be spent elsewhere. Why should I worry about losing some money? I know how to make more. Hell, even $200 may be too much for the land, for it's priceless after all. The boomers have offered you growth. They have offered to turn a town into a city. They have offered you more traffic, higher taxes, more pollution, a new frenetic pace of life, and an exponential increase in crime, drugs, gangs, and indigent ne'er do wells, all of which are guarenteed additions when towns become cities. I offer a parcel of land that can help one community retain it's reasonable prosperity, singular culture, and way of life. And who knows, maybe in time others will see the wisdom of what we have done. How 'bout it, Mr. Mayor, council members, citizens?"

I sat down and it was dead silent as everyone waited on the mayor and the mayor didn't say anything right away. I saw him look down the table at the council members, this way and that, and I'm sure one time I saw him role his eyes. Nor did anyone on the council respond by way of comment. But in the audience Toby Jensen did. I recognized him as Terri's friend, that I had seen at the Country Club months before, the man -- one of them anyway -- who had been cheated by Bingo Callahan. He stood and spoke.

"Mr. Mayor, Mr. Niles has made the town a very generous offer. This is clearly too significant an offer to be decided hastily...certainly not at this meeting. I recommend that the council at least place the purchase in abeyance for a time. Give the community a week or two to hear of the offer and to comment on it. Then the council can decide."

Jensen sat down and I felt that something awesome could indeed happen. Jensen's approach was perfect, it seemed; he made it seem so reasonable to give my offer some time, and thereby, a chance; so unreasonable to do otherwise. In the room as well, however, was Bingo Callahan. He was standing in the doorway, big and burly and he hadn't bothered to remove his cap, and he must have come in late, or I would have noticed him earlier. But he'd been there long enough to know what was going on.

"Mayor," he said, "let's not any of us be deceived by all this hot air about hiking trails and dead Indians and being sustainable, whatever that means. And if this person wants to sell the town 200 acres for $200 dollars I'd say he's more foolish than generous. I've heard other descriptions of this man since he came to our town and generous has never been one of them. Whatever he's really up to, this silly proposal is not a bargain for the town. The acreage is worth millions to this town, for the very things we have planned for it...the expansion to 18 holes which will give us the finest golf course in southern New Mexico, homes for our growing population of good folks, a new, safe highway coming into town, the RV park and all the rest. Once the developments are in you couldn't buy a fraction of that 200 acres for a mere $80,000 dollars. This man's proposal is from another planet. If not that, from another time. There's no future in turning the clock back. You can't stop growth. And nobody should want to try. It's coming, and we need to provide for it. I can't think of a town in the Southwest with a greater potential than our town right here, and the 200 acres that you will acquire will be a big part of that future. Anyway, Jensen's proposal is too late. The town voted at the last meeting an intent to purchase the land. Unless the council is prepared to rescind that intent, the vote must proceed. And I defy anyone on this council to vote against this important acquisition for our community."

The mayor, looking somewhat relieved, said, "Bingo, your point is well taken. We have voted to consider condemnation. So, public comment having been taken, I will simply ask the council:

all in favor of purchasing the Callahan Ranch as outlined at the previous meeting, raise your hand..."

Quintana, down at the end, was the only one who didn't raise his hand. He leaned forward to his microphone and looked almost like he was about to say something. I suspect he considered the futility of it. He hesitated, and presently he waved his hand in the air and sat back in his chair.

"Very well," the Mayor said. "I'll take that as a unanimous vote and we'll move on to..."

"Mr. Mayor," I said, standing up and reaching into my pocket, "there may be treasures on the land not yet discovered. I have these beans..."

"Mr. Niles, you've had your say and the council has affirmed their vote of the previous meeting."

"Mr. Mayor, these are rare beans. Each one is a jewel from the past. They are from my land and there may be more to that land than we know of. And there's a family of Mexican Black Hawks nesting down along the creek. They can't possibly survive the..."

"Mr. Niles!" he said, and this time he brought his gavel down. "The vote has been taken and the condemnation affirmed. And in fairness you've had your say. We are not going to change our vote over a bird's nest or a handful of beans, no matter where they came from. Now if you have further objections I suggest you seek legal council. The issue is closed here."

I sat down and the meeting droned on for a time. I don't know how much time but after a time I got up and left. I sensed that Jensen was looking to catch my eye as I left but I acted like I didn't notice. I walked right by where Bingo had been standing, but there was nobody there. I walked on back to the shop and when I got in there I recognized that smell you get when you've been in a bad nervous sweat. I was a little bad before but now after the meeting I knew I really didn't smell very good. It's a sick smell and it makes you feel sick when you smell it -- the smell of nervous fear -- and I knew I was losing it. I determined that in the morning I must bathe and shave and put on clean clothes and try to get it back. But for the moment, I couldn't. I couldn't do anything about tomorrow. I couldn't think that far ahead. And I knew I couldn't stop what was happening to me. I got undressed and into bed and lay there, hoping I would get sleepy. I really was very tired and needed very badly to get some sleep but I knew that didn't mean sleep would come. I waited and waited for the sleep to come. And I kept thinking of all I had done wrong to lose my land, and what all I might have done right to save it; and of how I lost Sarah, and what all I might have said or done to keep her, and what all Bingo had said or done to convince her not to be with me. And I tried to imagine things that I still had, things I could hold on to. I tried to be with Terri, tried to imagine that for a time. But that was futile, even to the unrealities of my imagination. We had been close for a moment or two...but now Terri Vinson was gone. Then I tried to be with Carla. She at one time had wanted to be with me, forever and ever. But that was futile, even to my incredible imagination. Carla Aguilar was gone. Terri was gone and Carla I had driven away and Sarah was the one I really wanted and couldn't have and now she was gone too. And there was no way, even with my bewildered mind and leaps of fantasy, that Claire could help me now. Claire was gone too. My head was spinning with all of this and all of them and I couldn't sleep. And so with sleep not coming like I'd hoped I thought of my new book, that I had just finished, and I tried to imagine that it was good. And I also thought of something else: there is still that hope that they will never find that village. I could picture in my mind how the land would change, with the expanded nine holes down in the valley, and the new housing up in the hills, and the highway and the other developments planned. That picture did not please me. I could picture it in my mind, how it was all going to change, and it hurt to look at it. But hidden away from it all, under the trees and brush along the high rock wall was that acre or so of land. I could imagine that they would never know what was there. Only three people really knew where it was, and I could not imagine that any one of us would ever tell. Toward the end I really started believing it and then I fell asleep.

Signal To Depart

Chapter 27

Late the next morning, bathed and shaved, dressed in clean clothes and looking more or less presentable, I went by city hall and got in to see the city manager and told him that I would accept their price for the Callahan Ranch. They apparently saw me coming from days before and they had the papers all ready. I signed, and the papers indicated I had 30 days to get the livestock and personal effects off the land. All generosity, I was told by the city manager that if I needed more time that would be no problem. I told him I wouldn't need more time, that I had already made a phone call that morning and made arrangements with a rancher for the sale and pickup of the cattle and the chickens and the horse and the milk cow, the tractor and implements and other accoutrements left over from the working days of the Callahan Ranch. I'd offered it all so cheap the rancher couldn't say no. The only thing left was to find a home for the dog. I'd offered the dog as a *pilón* to the rancher but the rancher said he didn't need another dog. I didn't tell the city manager about the dog, or that there was still a small crop out there that had never been harvested. I didn't figure that would matter to the city either way. Anymore, it didn't matter to me either way. He told me the money would be mailed to me by way of a bank check in about a week. I tried to think of where I might be or what I might be doing in a week's time and could think of nothing. So I gave him the address of my post office box in El Paso. He asked me what I was going to do with all the money. I told him I had no plans.

~ ~ ~ ~ ~

Still with no plans, I was sitting behind my desk one afternoon about a week later when Sarah Callahan walked in. She came right in the front door, rather like she half-way owned the place, and sat down in the chair by my desk in a way that had you noticing every little thing she did.

"Hello, Jason."

"Sarah."

"How's everything?"

"Life goes on."

"Sure. I guess we don't have much choice in that."

"Actually we do."

"Well I won't hang around to hear any of that kind of talk. You aren't the kind to feel sorry for yourself."

"Is that what it is?"

"I heard you did real well, actually. I heard you got $400 an acre for that little place."

"Yeah; great. Doubled my money in six months."

"That's what I heard. So you see, you did do real well, and it's all for the best."

"Guess I lucked out."

"Sure you did. And I guess you're wondering why I'm here."

"I've been expecting you. Only you're about two weeks late."

"Then I'll say that I guess you've been wondering why I'm too weeks late. And I'll guess that you've been blaming all this on Bingo."

"Blame? I don't know about blame. He won."

"He always wins, if you want to think of it as winning."

"It's a minor consolation to me that the town ended up with the land, and not him. But then I don't guess in the end it'll make much difference."

"It won't make any difference. The town ends up with the golf course, and the picnic area and such, which is what would have happened anyway. It's all pretty much what we'd planned all along, excepting it just took a little longer than what we wanted. What's important to Bingo is not who owns it, or even the money. He sees that land as important to the development of the town, and he wants to be a part of it, and he will."

"So Bingo is working it with the town to be the contractor for the new golf course and expanded country club and the RV park and the shortcut to Tobosa and that goddamn picnic area, and he'll be the developer for any new housing that goes in."

"You got it, Slim. You should know the truth of all this."

"Oh I think I can conjure up something pretty close to the truth...you leave me at the ranch on Saturday afternoon. Home, you get cold feet about just packing up clothes and daughter and leaving Bingo to face an empty house. Bingo comes back from Denver Sunday evening. Guilt overcomes you; it all -- or most all -- comes out. There's a big fight and then reconciliation. And everyone -- or almost everyone -- lives happily ever after. Married people go through those sorts of things all the time. In the end the cheating spouse generally goes back to the nest. The only thing I don't understand is why it took him all that time to get the town to take back the land."

"There's more than that you don't understand, Slim. And it looks like I'm going to have to tell you. The way you make things up about what's going on in the world, you'd never figure it out for yourself. You should know the truth of this. You should know this was all my idea. When Bingo found that Claire had left the land to you, he didn't take it all that hard...at first. He figured he could work some kind of a deal with you. And so he came by here and I remember he came home later that day and he was mad enough to spit, and he said, 'He's a purist; he's a damn purist,' and he said, 'He really believes that stuff,' like he couldn't believe it himself. You rejected him, and that was a mistake. What you did, that was a first for Bingo. He's always been able to work a deal for what he wants, and make it work to suit himself. But when he came home from talking with you he was sure crazy over what had happened. Or hadn't happened. I had to calm him down; I was afraid he was going to do something stupid, and ruin it for both of us. So I told Bingo to just get the town to condemn it or annex it or whatever they call it and get it that way. He and the town had it all planned anyway, for when Claire died. He said that wasn't enough, that he had to find where that pot came from. He'd known since he was a kid there was a Mimbres site on the ranch and it just drove him crazy to think you knew where it was and he didn't. He never could find it and Claire had told him again, right near the end, that it was all just a lost treasure story and there was no such thing and here that olla had turned up and she had evidently told you. It just drove him crazy; he can't stand something valuable like that just sitting there, hidden away, doing no good at all."

"You'd think he'd be content with the money he makes raping the landscape without having to make a killing pot hunting to boot."

"Highest and best use, Slim. Bingo has sold a bunch of pottery, mostly in the beginning, to get seed money for his business. That's how he got started. But anymore, my Bingo won't hardly sell a prime pot. It's a treasure hunt for him; mostly he just likes finding them. Then he sells the ordinary stuff, or gives it away. And he collects the best. We have the best collection in the Southwest, right in our basement. Sort of like you and your special books. You and Bingo are really a lot alike in some ways."

"Thanks so much."

Truth is best, Slim. You should know the truth of all this. You should know how crazy-wild he was that day. But I calmed him down. I told him I'd find out where the pot came from. I like to help Bingo in his business. I have helped him, lots of times in lots of ways. That's how all those rumors about me got started. And some of them are true. Bingo and I work real good together. And we know when not to ask questions. He just told me to find out, to find out where those people had lived, and find out quick, and then he would take care of the rest."

"It was that important to him?"

"Bingo believes in what he's doing."

"So you were working for him."

"Bingo and I work good together. You can't be surprised. Not after I didn't show up."

"I knew I'd lost. I didn't think I'd been betrayed."

"That's just like you, Jason, trying to keep everything all romantic, even when anyone else would see the truth. But now you should know the truth...it was my idea. You're always hiding from the truth Jason, and making things up in your mind. I don't want you making things up about me. I want you to know the truth."

"So you set me up and when you got what you wanted you handed it to Bingo on a plate."

"It wasn't so simple as that. I figured it wouldn't take me long to find out what I wanted to know for Bingo. Men are so easy to fool...show them something they've never seen before, and they haven't a lick of sense. And you were really easy. You're in a dream world, Slim. Once you'd been with me, I could have had that secret out of you anytime. Only, I must admit, I started liking you. I liked being with you. The way you are, Jason; you're different. You make such a thing of it. The things we did...you made such a thing of me when we were together. Any woman would be taken in. I could feel it happening and I knew that I was falling in love with you some way, and even you're crazy scheme a little bit. I knew I was in for a lot of trouble. Because you were after me to give up everything and be with you, and Bingo kept pressing me because I still couldn't tell him what he wanted to know. I knew I could find out anytime, but I kept putting it off. There was something about you. You made such a thing of it...and me. The way you put yourself into it, any girl would be taken in. And you would get me to do those things and make me feel special as a woman, and you'd tell me your plans and how you thought the world should be, and about our life out at the ranch, and I'll admit it got where I didn't know what was happening to me. You have a way about you, Jason. It's not real, it's all a kind of make believe, but you have a way of making people believe it."

"You have a way of making people believe it, too. You played it almost like you meant it."

"It won't do you any good to get nasty. I told you: men are so easy to fool. And you were a piece of cake. But by the time we had that last night together, I didn't know what I was doing. I was very confused; you had me believing everything you were saying. I wanted it to be as you said. And I didn't want it ever to end. I didn't hardly want to know where those pots are hidden under the ground. But in the end I knew it couldn't be. That's why, when you finally showed me, I had to cry, because I knew it was over."

"It didn't have to be over. You could have done just what you said you were going to do. And we would be together now, just like we planned."

"No Jason. That's just more of your make believe. You had me for a while. But you guessed right about some things. I did get cold feet when I got back home, and there was little Jill. And she went to bed that night and I was all alone and I had lots of time to think. And I knew it wouldn't work, because I know all about you. It's all in your head, Jason; it's all your make believe. That ranch was all in your head. You'd never do anything with it. You'd never have anything more than a few scraggly chickens and a few cows eating more than their worth and that potty little bean patch."

"That may not seem like much to you, but it meant something to me. And I wanted more than that, and with you, it could have been all that I dreamed."

"I can't help you with what you want. Mostly what you want is to keep that secret, hidden in the ground, where it will never do anyone any good. And you want to make the world go around you, and teach it a lesson it doesn't want to hear. And you want to take that ranch back to something you think it was. You like to imagine it that way. I don't know if it ever was what you imagine, even when Claire was young. I know that life myself; I've lived it. I'm not going back to smelling cow shit on my clothes all day and stooping over like a Mexican in the hot sun picking your silly beans. I like the life Bingo has given me. There's lots of new things all the time now, and with Bingo I can have whatever I want. And I don't want your make believe. You wouldn't ever really do anything with that ranch, anymore than you'll ever write a book. I know about your book, Jason."

I didn't move this time, or say anything, or attempt to intercede, as she got up from her chair and took a couple of steps with a grace I still couldn't help notice, and from behind my desk took my book from behind the glass and off the shelf.

"When you tried hiding it, I had to wonder why. And that last morning, I thought, well, surely we know each other well enough now. You were still in the back and so I came over and reached up like this and took it down. I didn't have to look for long because there's nothing to see. Congratulations Slim, until now, you had even fooled yourself."

And she held the book before me, and with her fingers she spun the pages before my eyes, and of course they were all empty, every one. And when she was done she tossed the book onto the desk.

"What about those wooden boxes under the shelves that you're so proud of. Are they filled with empty pages, too?"

"They're not empty; those are my writings."

"Are they books? Are any of them books?"

"No, they're drafts...they're not ready yet. And the novel I've been working on lately...I have draft of that now, too. I think it's pretty good. But it's not really finished. Not yet."

"Why not? You're supposed to be a writer. Why don't you finish something, and get it published?"

Signal To Depart

"I don't know. They're never quite right. I think, for every good book, there is that one beginning, a sentence, or maybe two, that starts that book and is right for that book. It may not be any sort of special sentence on it's own. But it's right for that book. I've read lots of great books. And when I finish I always go back and see how the author started that book, and I always see, that was the only beginning that book could ever have. I write, and I finish what I'm writing, at least a draft, and then I go to look at it again, and it's just not right. Not right at the start. And so I pile it in a box, thinking some day I will be able to start it right, and finish it."

"You won't ever make it right. You won't ever do any writing except your make believe. You won't ever finish and you won't ever find the sentence that's just right because you're afraid to have a book, a real book that's out there for everyone to read. And so you hide everything away in boxes and pretend you have a book on the shelf. You imagine it's a book that everyone would want to read, but it's really nothing at all. You're books are all make believe. And the ranch, and the thing with you and me, that was just another make believe thing in your head. When I found out about your book I was just real confused. But then, over the weekend, the more I thought about it, the more it made sense to me. It was just like you, really, and then I knew what it meant, and then all your other make believe began to make sense too. I thought, maybe I should feel sorry for him some way. But I didn't feel sorry for you at all. And then, the more I thought about it, I got pissed. You're sorry, all right. You're a sap. And you and I were lovers and you were offering up these *unspeakable intimacies* you called them and making me feel special as a woman and you said everything was special and secret and only for us and I found out you were still seeing that fat Mexican the whole time and you made believe to yourself I wouldn't know or care. And then we had our special night together. And we went out to the ranch the next day and you had created this whole little world for us. And you almost had me believing it. But I knew about your phony book and I knew you had been fucking that Aguilar girl the whole time, and then pretty soon I found out about that Blackwoman. I don't know who you think you're kidding...thinking a woman like that can strut her stuff around town with you and leave your place the next morning when everyone can see, and not have the whole town know about it."

"Well you were doing it. You were with Bingo every night."

"That's different. Bingo's my husband. And he's not a nigger."

"Would that he were; with a man like Bingo, he's got no where to go but up."

And I got my face slapped for that. I got my face slapped hard, and then she was over at the door, and she was almost crying, but she still had a handle on what she'd come for.

"And I'm going to tell you something else, Slim. For a while, when you had me believing it, it was hard to make love at home after being with you. But it's not hard anymore."

"Thanks so much."

"You should know the truth of it. I can't be what you want me to be, Jason. It can't be the way you want it. Those times are over. And you have me confused with someone else."

And then Sarah was out the door. I watched her walk away, down the walk, and then across the street in a half run; she had a way of moving that had you noticing every little thing she did.

Chapter 28

I hadn't been out to the ranch since I got the news they were taking it. I hadn't the heart for it. And there had been no reason to go out there.. The milk cow was near dry and I hadn't worried about her. The rancher I called had paid me cash for the cattle and the horse and the milk cow and the tractor and all the implements and everything else. He knew the place and had picked everything up. I had no heart for the little crop I'd raised. Harvesting it would just make me sad and I wouldn't know what to do with it now anyway. Anymore, it was just a potty little bean patch, like Sarah said. The only thing that had made me think I ought to go out there at all was that little blue-heeler dog. I had no use for a dog now either and the rancher, like I said, didn't want the dog. I really had no use for her anymore and I guessed she was still out there, hanging around the barn and eating out of the fifty pound feed sack whenever she got hungry. I didn't really know and hadn't cared much either. But Sarah had paid her visit and had given me the business, finally and permanently, and now I knew that nothing was safe or hidden out there anymore; and the day wore on to late afternoon and it came to me that I had to go out there; and maybe if she was still there I would allow the dog to follow me back to the shop. Then I'd run an ad in the paper and give her away to someone who wanted a dog.

It was getting late in the day and I closed up and put my hat and coat on and walked out to the ranch. It was clear and cool with the sun setting fast on a fall day. I went out by the Tobosa highway and turned off down the ranch road. Well before I got to the cattle guard and the ranch boundary I could hear the machinery at work over the hills, and instead of following the ranch road all the way in I turned off and hiked south over the hills, picking up that north-south cow trail, till I topped out on the largest hill overlooking and just west of the ranch headquarters and from up there I could look down and see everything...

...The barn was gone. You could see where it had been but it simply wasn't there anymore, just the outline in the dirt where the foundation had been. And the corrals and the loading chute and all the outbuildings, they were gone too. There was no sign of the dog. And the house was down, too, though it wasn't entirely gone. It was in a heap, what was left of it; much of it was in two dump trucks that stood idling nearby; as I watched a loader was scooping up the last of the rubble and filling the second of the trucks. Back a ways from this work Bingo Callahan sat on his own idling machine, the D-8 Cat I'd seen him use before in the work he did. Here his work was evidently done; he had leveled the barn and corrals and outbuildings days before, it had been scooped up and driven off, and now he had leveled the house. He could sit and watch and smoke a cigarette as the last of it was carried off, too. I sat down in front of a small juniper, where my outline wouldn't show against the sky, and watched. The trucks went and came back and were refilled and the trucks drove off again and the drivers were gone and the operator of the loader put the loader in road gear and left and the house was as absent as the barn. Only

Bingo was left. I watched as he got down from the dozer and walked over to where the house had been and he scratched around in the dirt a little with his foot. A couple of times he reached down and picked up some small remnant of that home. He would look at it and then toss it away. Then he went back and climbed up into the seat of the dozer, still idling. He lit another cigarette and then he seemed to be looking around. It was an empty sight all around by my eyes but I had to surmise that Bingo Callahan was now looking at what he would call good works -- no house, no barn, no corrals, no cattle or chickens, no milk cow or blue-heeler dog, a place cleared and ready for something new and better to take its place. The workers were now gone too, and Bingo would see himself alone at the end of this day; no one would notice me at this hour, sitting in front of a juniper up on the hill. Presently he came back to himself and he went into gear and braked one track and the other track walked the machine around in a jagged half-circle till it was facing south and then he started south, crawling and lurching over the ground and making tracks; and with the blade just skimming the surface he was also making a rough road, going parallel with the face of the cliffs. I stood and went back behind the hill and headed south, too. I knew where he was headed and I stayed behind hills and picked up that cow trail again and worked south; I could hear the machine running parallel to me just over the hill and I could see puffs of dark smoke from the diesel in the air. When I topped out I was right above the collection of trees and land that hid the ancient site of the Mimbres Indians. Once again I sat down in front of a juniper to hide myself and watch. Bingo was already there. His machine was still idling and he was standing above the seat and looking out over the grove and then he reached down and shut the machine off. Then he got down and walked off into the grove. He was in the shade down there and I lost him a couple of times in the trees and brush and then he appeared again, walking out of the grove. He would know now everything he needed to know, and he knew what to do with that machine. The day was fading fast and since he had shut off that diesel I knew he wouldn't start it again until tomorrow morning. I watched as he walked on back to where the house had been. His pickup was parked nearby. I waited and watched until he had gotten in his truck and then he drove off. I came down off the bluff and walked on through the grove. Once you knew it, it really wasn't that hard to see that they had lived here. I came back out of the scrub and walked through the dusk the near half mile back to the house. Only it wasn't there anymore, just some piece of wood and broken glass and a few crumbling adobe bricks they had not completely cleaned up. I whistled a couple of times but there was still no sign of that dog. I turned and went on down into the bottomland and over to my two and a half acres of crop. This at least stood undisturbed. I walked in and handled a few ears, peeling back the shucks. They had passed the stage of picking some for supper. They had matured and dried and the kernels were hard. They would still be good to feed to cows or chickens or hogs but I didn't have anything to feed them to. Or you could grind the kernels up and make corn meal but I had no reason to do that either. My black beans were past ripe and full and dry and hard in the brown pods and all ready to pick. I had no interest in picking them. I went over to my little patch of ancient beans. They were past ripe too, and full and dry and hard, and needed to be picked. I had no use for them anymore. And then I saw where one pod had broken open in the wind and the brightly colored beans had fallen out on the ground. I kneeled and picked them up one by one and put them in my shirt pocket. I stayed kneeling and opened more pods and collected several good handfuls of beans until my shirt pocket was full. I left the crop and walked on by where the house had been and whistled again for the dog. There was nothing, and I knew now what I had to do.

Chapter 29

I got to the shop and went back into the kitchen. I got a little old ten ounce soup can from the trash and rinsed it out and I put my beans in there. The beans had filled my shirt pocket and in fact I had to be careful to keep them from falling out and they just about filled the little can. I took the little can of beans to my bus in the alley out back and I got up in the bus and put the can of beans on the dash in front of the windshield where they certainly would be found, and then I sat down and turned the key on the ignition. I hadn't driven the bus in months but I closed the choke and it turned over with just a little persuasion and in time idled smoothly as I gradually opened the choke. I let it run a bit and then I shut it off and got down and checked the oil and the water and tires and all the fluid levels and made sure the belts were tight and made sure that the bus would be ready to drive in the morning. I wasn't going far but I wanted everything to work just right.

I went back into the shop and began to empty the shelves of books. I would fill a box full of books and carry it to the bus and then take the books out and fill a corresponding space in a book shelf in the bus. I had maintained my books, most of which could be put under the general heading of Western Americana, in a certain order by topics -- Ranch & Range; Mountain Men and Hunters; Natural History/Environment; Fiction and Literature; Agriculture and Homesteading, with each topic arranged by author, and I wanted this order maintained in the traveling library. When the bus was found, this would show that a man had had some feeling and regard for his books. This transfer of books was time consuming but I kept working. Where I ran out of book shelf space in the bus I emptied the wooden boxes that held all my writings, left the writings for the time in neat stacks of papers on the floor, and filled the boxes with the rest of the books. These boxes, too, maintained my order of arrangement and I stacked the boxes on the floor under the shelves in the bus where I had stored my writings before. I was ready to carry the last of these boxes of books to the bus when there was a knock on the door. I opened the door and Carla Aguilar was standing in the dark on the walk outside.

"Jason...can I come in?"

"Looks like I'm real busy. Why don't you come back tomorrow."

"It looks to me like you won't be here tomorrow."

"You're right."

"So can I come in now?"

I stepped back out of the way and she stepped in and I closed the door behind her. We stood there by the door looking at each other. She was very pretty, with her coat on and her hands in her coat pockets for it had gotten cold outside, and her long black hair down the back of her coat and she was looking through her glasses all around the room with a kind of frightened look on her face and she was kind of pretty that way too.

"Why are you leaving, Jason?"

"Oh, I think I've got plenty of reasons."

"You should stay."

"I'm not going to hang around here and watch this town outgrow all its goodness."

"I heard you said some fine things at the town council meeting the other night. It has gotten some people thinking about the future of our community. I've been talking to some of them and we want to petition the town council and the county commission to begin land use planning for our area, and work with private trusts like the ones I spoke about, to protect historic structures and valuable lands and retain some of the rural life and open space and the unique cultures of our community before it's gone. You could be a valuable part of that."

"Too late."

"It's too late for the Callahan Ranch. It's never so late you just give up."

"I'm not giving up yet. I'm going to make a difference before I give up."

"I don't like hearing you talk that way."

"*No le hace.* You go join the cause. I've got my own cause now. And I don't like ranting around with a group."

"With some organization, and some help from others, you could have saved the Callahan Ranch. No one in town knew you even cared. People just assumed you bought it for speculation."

"Bingo and the boys knew I didn't buy it for speculation. That's why they brought the hammer down like they did. They weren't taking any chances. But you were right. You were right about Sarah all the way; she played me for a fool. As cunt-struck as I was, it wasn't very hard. So it's my own fucking fault, just like you said. And maybe you were right about how to save the land your way, even with the goddamn government in on it. But I can't do it that way. I'm looking at the Big Horizon now, and I've got a vision. A personal vision. An inspired personal vision. It's time for a remarkable act, and the will to carry it out."

"I don't like hearing that, Jason."

"I'm seeing things for the first time the way they really are. I'm seeing the truth of it. Anyway, you said yourself you'd never forgive me if I lost that land."

"I didn't come by to forgive you. And I didn't come by to blame you either. I came by to tell you that you said some fine things the other night and that some good can still come out of this. And I came by because I needed to tell you that Santos died this morning."

"Well that just about finishes it, doesn't it?"

"Yes, I think it does."

"Well maybe he did the right thing. He didn't hang around to watch them tear his place down."

"Except it wasn't his place."

I didn't say anything to that -- I couldn't -- and she waited a bit and let it set. And then she went on.

"I'm sure his heart just gave out. It's just the way he was. His heart wasn't good and he wouldn't take his pills and the doctor had told me if he wouldn't take them it was just a matter of time and it was going to happen. But I know he had gotten his notice of what was going to happen, and he must have heard the work going on over the hill the last few days, and he would take his ride every morning up where he could see all around. And then, this morning after his ride, he left his horse saddled. I found her like that, grazing in the yard. That wasn't like him. And he must have felt cold because he had wrapped himself in a bright blanket and sat in his favorite chair on the porch in the sun where he could see the hills all around and nothing else. I just wanted justice for him and for our family before he died. And I didn't get it."

"You must hate me now. You must."

"I can't hate you for what you wanted with Sarah. Because I wanted the same with you. And now that's over, too. It's all over now."

"You and Santos wrote a book."

"That's what I hold on to."

"What do you hear about your book?"

"I got two rejection slips and one response from a publisher who is interested."

"How interested?"

"Well, they called it a *conditional* acceptance. They said it is a *vital oral history* but that some things in Santos' life, as they said, *do not reflect well on the Hispanic male.* They said if I would agree to certain changes they would consider publishing the manuscript."

"Are you going to do it?"

"No. If you take that out, it's not Santos anymore. And it's his book, his story, not mine. But I've already begun typesetting the book with a friend who has everything I need to do it myself. And I have contacted a printer and another friend is going to help me with the cover and it's just a matter of months and it's going to be a book."

"I believe you're going to do it."

"I am. It's what keeps me going with all that's happened with you and the land and now Santos."

"I'm glad you have a book to keep you going. You get it done, Carla. You publish it just the way it is, with all of Santos there. It's a good story, and when it's a book you're going to knock their socks off."

"I'm going to do it. And it makes me feel good to have it. It's the only thing that makes me feel good now. But it hurts me because I don't know how to be with you anymore. So much went wrong and so much of it was because of you. But it was only because of you that I ever had so much hope of how things could be. And Santos and I never would have done my book without you."

"Perhaps. But now you've done it. And you don't need me anymore. You're the writer now, and a good one, too. You're the one to carry it on."

"But you've written so much more than me. And you're the one who made me believe I could do it."

"Then I'm glad my self-delusions have done someone some good. But in fact, *I* have done nothing at all."

"But those must be your manuscripts over there on the floor."

"Those, Carla, are several neat piles of trash."

"Those are your manuscripts, that you kept in the boxes."

"Yes, and they're trash. The novels are verbose, circuitous, cautious, pointless, endless, and ultimately all unfinished. The short stories are vague, minimalist and pretentious. The essays are pompous and disingenuous, lacking any of the sauce and directness and wisdom I admire in the many good essays I've read. None of it has anything to say to the world, at all. They're all trash, and that's where they're going."

"Well if they need work, you can work on them and make them better. My book needed work, and with your help I made it better. You can't expect perfection. And what about the novel you've been working on? You were almost finished."

"I did finish it. And I've looked at it since. And it's trash. It was written by a make-believe man living in a dream world, and with all the attendant flaws of everything else I've ever written. It also has no good beginning. If I could ever write a good sentence, one good sentence to start one good book, then I could write that book. But I can't do it; I can't even write one good sentence. Nothing I've written is a book."

"But you have written a book. You showed it to me."

"Then I'd better show it to you again."

And I stepped over to my desk and picked up the volume in its fine binding and brought it over to her, and I opened it in front of her and spun the empty pages by her with my thumb.

"There, you see, it's a nice package, isn't it Carla. A custom designed, one of a kind, hand-bound book, and it's all a facade. It's empty as a deadfurrow."

And she turned away and yet I could see that the tears were already on her face. And it interested me to see the difference in her response from that of Sarah, who was made furious by my make-believe book. For Carla was all sympathy and empathy and hurt. Hurt for me. It was sympathy and empathy and hurt misplaced; poor thing, she still couldn't see she had fallen in love with a joke. A bad joke, hardly worth the telling.

"It's good I showed it to you, Carla. It's good that you know. And I promise you this will be the last time I disappoint you. I want you to go on now. And I don't want you losing anything of yourself over me. You're the one good thing I can leave behind here, you and that book you wrote. I'm going to leave thinking maybe I helped you a little bit there. I can leave feeling good about that. And you're even more beautiful now than when I met you. You have that something now that all men love and all women want. You've got it now, Carla. You were always so pretty, but now you have that something else too; and you ought to know you made Sarah Callahan jealous as a cuckold bitch."

She tried to smile and said, "You gave me that, too."

"That's good. That makes me feel good. I'll take that with me, too. You'll always have that now, Carla. And women will envy you, and men will love you. They'll want you, and when the time comes, you'll have the one you want."

"They already want me. But I wanted it all to be with you."

"Too late. I ruined all that. You go on now; I've got lots to do before morning. You go on and make it all happen for yourself, and don't you dare look back."

She turned to face me now and there were those tears behind her glasses, coming down her pretty brown face. "I do worry about you. I know you are planning something horrible."

"Don't worry about me. I can see your success now. I can see the triumph of Carla Aguilar. That makes me happy. And for myself, my mind is clear. I can see the truth of it now, and I know what I have to do. I've never felt this good. This isn't any dream anymore. I've got a vision, a personal vision, and I shall commit a remarkable act."

"Will you come back?"

"That's not the way the story ends."

She started to say more but I put my arms around her and held her close for both of us and then I was urging her to the door and she was teary and reluctant and yet compliant and then she stood just outside, looking at me.

"I still think you can do it, Jason. I think you can fill those pages with a book -- all ornery and saucy and even a little bit mean, and still full of heart and sensual and raunchy and wise, and one I'd love to read."

She was strong and had a certain dignity and she had the last word between us for before I could rebut her she was gone.

Chapter 30

I couldn't stop now. This was a story I could start and create and finish. I began by carrying the papers stacked on the floor out into the alley behind my apartment. There, just down the alley from where the bus was parked, was the burn barrel where I and several others who used the building, burned our trash. I had a lifetime of accumulated trash and self-delusions on paper and I commenced to burn it all. It was a pleasure for me. Every writer has produced works that they hope no one will ever see. We are too vain to destroy them, yet we worry that after we're gone they will be discovered and published to our everlasting shame. I had a life's work that I hoped no one would ever see and as I set the first pages afire, and fed others in by the handful, my worries there ceased. Rather like prolonging a satisfying meal, I continued to feed the pages into the flames in small bunches. There were a great many of them and it took time but in time they were gone. Then I went to my desk and took out the draft of my latest novel. I had believed in it once, but I knew now it was trash. A pleasant enough story, readable I suppose, carefully constructed and competent, but nothing my friend Carla would want to read. Certainly it was neither ornery nor saucy nor even a little bit mean; nor full of heart nor sensual nor raunchy nor wise. It took no chances. It's characters were not authentic; in fact, lacked character. They, too, took no chances. The story had nothing to say to the world. It was trash and I took it out to the burn barrel in the alley and fed it by handfuls into the flames. Thank God I had never made copies of my work; there could be no other drafts out there, floating around, that someone might find. My mind was clear on that score.

I proceeded then to pack my clothes and all personal items as though I were preparing to leave town for a long journey. Indeed I packed everything up and placed it into my roving home just as it had been when I arrived some nine months before. I was precise and neat and got everything put up just as I wanted it. In the end, the only things of mine left in the shop were my revolver in the desk drawer, my empty book on top of the desk, and the bow and arrows, modeled from an ancient design, hanging on the wall. I gathered these items up last and took them to the bus. I hung the revolver on the hook by the bed in the back of the bus and then I placed the book on the seat where a passenger would have sat up front. I took my pencil from my shirt pocket and placed it on the book. I set my ancient weapon on the floor between the seats. Then I sat down behind the wheel and started the bus. I let it idle a bit and as the engine warmed I opened the choke and idled it down. Then I put the shift into reverse and backed out of the alley and into the street. I shifted into first and drove slowly down Chihuahua Street to the corner, turned and went east on Main to the light at Main and the Tobosa Highway. It was very late at night now, in fact well into early morning, and the town was very quiet indeed. I waited at the light and a cop making his rounds came along the highway, coming into town, and drove slowly though the intersection on the green. I lifted a partial hand in the usual small town greeting from passing vehicles and he responded in kind and then, having made my stop at the red, I turned right onto the Tobosa Highway. I watched his lights disappear in the mirror as I drove out of town. Of course he could have no idea what I was going to do.

I drove on past the turnoff to the Callahan Ranch. A half mile beyond was the turnoff to the country club, as it currently stood, and, as well, the county dump. I made that turn to the left and drove in. A half mile in, the road to the country club went south, opposite the turn-off to the dump, which went north. I slowed and turned north onto the road to the dump. Directly, well before the dump, I slowed and turned east and drove the bus slowly down the little dirt road that led to the boundary fence and gate and one of the dirt tanks of the Callahan Ranch. I stopped shy of the fence and turned off the engine and sat in the dark and quiet of the night. There was not a sound of wind, it being a very still night, and the stars shone clearly, it being a cloudless night, and there was no sight or sound of other vehicles or people or any signs of activity at the club or the dump. There was a three-quarter moon which would aid my final access in, and I considered that I was well positioned and perfectly prepared for the final act. I would presently leave the bus and cross the fence and hike over the hills, not far, east and north of the bus and the dump, to the bluff overlooking the site of an ancient village. There the dozer was parked. And there, just past dawn, I would silently kill a man at plunder and sacrilege over an ancient culture. Afterwards, I would return here, to lie down on the floor in utter calm and contentment, well placed between my shelves of books, and pull the trigger. By evening the story would be moving rapidly, not only around town and into the news statewide, but perhaps further, into the history and mythology of the West: the arrowed, bloodied form, gut shot, obviously a homicidal killing; the gunned, bloodied form, head-shot, obviously a suicidal killing; the incredibly sinister, hateful, pathetic and lurid connection between the man who died by his machinery, and the man who died surrounded by his books; the contrary purposes, goals and dreams that each man held; the ironic victories of each; the empty book with the pencil lying vacantly beside; the soup can of colorful ancient beans. It would take time for the whole story to come out, but I could hope that in time someone who could write would tell it. I couldn't write the story, but I could create it. This was a story that had something to say to the world. This was something I could do. I considered that I contemplated a inspired act, and that I was surely mad. And I couldn't wait.

Armed with a weapon of the ancients, I left in the dark with just the faintest hint of dawn in the east. I went through the gate to the stock tank and set off across the hills, picking up the cow trail headed south. I knew where to go and could see quite well in the moonlight. At the bluff I stopped, looking down on the ancient village, still intact. Nearby was the dozer, a silent monolithic machine. It squatted there, harmless enough in itself, useful enough in the right hands, but potentially destructive of great cultures and the fragility of the natural world. A long step back from the edge of the bluff were two boulders you could just get your arms around with a scruffy little Piñon Pine growing out of the rocky soil in the space between them. I sat down behind the natural curtain; it was the perfect spot to hide and bushwack someone who needed killing; I would not be seen yet I could see and when the time came I would rise to a crouch and draw a primitive yet deadly bow. The bluff was not high here, I would hold a little low as I released, and when he was working his machine along the bluff he wouldn't be twenty yards away. I could hit at that distance and the fine black point would penetrate. I strung the bow and notched my best arrow, the one that had neatly killed a hare. I rose to a crouch several times, drew back and held on the seat of the machine. It was too far where it was parked for a shot. But the village ran right up to the edge of the bluff and as he uncovered it he would move closer. It was the perfect spot to bushwack someone who needed killing.

I sat back down and waited. Gradually light in the east became less faint and grew more real. It was cold. I could see my breath and feel that the air was near frost yet I didn't feel cold and would not shiver. Not long before I had waited in a cold nervous sweat and rank nervous smell for my time to talk. But that was ineffectual verbiage. This was real, this was doing something; this would make a difference. She had called me a sap; well, we would see about that. I was calm, warm in the cold, contained. I couldn't wait.

And I didn't wait long. I saw his headlights first, coming down the ranch road, bouncing in and out of the trees and turning my way as he drove by the ranch, picking up the just-made rough road the dozer had scraped out the day before, and on up to a stop by the big machine. Clemson "Bingo" Callahan got out. In the half light of the early dawn, before the sun itself had appeared, you still couldn't miss who it was. He was ensconced against the cold in brush-brown coveralls, gloves, and a wool tractor cap. He climbed up on the machine and the diesel shook mightily as it turned over, belched dark smoke, then, gradually, settled into a steady rumble in its tracks. Bingo let it warm. Then he went to work.

He moved the dozer and gently dropped the massive blade. You could see he was an artist, of sorts, with this machine, as he precisely sheared off the grass-held topsoil and knocked down the brush and the occasional small tree here and there. He lurched slowly forward, not far, until he uncovered the first foundation blocks of what had been an outside wall. He backed up and could see, as I could, that this wall ran perpendicular to the face of the bluff. He backed up and moved in against this wall again and again, each time just shearing the surface and each time moving the blade one blade-space further east. He was moving slowly away from me and uncovering the outline of the wall. At the point where the wall made a right angle turn to the south he braked and tracked and lurched his machine around and similarly uncovered the outline of the east end the room. At that point he, and I, could anticipate that this room was quite large and rectangular in shape and came out from near the base of the bluff towards the east, with its long sides running east and west. He braked and tracked around till he was positioned at the northeast corner of the room and, lowering his blade to just shear the surface, began to uncover the room itself, moving east to west. He was now moving toward the bluff, and me. He came half way across, then backed up and made another pass, cutting a little deeper. He did it again and this time signs of what had been life began to appear. He really was good with the machine and I could see it wouldn't take him any time at all to uncover the village, get most of the prime pots he wanted, then declare the discovery was all happenstance. He had the first of these discoveries revealed now, and he stopped and backed up and got down and went and got a shovel from his truck. He came over with the shovel and dug out the first of the treasures and kept digging and in time produced two pots that had not survived the weight of the machine and surfaced in pieces, and three that did. He examined these items with interest, then took them, broken and intact, over to his truck and got a cardboard box from the cab of the truck and put the items inside the box. He carefully folded the box closed and put it into the cab of the truck. He came back and climbed up into the dozer and this time he did not back up for another pass over the same portion of the room but continued on, setting his blade for a fresh cut over the intact surface, moving towards the base of the bluff. For me, this had gone on long enough. As he approached inside my twenty yard range I determined to take him head on. I would rise to a shooter's crouch at full draw, and as he lifted his startled eyes to the movement, I would grant him an instant of recognition, so he would know what was going to happen to him. Then release, and take him high up in the gut, just below the brisket. He was a big man and it might take more than one shot to finish the killing; I had two more arrows I wouldn't hesitate to use. The machine crawled slowly forward, its skilled operator just skimming away the revelations, not ruining more than half of what was there. I got my legs underneath me, placed the first tension on the string, and prepared to rise...

...It was still not the good light of morning and so the first I saw of the second vehicle was the headlights running in and out of the trees and bounding along over the ranch road in the distance. I had determined that Bingo sent all the workers home for a few days, the buildings having been demolished and cleared, and so I did not expect that he would have company. Certainly not this early in the day. But the vehicle came on down the road and on by where the house and barns had been, and bounced on over the rough road to the site as I took the tension off the string and dropped back down into a sitting position behind my sheltering rocks and tree. It was the 4 x 4 power wagon that Sarah Callahan drove, though with the early sunlight reflecting off the windshield I could not see who drove it. Then the wagon came to a stop by the pickup, and Sarah got out one side with a basket, and as little Jill hopped out and came running from the other side I knew at the sight that I would never be able to kill that little girl's father. The little girl came running up to the big machine and her father stopped it's crawling, rested the blade, and climbed down. He hefted the child up and I could tell much of what was said though with the engine still running there was no hearing their words. He carried her part way over to where Sarah waited by the truck and when he set her down she ran ahead to Sarah and then back to her father and then back to Sarah with great joy. And there they all stood for a time by the vehicles and talked and I could tell much of what they said though I couldn't hear. Sarah looked very fine; just as I'd known her. She had brought his lunch in the basket and they talked about that and she took a thermos out of the basket and poured him some coffee and she got some cookies out of the basket too and he ate the cookies and drank the coffee as he pointed over to where he had dug and told Sarah all about it and she would nod and smile approvingly and the child leaned against him and looked up and stood enraptured by this adult work and world. When he finished the cookies and coffee he went to his truck and brought the box and set it on the ground and opened it and showed Sarah and the child. These were great treasures from an ancient time and they showed great pleasure in having them. In time he put them back in the box and took them back to the truck and she went with him and put his lunch basket also in the cab of his truck. There was apparent great fondness in their family farewell and I watched everything until Sarah and little Jill had gotten back into her vehicle and had driven off and disappeared finally in the trees of the ranch road headed to town. By that time Bingo Callahan was back up on his machine but I didn't watch him dig the rest of the Mimbres village. As the machine went back into gear and commenced to belch smoke and grunt its power over the ground I lay back from my seated position to stretch out on my back and cover my sight from the rising sun with my arm draped over my eyes, and I wept. I wept quietly but thoroughly for I had found my final and permanent defeat. This story, too, would have empty pages. I lay for a long time it seemed in hopeless shameless almost silent weeping with the dozer grunting and belching and doing its work just over the rise, and I wished I could stay forever here and just like this, ensconced in wild hills so close to town, hidden from the past and sheltered from the future and out of sight of the work nearby; but I knew it could not last. For one thing, my bed of rocky soil was becoming decidedly uncomfortable. And increasingly I had the feeling that someone was watching me. I had seen the power wagon drive off, and I could hear that other machine still moving and grunting and working over the cliff and out of sight, and what person could find me anyway in my sheltered bushwack hideaway? Yet the sense of it would not leave and only grew with the discomfort of rocks underneath me, and in time I lifted my arm from my eyes and it was Claire's little blue-heeler dog. She was curled up nearby and when I lifted my arm and acknowledged the world she lifted her head from where she rested it on her paws and looked at me with two bright eyes, one brown, one blue, and ears raised in recognition.

I stayed low leaving that place, till I topped the first rise, and then I followed my trail in on the way out. The dog trotted obediently at my side, looking a little gant, for she had been forced to hunt when the barn came down and the food was gone; she looked up at me from time to time, waiting for my usual directive to... "Go to the barn!" But there was no barn, and after I went through the gate and as we approached the bus, I said, "Okay, you can come along." At that she went into her silly run and jump and spin and lots of frantic barking outloud, then racing ahead to the bus, then back to me and she circled me at high speed and went into her jump and spin again, and again, and again as she yapped at the sky in joy. I opened the door to the bus and she was in there before me and tried her run and jump and spin in the front of the bus. She went from seat to seat and across the dashboard in frenetic circular joy and knocked over my soup can of Mimbres beans; they scattered on the floor and I hollered, "Enough Goddamnit!" She stopped, and there she sat on my seat behind the wheel. I said, "Get in the back!" And she hopped down and scurried to the back of the bus and lay down on the rug by the bed, looking at me. I got in behind the wheel and placed my weapon on the floor between the seats and considered that I would have to give the dog a name somewhere down the road, and maybe in time let her ride on the seat beside me as we traveled and viewed the fading myths of the West...

...For indeed it seemed I could see most all of the West from where I sat, the mountains to the north and the deserts going on south to Mexico; and the hills and the valley closer in and the trees along the creek; and even including puffs of dark smoke rising from a spot over the hills not far away. And I thought that I was condemned to witness the last of what an ancient people had first seen not two thousand years away. It must have seemed a glory of a find. And for centuries on end they had hunted the grassy hills, and reveled and nurtured and cultivated along the sweet inviting valley streams, between the forbidding forests and heated deserts, fertile, fervent, lusty, struggling lives, that built through the generations to an artistic climax that spoke of all the lively mysteries a world would never know until they were gone. It was certain that I would never know a land or life that could yield such perfect aching wonder. But I had known a measure of it, made all the more wondrous by its fading fragility, its confounding myths, its urgent ineluctable loss in the face of the time which has come. Will any spread of people ever know in time when the best is going by, or realize but little of what was lost and gone before...?

Signal To Depart

...There was a story here all right. And while I had the beginning of it in my mind, I picked up the pencil and book from the seat beside me, and opening to the first page I wrote:

They came into the valley as a tattered band just ages ago

I considered the sentence briefly, then placed a period at the end of it. Then I replaced the book and pencil on the seat beside me and stooped without abjection to the floor of the bus where I gathered one by one as many of the colorful ancient beans as I could find, and put them in my shirt pocket.

It was time to move on.

M. H. Salmon is the author of the non-fiction books *Gazehounds & Coursing*, *Gila Descending*, and *Tales of the Chase*; and the novel *Home is the River*. He lives with his family near Silver City, New Mexico.

HIGH-LONESOME BOOKS

"Published in the Greatest Country Out-of-Doors"

At *HIGH-LONESOME BOOKS* we have a great variety of titles for enthusiasts of the Southwest and the great Outdoors -- new, used, and rare books of the following:

Southwest History

Wilderness Adventure

Natural History

Hunting

Sporting Dogs

Mountain Men

Fishing

Country Living

Environment

Our catalog is FREE for the asking. Write or call.

HIGH-LONESOME BOOKS
P. O. Box 878
Silver City, New Mexico
88062
505-388-3763

Also, please call for directions and come visit our bookshop in the country at High-Lonesome Road near Silver City